"DEAD IN THE WATER"

DAN DEADMAN SPACE DETECTIVE BOOK 3

BARRY J. HUTCHISON

ZERTEX

ALSO BY BARRY J. HUTCHISON

SPACE TEAM SERIES

Space Team

Space Team: The Wrath of Vajazzle

Space Team: The Search for Splurt

Space Team: Song of the Space Siren

Space Team: The Guns of Nana Joan

Space Team: Return of the Dead Guy

Space Team: Planet of the Japes

Space Team: The Time Titan of Tomorrow

Space Team: The King of Space Must Die

Space Team: A Lot of Weird Space Shizz

DAN DEADMAN SERIES

"Dial D for Deadman"

"Dead Inside"

"Dead in the Water"

SIDEKICKS SERIES

The Sidekicks Initiative

EVERYTHING ELSE

The Bug

CONTENTS

ONE

IN SOME CIRCLES, the Jonta Exodus was considered to be one of the planet Parloo's all-time classic automobiles.

These circles, however, were populated entirely by the deluded and the deranged, and their opinions were widely ridiculed. In truth, the Jonta Exodus was arguably the worst car ever produced on any planet anywhere in the universe, and after successfully managing to get rid of one of the fonking things, Detective Dan Deadman was dismayed to have recently found himself the unlucky recipient of a second.

Right now, the car was stopped in a 'No Parking' zone outside one of the more disreputable drinking establishments in the city of Down Here. The driver's seat was empty. The passenger seat and an indented tray in the dash were not.

"Think he'll be OK?"

According to her fake ID, her name was Oledol Lodelo, but everyone in her extremely limited social circle called her Ollie. She squirmed anxiously in the Exodus's rigidly unforgiving passenger seat, her eyes flitting from the door of the bar to the six-inch-tall man sitting in the dash indent.

Artur was... well, she wasn't really sure *what* he was, exactly. He was small and bearded, swore a lot, and spoke with a funny accent. He owned an impressive range of doll-sized dresses and was currently wearing a cheeky off-the-shoulder black number with a white bow tied off at his hip. Hairy toes poked out of his plastic sandals, the pinhead-sized toenails yellow with fungus.

"Who?" he asked.

"Dan."

"Oh, that big gobshoite. Yeah. Course. He'll be fine, Peaches. Sure, he does this sort of thing all the time."

Ollie nodded and tried, once again, to get comfortable. The car refused to allow it, though, and she searched for something to keep her mind off the growing stiffness in her legs, neck, and lower back. And, slightly less so, her upper back, forearms, and feet.

Nothing much was happening in the bar itself from what she could see through the grime-encrusted window. Dan had gone inside to look for someone a few minutes ago. Reassuringly, there had been no shouts, screams or gunshots since then. This was in quite stark contrast to the three other bars they'd visited that night, and she was taking it to be a positive sign.

"How did you two meet?" she asked.

"Me and Deadman?" said Artur, shimmying around in his indent. He laughed behind his beard. "Ha! Now there's a tale for the tellin'!"

Ollie's eyebrows raised as she leaned in, intrigued.

"We met in a pub," Artur said.

Ollie nodded and bit her lip, waiting to hear the rest. She giggled in anticipation. "Right..."

"Actually, that's pretty much the whole of it," Artur said. "In hindsight, I may have oversold it to ye a little bit."

Ollie leaned back. The Exodus's seat punished her accordingly.

"Oh."

"Aye, not all that exciting a story, really," Artur admitted. He clicked his tongue against the roof of his mouth. "Mind you, he *was* on fire at the time..."

The window of the bar exploded outwards and a corpse in a brown overcoat crunched onto the sidewalk.

"Oh-ho. Would ye look at that? Speak of the devil an' he's sure to appear," Artur announced. He leaned forward, rapped his knuckles on the windshield, and raised his voice. "Ye alright there, Deadman?"

Dan clambered to his feet, accompanied by a tinkling of falling glass. His left arm was facing backward from the elbow down. He twisted it into place with a grunt. "Fine," he said.

"It's just that ye appear to have been thrown arse-first through a window."

Ollie opened the Exodus's passenger door, but Dan jabbed a finger at her. "Don't. Stay in the car," he barked.

Nodding, Ollie jumped out and stood to a perky sort of attention in front of him. Dan glowered at her. "What are you doing?"

"You said 'don't stay in the car,'" she reminded him.

"No, I said, 'Don't,' end of sentence, then, 'Stay in the car,' new sentence."

Ollie gazed back at him blankly, her face fixed in a vacant sort of half-smile. Dan sighed.

"Forget it. Just get back in the car. I've got this under control."

"OK," said Ollie. "It's just... You were thrown through a window."

"And?"

"And so, it doesn't look like you've got it under control."

Dan ran his gloved fingers through the few remaining wisps of his hair, which made him realize he'd lost his hat. He grunted out a reply. "Did you ever consider that maybe I *wanted* to get thrown through a window?"

"No," Ollie admitted. She considered it now. "Did you?"

Dan briefly considered lying and confirming that yes, it had been deliberate, but then changed his mind. He sighed. "Doesn't matter. Just wait here, while I..."

He turned back to the bar door just as an enormous armor-plated figure ducked through it.

Living thousands of light years from the planet Earth, Dan had never seen an armadillo before. If he had, he might have spotted some similarities between that creature and this one, although any likenesses were passing ones at best.

Even partially ducked, the figure stood almost eight feet tall. Interlocking armored plates covered its torso and its upper arms. Each of its spiked fists were larger than Dan's head, while its own head was a neckless bump between its shoulders, heavily protected by yet more of its organic armor plating.

"Holy shoite, he's a big lad," called Artur from the relative safety of the car. "I don't fancy yer chances against that thing."

The giant armadillo lumbered towards Dan, cracking his knuckles. "Get going," he spat through his scrunched up little mouth. "We don't want you bugging our clients."

Dan shrugged. "OK. OK. Fine. You made your point.

But I left my hat in there. I'll just go get it."

The armored chest blocked his path, giving Dan a close-up view. Each interlocking plate had to be thick enough to stop a blaster pistol, never mind a fist.

"I told you to get going."

"And I told *you*," Dan began. He kicked out sharply, snapping the armadillo-thing's knee outwards. Those big hands grasped at Dan as the guy fell, but he stepped smoothly back out of reach.

The sidewalk shuddered as the armadillo-thing hit it, his leg buckled unnaturally outward, a hiss of pain whispering from his lips.

Dan stepped around him. "I'm getting my hat back."

"Should we come?" Ollie asked.

"No," Dan said, in a tone that suggested this wasn't open to discussion. "Stay here. Watch that thing. If he tries anything, take care of him."

Ollie looked down at the fallen brute, then back to Dan. "OK," she said, resolutely. She gave Dan a double thumbs-up. "We will!"

Dan hesitated. "Uh... OK, then," he said, then he *cricked* his neck a couple of times, adjusted the collar of his coat, and stepped back into the bar.

The inside of the place was relatively quiet, which was a change from the other places he'd been that night. It was also a complete shizzhole, which wasn't.

For the most part, the clientele here hadn't come to celebrate or socialize. They were here because they wanted somewhere dim and dank where they could sit alone and drink their memories away. Of all the places Dan had visited that night, this was by far his favorite, and there was a shadowy booth in the back corner that practically had his name on it.

That wasn't why he was here, though. Ignoring the dirty look and muttering from the barman, Dan retrieved his hat from the spot on the floor where it had been knocked off, dusted it down, then deposited it back on his head. It was a little battered and out of shape, but no more than the rest of him.

"Let's try that again."

He pointed to a ratty-faced little bald guy sitting hunched on a stool at the far end of the bar. "Bonbo, you and I need to talk."

Bonbo nodded. "S-sure thing," he said, his hand trembling as he raised his glass to his lips and tipped the contents down his throat. His already scrunched-up features became momentarily more so, and he coughed as the fiery liquor scorched the back of his throat.

And then he was off and running, the stool clattering to the floor as he raced in the direction of the only door not currently blocked by a corpse in an overcoat.

"Mindy, stun shot," Dan said, drawing a blaster the size of a miniature cannon from inside the coat. The weapon's lights illuminated and its chamber spun, but before Dan could pull the trigger, Bonbo was through the door and safely in cover.

"Why do they always fonking run?" Dan grunted, giving chase. Something big and ugly attempted to block his path, but the butt of Dan's gun cracking across the bridge of its nose promptly gave the thing pause to reconsider.

Dan didn't bother to take it slowly at the door. Being dead brought with it a number of advantages, the main one being that it was difficult to become deader. If Bonbo was waiting through there with a gun, as long as the shot didn't take Dan's head off, it wouldn't really slow him down.

Beyond the door was a room that was balancing on the

cusp between 'bathroom' and 'biological weapons testing site'. As far as Dan had been aware, he no longer had any sense of smell, but the stench wafting through the open doors of the bathroom's six stalls forced him to reassess this.

There was a single small window in the place, but it was too high for Bonbo to be able to reach. Dan was pretty sure of this, as Bonbo was currently jumping to try to catch the ledge but falling short by several inches.

"I just want to talk," Dan said.

Bonbo, suddenly alerted to the detective's presence, screamed briefly, then shot into the closest stall and slammed the door shut behind him.

Evidently, there was no lock on the door, as he immediately jumped back out again, before darting into the next one. This time, once the door had slammed, there was a definite *clack* of a locking mechanism being activated.

Muttering below his lack-of-breath, Dan holstered his gun and crossed to the cubicle door. The paintwork had been etched and sketched with graffiti in various symbols and languages, all of which were quickly translated by the chip implanted in one of Dan's eyeballs. None of it was of particular literary merit, though, and he kind of wished the chip hadn't bothered.

"You're not in trouble," Dan said. "I'm not after you. I just want to talk."

"Then why did you chase me?" Bonbo whimpered through the door.

"Because you ran away. I can't talk to you if we aren't in the same room."

Bonbo didn't have an answer for that.

"Open the door."

"N-no. We can talk like this. You out there, me in here."

Dan pinched the bridge of his nose and inhaled slowly.

The urge to kick the door in and waterboard the son-of-a-bedge with toilet water was almost overwhelming, but he'd been trying to resist such temptations of late. He blamed Ollie.

Mind you, he blamed her for pretty much everything.

"Fine. We'll talk like this," Dan said.

"You're going to shoot me through the door," Bonbo replied, his voice cracking.

Dan raised his hands so Bonbo could see them above the stall. "The gun's away. Like I said, I'm not after you." He brought his mouth closer to the door. "I'm after Krato."

There was no reply from the stall, but the way Bonbo's breath changed told Dan he had the man's attention.

"Word on the street is he's behind what happened at the mall on Eighteenth," Dan continued.

"I... I don't know anything about that," Bonbo said.

"I do," Dan said. His voice dropped into a growl. "You want details? I can give you details. Ninety-six adults. Thirty-eight children. Least, that's what they think. I'm told that piecing them together has been challenging."

"I don't know anything about it," Bonbo repeated, the words choking him. "I swear."

"I know you don't, Bonbo. I know you aren't mixed up in this. If I thought you were, this door would not still be standing," Dan said. "But I need to know for sure it was him. I need to know he sold the weapons. That's all. Just a yes or a no."

There was a *clank* from beyond the door as Bonbo's legs gave way and he landed heavily on the toilet seat.

"He'll kill me."

"He won't have a chance," Dan said. "One-hundred-and-thirty-four people, Bonbo. One-hundred-and-thirty-four."

The bathroom door squeaked open. Something with tusks and facial piercings shuffled in, fiddling with his belt.

"Occupied," Dan barked, snapping his head in the newcomer's direction. "Fonk off."

"But..."

Dan pushed back his hat, revealing the full horror of his decaying face. "Hold it in," he said, then the door squeaked again as Tusks beat a hasty retreat.

"Still with me, Bonbo?" Dan asked.

A cheep from inside the stall confirmed he was.

"Yes or no. That's all I need."

"N-no," Bonbo whimpered.

Dan clenched his jaw, both fists and, to a lesser extent, his buttocks. "Don't jerk me around, Bonbo," he warned, but he was barely halfway into the sentence when the voice from the stall became a shrill squeal of panic.

"*No, no, no, no, n—*"

Bonbo exploded. At least, that's how it seemed from the other side of the door. There was a visceral meaty sort of sound, then the filthy ceiling above the cubicle was pebble-dashed with blood, flesh, and fragments of bone.

Something black and pointy, like a blade fashioned from darkness itself, stabbed upwards, appearing briefly above the top of the stall door. Bonbo's head – or possibly just the top sixty percent or so of it – was impaled on the spiked tip. His eyes rolled forward then flopped out onto his cheeks. The top of his skull flapped open and closed as if on a hinge, then the head and the blade jerked sharply downwards out of sight.

Dan kicked open the door, his hand already reaching into his coat for Mindy. He caught a glimpse of an empty Bonbo-sized sack of skin just as it was yanked down into the toilet bowl. Blackish-brown water burbled up from the plumbing, then poured out over the seat. The liquid sloshed over the floor and into the one remaining shoe that sat upright on it, and which was now the only evidence that Bonbo had ever even been there. Unless you counted the blood, guts and brain matter on the ceiling, of course, in which case there was probably a good pint and a half of proof to confirm his presence at the scene.

Dan stepped back from the slowly expanding puddle. "Shizz," he muttered.

And he was right. It was.

DAN STEPPED out onto the street and found Ollie kneeling beside the fallen armadillo-thing. She had torn a strip off the bottom of her t-shirt, and was wrapping it around the armadillo's knee. The t-shirt itself had the slogan, *I'm Smiling Because I Have No Idea What's Going On* printed across the front. Artur had spotted it in a shop window and insisted on buying it for her. Or, more accurately, had insisted Dan buy it for her.

Ollie, for her part, didn't really get the joke, but she did like the color, so that was fine.

"What are you doing?" Dan asked.

Ollie and the armadillo both looked up. "You said to take care of him," Ollie replied.

Dan tutted. "No, that's not..."

"I tried to tell her, Deadman," said Artur. He was standing on the grille of the exodus, looking for all the world like a hood ornament. "I said that's not what ye meant, but she wouldn't listen. He means 'shoot him in the face' I said, not mollycoddle the big bastard. Am I right?"

Dan caught Ollie by the arm and hoisted her to her feet. "Come on, get in the car," he said.

"Oh. OK," Ollie said. She flashed a smile and a wave to the injured armadillo. "Get well soon."

"Uh... Thanks," he replied.

Dan bundled Ollie into the passenger seat, then walked around to the driver's side. Artur hopped into his coat pocket as Dan passed, and gave a little cheer of triumph when he landed safely inside.

Pulling open the door, Dan hesitated. He looked down at the armadillo-thing, then pointed to the bar. "The mess in the bathroom? Just so you know, that wasn't me."

The armadillo grunted with distaste. "Yeah, sure," he muttered. "That's what they all say."

TWO

"Exploded? What d'ye mean, he exploded? In what way did he fecking explode?"

"Outwards, mostly," said Dan.

"Ye know what I meant!" Artur replied. "*Why* did he explode?"

Dan shrugged and wrestled with the wheel of the Exodus until the car begrudgingly agreed to change lanes. As a general rule, the streets of Down Here were busy around the clock, but the sector Dan's office was located in was considered too dangerous for most people to go roaming around after dark, so traffic was lighter here.

"I don't know," Dan admitted. "One minute he was sitting on the toilet, the next, his insides were on the ceiling."

"Holy Father, that's an unfortunate way to go," Artur muttered. "I mean, I have had some *brutal* shoites in my time, but never to that extent."

"Something stabbed up at him out of the toilet," Dan said. "It... I don't know. It gutted him, or burst him, or something. Then it pulled him down."

"Down the bog?" said Artur. He whistled quietly. "No, that's a new one on me."

"Will he be OK?" Ollie asked.

Dan shot her a sideways glance. The Exodus took advantage of the momentary distraction and drifted into oncoming traffic. The blaring of horns forced Dan to face front again.

"No. No, he won't be OK," Dan said.

Ollie seemed saddened by this. "Are you sure?"

"He exploded, then his empty skin was dragged down the toilet," Dan said. "So yes, I'm pretty sure."

A cargo ship rose noisily from behind a building on the right, then roared up towards the blue glow of the floating cities far overhead. Everything inside the car rattled and squeaked until the din of the ship's engines faded into the general soundtrack of the city.

"It's a damn shame," Dan said, crunching down a gear and turning onto a side street that ran between two rows of crumbling old office blocks.

"Such a sad waste of life," Ollie agreed.

"No. I meant he was my only lead. Krato's got to have a bunch of guys working for him, but I'm fonked if I can find out who they are. I really thought Bonbo was going to talk."

He caught the look from Ollie.

"But sure, the waste of life thing, too."

The Exodus's brakes screeched in protest as Dan kangarooed the car to a stop behind a row of parked mag-levs. He cut the engine, but it chugged and rattled for several more seconds before spluttering into silence.

"Man, I hate this fonking car," he muttered, throwing open the door.

"Hold up, wait for me," Artur said, sliding down the dash and landing on Dan's lap. He clambered into the detective's coat pocket, then gave a thumbs-up. "All aboard."

Dan and Ollie both maneuvered their way out of the car and onto the sidewalk along the street from the office. It was only thirty feet or so to the door, but Dan unbuttoned Mindy's holster, just in case. It had been a while since anyone had tried anything around here, although after what he'd done to the first guy, that wasn't really a surprise. Still, there was no harm in being careful.

"Ye think yer man, Krato, did it?"

Dan shrugged. "Maybe."

"You think he came out of the toilet?" Ollie asked.

"Not him personally, no," Dan said. "But, I don't know. Maybe he arranged something. Or maybe Bonbo was just unfortunate."

"That's a fecking understatement," said Artur. "Impaled up the arsehole while doing yer dirty business? I'd call that more than a spot of misfortune."

Despite everything, Dan snorted. It wasn't a laugh, not really, but it was about as close as he was likely to get. He had no idea what it was about Artur's accent that made the translator chip's censorship function fail to sanitize his bad language, but on nights like this he was grateful for it.

"You have a point," he agreed, as they reached the door to the office block and Dan shoved it open.

Or tried to. The door was locked. This was unusual, to say the least. The door was never locked. Sure, it gave the impression of being locked to the casual onlooker, but one solid shove had always been enough to throw the thing wide open. Now, though, it held fast.

"It's locked," Dan said. It wasn't a particularly insightful observation, but it was the best he could currently come up with.

"Oh," said Ollie. She looked the door up and down. "What happens now?"

"We unlock it," said Artur, popping his head out of the pocket. "Ye do have a key, right, Deadman?"

Dan shook his head. "Never needed a key. Not for this one."

He put a shoulder to the door, in case it was stuck. It *thudded* in the frame but didn't budge.

"No, it's definitely locked."

"I can see now why ye went into the detective business," said Artur. "Sure, a steel trap mind like that'd be wasted in any other line of work."

Dan bent and examined the row of buttons next to the door. His name was up there near the top, but there was no point ringing that buzzer. "The building manager's on here somewhere," he said, struggling to make out the scratchy hand-written notices in the dark.

"Uh, there are some people watching us," Ollie said.

"Where?"

"Across the street," Ollie told him. She waved.

"Don't do that," Dan told her, still not looking.

She stopped waving.

"How many?" Artur asked.

"Three," she said, and Artur looked a little disappointed at that.

Dan shrugged. "Nothing to stop them looking. Last I checked, that's one of the few things still legal in this city."

"They're just three muggers, or what have ye," said Artur, leaning out of Dan's pocket so he could follow Ollie's gaze. "They're harmless enough. Nothing to worry about, Peaches."

"They look pretty serious," Ollie said.

"Sure, it's like me old mammy used to say, 'They're

15

more frightened of you than you are of them.'" His brow furrowed. "Or was that spiders? Whatever, I'm sure the same thing applies."

"Found it," said Dan. He pressed a button with his thumb and held it. From somewhere in the building came a faint but insistent *bzzzzzt.*

"I think they have knives," Ollie whispered.

"Good for them. Sensible," said Artur. "Ye certainly don't want to be wandering these streets at this time o' night without a weapon."

Ollie looked down at herself. "I don't have a weapon."

"Ye don't need one, Peaches," said Artur, winking at her. "Ye've got us. Also, ye're a feckin' demon-monster who nearly destroyed the entire city, so I reckon ye'll be fine. No offense, like."

"Keep an eye on them," Dan instructed, briefly meeting Ollie's gaze. She nodded.

"Will do."

A voice hissed from the door intercom. "What? For fonk's sake! What is it? Do you know what time it is?"

"It's Deadman," said Dan. "Top floor. We're locked out."

"Oh. *Deadman,*" said the voice, spitting out Dan's name like it had left a bad taste.

"Can you buzz us in?"

"No."

Dan looked from the intercom to the door and back again. "What?"

"You're evicted," the voice explained.

"Evicted?"

"That's right. E. Vic. Ted."

"He can't do that," Artur said. "Ye can't do that!"

"Wasn't me," the voice replied. "Government orders."

Dan frowned. "The Tribunal?"

"No. Big government. Higher up." His voice dropped to a whisper, as if just saying the word aloud might get him into trouble. "Krone. He's building an outpost."

Dan's eyebrows, which had been bunched around his nose, climbed all the way to where his hat met his head. "Krone? Why would Krone want to build an outpost here?"

"Again, you think I asked?" the voice hissed. "Point is, we're all out. They're taking over this whole street."

"Why?" Dan demanded.

The voice snorted. "You think I asked? You think they'd tell me if I did? We're out. Shut down. Everyone's stuff has already been shipped out."

"Deadman!" Artur said. "It's getting late. I need locking up for the night before I start getting too lairy for me own good."

"Shipped out? Shipped out where?"

"The Stagnates."

"You have got to be kidding me," Dan groaned.

"Anyone using the office space for habitation purposes – that's losers like you and me, Deadman – has been relocated to the Stagnates by order of the Tribunal."

"Oh yeah?" snapped Artur. "Then how come ye're still in there?"

"I'm not," said the voice. "The Tribunal hooked up a comm and told me it was my responsibility to answer it. I'm already in the Stagnates, and unless you want the city's finest hunting you down, I suggest you do the same."

"Now hold on—" Dan began.

"Goodbye, Mr Deadman," the voice said. "And good luck."

There was a soft *click* from the intercom.

It was followed, a moment later, by a second.

"And don't contact me again. I won't answer."

The intercom clicked for a final time.

"Hello? Hello? Damn it!"

Dan jammed his thumb against the button again and held it until it was clear no-one was going to respond.

"Son of a..." he grunted, releasing the button. He shook his head. "Could tonight get any worse?"

From behind him, Dan heard the unmistakable *shick* of a flick-knife opening.

"OK, give us your wallet and nobody gets hurt."

"Those men are here," Ollie whispered.

Dan sighed. "I told you to keep an eye on them."

"I did. They walked across the road."

"She's observant, all right," said Artur.

"The wallet. Hurry up, pops, or we start slicing!"

Dan looked down at Artur in his pocket. "Did he just call me 'pops'?"

Artur cracked his knuckles and sniggered. "He did that, Deadman. Ah well, at least the night's not a *total* write-off, eh?"

———

ONCE SOME PAINFUL lessons had been learned by the three knife-wielding men, Dan filled Ollie in on what he knew of the Stagnates.

The concept itself was sound enough. Down Here mostly existed to provide for the floating cities of Up There, and to do so it depended on a thriving workforce where everyone pulled their weight. As a result, being unemployed Down Here was punishable by imprisonment or death, and anyone without a job needed to have a damn good scam in place to ensure they didn't get found out.

The majority of the jobs available in the city were of the low-paying variety, and despite Down Here being a cancerous shizzhole, property prices were beyond the reach of many people.

That was where the Stagnates came in.

Squeezed between the sewer system and the city above, the Stagnates was a vast underground warren of undersized habitation pods, designed to house Down Here's working homeless. It had been a political points scorer back in the day – a shining example of how the Tribunal really cared for the city's less fortunate.

Forty years later, it was a cesspit – overpopulated to bursting point, and overflowing with the city's detritus. Riots broke out every few days. Fire ripped through whole sectors on a monthly basis. The official reports on the blazes were that they were all accidental, of course, but rumors persisted that the Tribunal set them deliberately to thin out the populace. Either way, it didn't make for a great living environment. And this was coming from someone who had, until half an hour ago, lived in a sparsely-furnished office.

"Can't we go somewhere else?" Ollie asked, as they approached a heavily-guarded gate in a tall fence. The fence ran for just five feet or so on either side of the gate, then turned at right angles, forming the sides of a small square. Inside the fenced-off area, a circular metal hatch stood open, revealing a dark hole in the ground.

The fence itself hummed with electrical energy, and while it appeared to be designed to keep people out, it was worth noting that the armed guards both stood on the inside of the fence.

"I want my stuff," Dan said. "Besides, short of sleeping in the car, we don't have a lot of choices. It'll just be for tonight. We'll find a new office tomorrow."

"Me arse," Artur said, but Dan folded the flap of his pocket closed, muffling him.

"Stay quiet," Dan instructed. "And don't move."

"Oho. Boss me around, would ye? Ye big bollock-headed gobshoite," Artur retorted, but to Dan's relief he didn't say any more.

Ollie took a deep breath and stumbled on behind Dan. She'd made the mistake of staring straight at the powerful spotlights shining down on the Stagnates entrance, and was now half-blinded.

There were entrances all over the city, some of them protected, like this one, others far less so, depending on where they were situated.

The guards moved behind the fence as Dan and Ollie approached. A blue trim illuminated along their armor and an opaque visor snapped down from each of their helmets, covering their faces. Officially, they were a division of the Tribunal, but the similarities between the armor designs were minimal. Power outages were common down in the Stagnates, and the glowing outfits came in handy sometimes. Riots were common, too, so the armor was heavy enough to take some serious licks, but flexible enough to allow for some strategic running away.

The guns they carried were the size of sawed-off shotguns, but with battery packs sticking sideways from each barrel. The elongated packs acted as second handles, giving the shooter a fighting chance at controlling the weapon's powerful kick, while providing enough charge to shut down one of those riots without having to switch batteries.

Both weapons whined as they were switched to *Ready Mode*.

"Halt!" barked one of the guards. The voice was female,

Dan thought, although the way the helmet amplified it made it difficult to say for sure. "State your business."

Dan kept walking for a few paces, then stopped when both guns took aim at him through slots in the gate. Up close, he could see a faint shimmering across the fence. Energy shielded. Made sense. Physical objects could pass through. Blaster bolts couldn't.

"We've been relocated," Dan said.

"At this time of night?" the female guard demanded.

Dan resisted the urge to point out that most relocations took place in the middle of the night, when the relocatee was too shocked and exhausted to put up much of a fight.

"We just found out," Dan said. "Came here as soon as we were informed."

The guard grunted in a way that suggested she was dissatisfied with this answer, but she didn't press it. She motioned to a scanner built into the gate and tapped a screen on her side a few times.

"How many?"

"Three," said Ollie.

"Two," Dan corrected. He held the guard's gaze through the mask. "Numbers aren't her strong point."

Neither guard moved for several painful seconds, then the tapping resumed.

"OK. Retina scan." The female guard pointed to Deadman. "You first."

Dan pushed back his hat, earning a little gasp from the other guard that he found both pleasing and just a tiny bit devastating. He had to bend forward a little to bring his left eye in close to the scanner.

"Hold still."

Dan did as he was told. His ID had been expensive, and

he'd been told at the time that it'd stand up to full Tribunal scrutiny. Guess he was about to find out.

The scanner emitted an angry-sounding *buzz* that made Ollie jump. A screen the size of a credit card snapped out of the scanner, a red X illuminating as it unfolded.

Shizz.

Still not moving his head, Dan unfastened one of his coat buttons.

The female guard tapped her screen a few more times, then looked Dan up and down. Beside her, the other guard adjusted the grip on his gun.

Dan unfastened a second button, and subtly slid his hand into the coat.

"Other eye," the guard barked.

Dan blinked. "Huh?"

"You used the wrong eye, dummy," the second guard said. It was the first words he had spoken, but Dan disliked him already.

Dan slipped his hand out of his coat, then shuffled sideways until his right eye was lined up with the scanner. It *bleeped* almost immediately, and the red X was replaced by a green smiley face.

"Now you," the first guard said, indicating Ollie with a tilt of her head.

Dan stepped aside and motioned to the scanner. Ollie, who was still suffering the effects of the spotlights, blinked rapidly and tried to study the device.

"Hold still."

Ollie looked at the guard. "Huh?"

"Don't look at me, look at the scanner."

"The what?"

Dan indicated a circle on the front of the device. "Stare into that part."

Ollie stared into it, then glanced at Dan. "Why, what's it going to do?"

"Just look at it."

Ollie looked at it.

"Closer," the first guard barked.

Ollie stepped back, suddenly alarmed. "Why is it going to get closer?"

Dan shook his head. "No. *You* get closer to *it*."

Ollie visibly relaxed. "Oh. OK. Got it."

She took a half-step closer. "Like this?"

"Bring your eye nearer to that part," Dan instructed, pointing again.

Ollie leaned forward and pressed her forehead against the cold metal of the scanner's front.

"Not that near," Dan sighed. He caught Ollie by the neck of her t-shirt and pulled her back a little. "There. Hold it there."

Ollie turned to Dan. "Here?"

"Face front!" the second guard snapped.

Ollie turned to him, startled.

"Don't look at him! Look at the scanner!" the first guard ordered.

"I *was* looking at the scanner," Ollie protested.

She looked at Dan.

"I was, right?"

"Ma'am, we're going to shoot you," the first guard warned. "We are going to shoot you if you don't look at the scanner right now!"

Ollie turned to the woman, but Dan caught her head and turned it back to the scanner. "Look there now," he instructed, pointing to the lens again.

"Like this?" Ollie asked, then the machine *bleeped* and the smiley face flashed up again. She smiled back at it. "Did

I win?"

"There are no winners here," Dan grunted, then the guns withdrew and the gate slid aside.

"You're free to enter," the first guard said. Her tone hadn't changed, despite the system granting its approval. If anything, she sounded even less amused than she had done a moment ago. "Take the ladder and pass through the security checkpoint. Your living areas have been assigned."

Dan stopped just inside the gate. "We're together, right?"

"Take the ladder. Pass through the security checkpoint," the woman reiterated. She pointed her gun at Dan, then motioned with it to the hatch. "All questions will be answered below."

Dan tapped the brim of his hat, then took Ollie by the arm and led her to the hatch. The gate closed heavily behind them.

"We will be together, won't we?" Ollie asked.

Dan tried a reassuring smile, but he was out of practice and, if he were honest, had never been great at them in the first place. "Guess we'll find out, kid."

He peered down into the shadowy corridor of the Stagnates below.

"I guess we'll find out."

THREE

Dᴀɴ ʀᴇᴀᴄʜᴇᴅ the bottom of the ladder first. A set of motion-activated lights blinked on, flooding the passageway with a clinical white glow. Two Sentinel Hoverturrets rose from charging docks in the floor and circled around, searching for something to lock onto. It wasn't until Ollie clambered down the ladder that they found a target. They set up an orbit around her, guns trained on her head.

"What are they doing?" she whispered.

"They track heat," Dan explained. "Just don't make any sudden movements."

Ollie froze.

"Regular movements are fine," Dan assured her. "Just don't try running. Or jumping. Or waving your arms around. Or..."

He frowned. "Actually, no. Just do what you were doing and stand still."

The passageway was approximately round and gave the impression that it had been drilled out with a lot of hurry and very little care. The floor had been flattened out a little, but it had been done so inexpertly they may as well not have bothered.

The area they stood in was fifteen feet long, with floor-to-ceiling mirrors blocking the corridor in both directions. The same smiley face they'd seen on the scanner flashed steadily near the top of one of the mirrors, while the other sported a solid red X.

"Looks like we go this way," Dan said, stepping closer to the mirror. The surface was slightly warped, deforming his already less-than-perfect features, and bloating him around the middle.

"Ha! Look at you," Ollie said, joining him at the mirror. She gasped. "Look at me! I'm fat. Now I'm thin! Now I'm fat!"

Dan let her wiggle and shimmy in front of the mirror until it became annoying. Or, to put it another way, he let her wiggle and shimmy in front of the mirror for four and a half seconds, then ordered her to cut it out.

"I told you, no sudden movements," he reminded her.

"Oh. Yeah. Forgot," said Ollie.

She leaned left and laughed as one of her arms briefly developed Elephantiasis, before Dan yanked her back upright again.

"Sorry. Forgot again."

"Weapon detected," chimed a voice from somewhere in the mirror. The smiley face's mouth moved in time with the words but remained fixed in its ridiculous grin.

A hatch slid open in the mirror, revealing the inside of a scratched and dented metal box. "Please deposit weapon for safe-keeping."

Dan hesitated, but there was no point in trying to argue. Weapons weren't permitted in the Stagnates. Not for the residents, anyway. The gun was registered – more or less –

so he'd get it back. Still, he felt a twinge of something like grief as he took Mindy from her holster and gently rested her inside the box.

"I want that returned when I leave," he said, but the cartoon face just smiled in reply. "And fully charged."

The hatch snapped shut as soon as his hand was out, and it was impossible to tell where the opening had been.

"Place hands on the indicated areas," the smiley face instructed.

The glowing outlines of four hands appeared on the mirror, two in front of Dan, the others in front of Ollie. Ollie lunged for them without hesitation, earning two *cheeps* of concern from the Hoverturrets.

Dan placed his own hands in the marked areas. A flurry of activity lit up the mirror as readings were taken and databases were accessed. Dan and Ollie's names appeared, along with several different serial numbers and codes.

Finally, two lines of text appeared, both different.

"Corridor eight-four-seven, pod nine-nine-four," Ollie read. She looked at the writing on the mirror in front of Dan, then to Dan himself. "What does that mean?"

"It's the location of your living quarters."

"Yours is different."

"I'm in eight-four-nine. That sounds pretty close. You'll be fine."

Ollie bit her lip. The one and only time she'd tried living somewhere Down Here without Dan, it hadn't ended well.

"What if someone tries to hurt me?"

"They won't," Dan said, doing his best to sound convincing. "You'll be fine."

The outlines faded. Ollie and Dan both removed their hands from the glass. "But what if they do?"

"Then hurt them back," Dan instructed. "Just try not to bring the whole place down when you do."

The mirror split down the middle and partially retracted into the walls, revealing two uniformed men standing at attention on the other side, who had presumably been there all along. Compared to those upstairs, the armor on these two was less obvious, and was built into something that resembled a Tribunal officer's dress uniform, but without the medal strips or the shiny buttons.

"You will follow us," they instructed in near-unison, then they both performed complicated about-turns and set off along the corridor, arms swinging with perfect, clock-work-like precision.

Another door slid open ahead of the escorts, and the Stagnates was revealed in all its glory. The featureless corridor was now lined with metal doors on both sides, all of them scorched and scratched and stained with things that didn't really warrant further investigation. Garbage bags were piled up outside most of the doors, and even though living with Dan had helped Ollie build up an impressive resistance to bad odors, she visibly flinched as the stench of the place hit her.

It was noisy, too. From behind every door came shouts, screams, coughs, crashes and cries. No laughing, though. Never laughing. There was no laughter here.

"It's hot," Ollie said, blowing upward over her own face. Beads of sweat stood out on her pinkish-purple skin, then meandered down the tapestry of alien patterns on her cheeks.

"Is it?" Dan asked. He shrugged. "You'll get used to it."

"She won't," said one of the escorts, although it wasn't clear which one. "Now keep up."

The escort on the left, who was ahead of Dan, turned sharply into a side corridor. "Eight-four-nine this way."

Dan stopped at the junction. The other escort marched on, but Ollie hung back.

"What if I never see you again?" she fretted. "What if something bad happens?"

"Nothing bad is going to happen," Dan assured her. He glanced around at where they'd found themselves. "Nothing worse, anyway. I'll find you in the morning and we'll get out of here."

"But what if you can't?" Ollie asked, her voice fraying a little at the edges.

Dan pulled his hat off his head, fiddled with it in front of him for a moment, then deposited it on her head. "Here. Take this. You know I always come back for my hat," he told her. "It'll protect you. Think of it as a lucky charm."

"I'll 'lucky charm' ye, ye racist bastard," mumbled a voice from inside the hat.

Dan winked. "You're going to be OK, kid. Trust me." He jabbed a thumb in the direction of Ollie's escort, who was already forty feet along the corridor. "Now go catch up. Keep your head down, play it cool, and everything will work out just fine," Dan said.

She hugged him. He wasn't quite sure how to react, so he just stood there, staring impassively at the wall ahead of him.

He watched her dart off after the escort, holding the brim of the hat to stop it falling off her head.

"I hope," he mumbled, then he turned and plodded into the half-darkness.

DAN'S CELL – BECAUSE 'ROOM' would have been an overly generous description – wasn't too far from the junction. This was its one and only redeeming feature. It didn't come close to making up for the rest of it.

The escort had told him to report to the nearest 'Education center' in the morning, then left him to grapple with the voice-activated door. It was either malfunctioning, or it didn't like him, and it took six attempts at getting the thing to recognize his voice pattern before one of his bunkmates got fed up of listening to the fonking thing and opened it from the inside.

The guy who opened the door was short and stocky, with the most pointed nose Dan had ever seen. His head and face were a tangled nest of hair, beard and eyebrows, and his red-raw skin looked like someone had recently set about him with an industrial sander.

He wore a cashier's uniform from one of the big supermarket chains, and from his expression he'd either just got off a long shift or was dreading the thought of an upcoming one.

"Thanks," Dan said, nodding down at the four-feet-tall figure. He gestured to the door. "Is it broken?"

"What am I, maintenance?" the cashier spat. "Just get in before you attract attention."

Dan looked along the corridor in both directions. There were at least three people watching him from other doorways, tucking themselves in to try to stay out of sight. He raised a hand in a wave of acknowledgment, then stepped into the cell.

Something cracked him on the back of the head and the floor became quicksand beneath him. There was a set of metal bunks on the wall on the right. He grabbed for the frame and stopped himself falling, but the cashier was suddenly on Dan's back, fists hammering him around the head and face.

Dan turned sluggishly. Something fat and semi-naked advanced on him, fists raised. Its skin was ice-white but patterned by a network of blue veins running just beneath it. A pair of tight red trunks covered its modesty, but only just.

While lacking in clothes, the guy wore a determined expression and two sets of *Knuck'em-ups* – metal knuckles with an added electrical kick. They were mostly illegal in the city, even more so in the Stagnates.

Stepping forward, Dan raised his arms to protect his head, completely exposing his torso. A flurry of surprisingly fast body blows pounded his stomach and ribs. If he'd needed to breathe, or had any functioning pain receptors south of his neck, it would've been a punishing attack. As it was, it just bought him five seconds to pull himself together.

Clutching at his ribs, Dan left his head wide open. One of the fists came up fast, barely giving him time to duck. He both heard and felt the immensely satisfying *crunch* of the knuckles connecting with the cashier's face. The little fonker tried to scream, but the electricity had tightened his muscles and clamped his jaw tightly shut.

Bending sharply, Dan launched the cashier at the other guy. Their heads *clonked* pleasingly, and Dan took advantage of the flailing and confusion by introducing his boot to the fat thing's (mercifully covered) testicles.

Both men hit the floor at pretty much the same time. Neither looked pleased by this turn of developments. Neither looked like they could breathe properly, either, which was a bonus.

The fat guy clutched at his groin, apparently having forgotten he was wearing electrically charged weapons on both hands. His flabby body went briefly rigid, and a howl whistled down his nose.

Dan smoothed a crease on his coat lapel, then crossed his hands behind his back, waiting for the groaning, sobbing, and involuntary urination to stop.

At first glance, he'd thought the larger of the two men was merely obese, but now he was able to look more closely, Dan realized a lot of the guy's bulk was muscle, albeit with a layer of blubber on top.

His face was concave, his eyes set deep below his over-hanging forehead, his chin jutting upwards to a squared-off point. There was a lump just above one of his eyes, although from the way it was growing Dan guessed that was a recent development.

"Thanks for the welcome," Dan said. He looked around the sparse cell and sighed. He'd thought being both home-less and dead was depressing, but this place really upped the ante.

Aside from the bunkbeds he'd already encountered, the room contained a single slop bucket in the corner, a small stool that even from this distance looked agonizingly uncomfortable, and a lingering aura of misery.

A poster had been fixed to the bare stone walls. It read: *Work is Necessary.* That was it. No cute wordplay. No motivational images. Just those three words in stark black text on a white background. Incredibly, as an attempt to brighten the place up, it mostly succeeded, which said more about the cell than the poster itself.

The two beds thing was going to be a problem. Although, it should be said, not for him.

"Top bunk's mine," he informed them, not keen on the idea of having the big behemoth on the bunk above. "Any objections?"

He took their grunts and groans as acceptance. "Wise move," he said.

The big brute found the strength to sit up. Dan's foot sent him back to the floor. "Now," Dan said, towering above them. "How about you tell me where I can find my stuff?"

"QUARANTINED? What do you mean it's quarantined?"

"I mean it's quarantined. Quaran-*tined*. You want me to write it down, dummy? It's an awfully big word for that little brain of yours."

Dan stared at the curly-haired old woman behind the screen. She was sitting back in a wooden chair, one hand half-buried in a bag of mints. Dan could hear one of the hard candies rattling against her teeth whenever she spoke.

"And wipe that stupid look off your face," she instructed. "And close your damn mouth before I close it for you."

Dan hadn't realized his mouth was hanging open. He was fairly sure the five feet tall blue-haired senior citizen sitting in the chair would be unable to carry out her threat, but he closed it anyway.

"Ha! You always do what you're told like that, dicksticks?"

Dan blinked. "Dicksticks?"

"Hey!" the woman barked.

She leaned forward and tapped the back of a sign that had been taped to the transparent screen. It read: 'Verbal or physical abuse will not be tolerated.'

"Consider that your one and only warning," she told him. She reclined and waved the back of her hand at him. "Now go. Shoo. You're uglying the place up."

To his annoyance, Dan found himself turning. It took some effort to make his feet stop.

"Look..." he squinted until he could read the badge on the woman's lapel. "Notty. I want my stuff."

The chair creaked as Notty leaned forward again. "And I told you, you animal-fondling shizz trumpet, you can't have it. It's in quarantine."

Dan pointed to a battered filing cabinet and a couple of cardboard boxes lined up against the wall behind her. An overcoat, identical to the one he was wearing, and a battered old hat could just be seen at the top of one box.

"Then what's that?"

Notty looked back over her shoulder, then gasped. "Oh! That? You know what that is?"

She faced front again.

"It's none of your fonking business, that's what." She smiled sweetly. "Got that? You colon sniffing tit hole."

Dan found himself blinking again. His eyebrows formed a knot above his nose. "Tit hole?"

"Right! That's it!" Notty announced. "You had your warning. Language like that isn't acceptable."

She jabbed a button under the desk. A klaxon sounded and the room's lights blinked out. "What the fonk is this?" Dan demanded, but then he became aware of movement behind him.

And on his left.

And – yep – there it was on his right, too.

His night vision was good enough for him to make out the shapes of several figures, although he couldn't tell what they looked like, or even where they'd come from. He got the impression they wore masks, though, and hazarded a guess that no matter how good his night vision was, theirs would almost certainly be better.

"Hang on, not so fast. I like to watch," said Notty. There was a rustling sound, and when she next spoke her voice was muffled by a mask of her own. "There. On you go."

Dan felt the buzzing of a shock-rod against his back, but it barely registered as information, let alone pain. He turned, caught the weapon, and drove an elbow into the mask of his attacker, crumpling it into the guy's face.

Twisting, Dan jammed the shock-rod into the stomach of one of the other figures and felt the vibration rattle through his skeleton as it unleashed its charge. He allowed himself just a moment to enjoy the guy's gargled cries, then immediately regretted it when something hard hit him even harder on the back of the head.

"That's it! Get the fonkfaced sock stuffer!" Notty hissed as Dan's legs were swept out from beneath him, sending him partly horizontal in the air, then fully horizontal on the ground.

A baton went *crack* just above one eyebrow, filling Dan's head with light and noise. He raised his hands to protect himself, but four arms wrenched them away, and a boot stamped his face into the floor.

Brain fogging, he reached into his coat for Mindy, and was briefly surprised to find the gun missing.

"Shizzzzz. F-forgot," he slurred, then something hit him across the bridge of the nose. The last thing he heard was the excited squeals of the woman behind the screen shouting something about a 'leg-humping spunk nugget' and then the already darkened room became marginally darker, and silence poured in through his ears.

"PSST."

"Wha—?"

Dan's eyelids scraped open, saw that everything was blurry, so closed again.

"*Psst!*"

Dan grunted.

Psst. Someone was saying, 'Psst' at him. Not making a *psst* sort of sound, but saying it like it was an actual word.

Idiot.

"Dude. Psst. Wake up, brah."

"I'm awake," Dan said.

Or... had that just been in his head?

"I'm awake," he said again, being sure to voice it aloud this time.

"Oh, dude. That's awesome! I was starting to think you were dead."

"I am dead," Dan confirmed.

There was a moment of silence.

"Oh. Well, my condolences, brah."

Dan forced his eyes open again. This time, the world was less blurry, but only just. With some effort he shuffled himself onto his elbows. Pain flashed like lightning inside his skull, but he gritted his teeth and ignored it.

"Hey, I wouldn't sit up, dude. Those goobers did a real number on you. You're lucky they didn't kill you."

"Again, already dead," Dan replied. He rubbed his eyes with a finger and thumb, then blinked a few times. A bronzed young man with dirty blond hair tied back in a loose ponytail squatted beside him, his facial expression slap-bang in the sweet spot between 'confused' and 'concerned'.

"Who the fonk are you?" Dan asked.

"Name's Finn. Finn Cariss," the guy replied, smiling and showing off one of the most impeccable sets of teeth

Dan had ever seen. "Well, technically it's Finalan, but most folks call me—"

"Alright, alright. I didn't ask for your life story," Dan muttered. He started to get up, and shrugged off Finn's attempt to help.

They were still in the room where Dan had taken the beating, but the screen the old woman had been sitting behind was now encased in the same mirror material he and Ollie had encountered when they'd first arrived. The word 'closed' flashed on the surface.

"Damn it," Dan grunted.

"Yeah, they shut up shop maybe an hour ago."

"An hour? How long was I out?"

Finn shrugged. "Ninety minutes. Give or take."

Dan rubbed his head where it ached. Which was every-where. "And what? You waited here the whole time?"

"Couldn't just go leaving you, brah," Finn replied. "Some of the people down here... Well, they're not very friendly. No saying what they'd have taken."

"I haven't got much of anything to take," Dan said.

"Arms, legs, teeth, eyes," Finn said, pointing to the various parts of Dan's body. "You've got enough."

"Seriously?" Dan winced. "This place is worse than I thought."

Finn nodded. "You can say that again, brah. Most newbies are lucky to survive the first couple of nights these days, but once you get past those then things tend to get..."

He stumbled as Dan shoved past him, the detective's coat swishing out behind him as he broke into a run. "Hey, where you going, brah?"

Ollie.

Dan barreled through the door and out into the corridor, where he immediately stumbled over a garbage bag, ripping it open and spilling the contents across the floor.

He kicked through the debris and ran on, frantically searching the fog of his aching head for the address that Ollie had been given. Behind him, Finn shouted a, "Take it easy, dead dude," but Dan ignored it and pressed on past the doorways and the garbage and the impending sense of dread.

What had the address been? Pod nine-nine-four. Corridor... what? Eight-four-seven, he thought, although he had no idea what corridor he was in now, so that information alone didn't help him much.

He raced on, following what he hoped was the route back to his own place. At least from there he'd have a starting point to work from, although he'd wandered for so long trying to find Property Storage he couldn't be sure he was headed in even vaguely the right direction.

His boots scuffed along the rough stone floor as he hurtled around a bend in the passageway. A group of prehistoric-looking creatures were bunched together around a doorway up ahead, laughing and jeering as they passed around a cigar-shaped metal pipe.

One of them – a rough-scaled yellowish guy in a gray jumpsuit – spotted Dan approaching and nudged the others. By the time Dan reached them, all five of the figures were watching him, their chests puffed out, their bony neck frills raised.

The largest of the five had the end of the pipe clutched between his teeth. His beady black eyes looked Dan up and down as he stumbled to a stop.

"What corridor is this?" Dan demanded.

"Why the fonk should we tell you?" the guy with the pipe snapped back, squaring his shoulders.

Dan slammed the heel of his hand against the end of the pipe, sending it straight to the back of the guy's throat, making his eyes bulge.

"What corridor is this?"

"Shizz, OK, OK!" said the guy in the jumpsuit. "It's eight-four-six!"

The leader hacked and wheezed while various members of the gang frantically pounded his back.

"Where's eight-four-seven?"

"Up there, next right," explained Jumpsuit. "Can't miss it."

"See, that wasn't so hard, was it?" said Dan. He drove a fist into the choking guy's stomach and the pipe was ejected in one sharp, sudden cough. "Next time, less of the attitude," he warned them, and then he was off running again, barely able to believe his luck.

Ollie was in the next corridor over, pod number nine-nine-four. He'd be there in no time.

Dan took the next turn on the right and stopped outside a pod door. Half-hidden by all the scratches, scorch-marks and graffiti was a number.

It read: One.

Turning, Dan looked along the passageway ahead of him. It stretched off for half a mile or more before curving out of sight.

"Oh, you have got to be fonking kidding me..."

FOUR

As SOMEONE who didn't breathe, it was physically impossible for Dan to get out of breath. Clearly, no one had passed the message on to his lungs, though, and by the time he'd reached the door to pod nine-nine-four he felt like his chest was about to implode.

"Ollie! Artur!" he wheezed, hammering a fist against the metal.

"Please state your name," the door panel chimed.

"Oledol Lodelo," Dan said.

"Voice print not recognized."

"Damn it. Ollie! Artur! You in there?" Dan cried, hammering again.

No reply.

Fonk! He'd told her she'd be OK. He'd told her nothing bad was going to happen, and now—

The door slid aside revealing Ollie sitting in a plastic chair. A hulking multi-limbed figure was behind her, its tentacle-like arms snaking across her shoulders and around her neck. Dan caught a flash of two silver blades, then he was charging across the room, fist drawing back.

He connected with the thing right between its disproportionately small eyes. It crumpled to the floor, its arms immediately going limp, the blades clattering across the rough stone.

"What are you doing?" Ollie yelped, jumping up.

"What do you mean, *what am I doing*? I'm saving you," Dan said. He glanced at her, then did a double-take. Her hair was shorter on the right side than it was on the left.

Dan looked down at the blades on the floor.

Scissors.

"Saving me from a haircut?"

"Smooth, Deadman. Real smooth."

Artur was sitting on the edge of the bed, blowing gently on his brightly painted fingernails. He had a white facecloth wrapped around himself like a towel, and his own hair had been neatly trimmed at the sides.

"I mean, if ye didn't approve of the style, ye could've just said something."

Ollie squatted beside the fallen... whatever it was.

"Banbara? Banbara, are you OK?"

Banbara emitted an inquisitive sort of groan.

"Are you hurt?"

Barbara moaned in the affirmative.

"I thought she was trying to kill you," Dan explained.

Ollie looked up. "Why would she be trying to kill me?"

"Pretty much everyone I've met since we got here has tried to kill me," Dan said.

"Is that why ye look like a big bag o' shoite?" Artur asked. "More than usual, I mean."

Ollie gave Banbara a shake, but the response was limited to another couple of groans.

"I think ye've properly messed the girl up there, Deadman," Artur said. "I mean, I'm no expert on the subject, but

I think we can safely say she's brain-damaged. Well done. Ye've made her a vegetable. And with poor Peaches's hair only half-finished."

"She had a weapon. Weapons. Plural. What was I supposed to do?"

Artur gave his fingernails another blow. "It's a tricky one, alright," he admitted. "But maybe *not* punching the poor cow unconscious might've been a start. I don't know, d'ye think that might've been an avenue worth exploring, maybe?"

Banbara's tentacles all jerked at once. Her marble-sized eyes fluttered open. "Ow! What the *fonk*?"

"She's OK," Dan said, visibly relaxing. "She's fine. No harm done."

"My legs! I can't feel my legs!"

Dan shuffled uncomfortably and very deliberately avoided Artur and Ollie's gazes. "They'll be fine. The feeling, that'll come back," he said. One of her feet twitched and Dan cried out in triumph. "See? Her foot moved. She's fine."

"Uh, can I be the judge of that?" Banbara snapped. She prodded gingerly at her face, which sported a fist-sized indent. With some concentration, she managed to 'pop' the dent back out again.

One of her tentacles pointed accusingly at Dan, while the others raised her into a sitting position. "Give me one good reason why I shouldn't get security in here right now, mister."

Dan opened his mouth to reply, then sighed. "No. I got nothing." He held a hand out to her. "Sorry, I guess that was my fault."

"You *guess* it was your fault?" said Ollie. "You punched her in the face."

"Or was it partly her fault for having her face right there in front of yer fist?" Artur asked. "Is there shared blame? Is that what ye're sayin'?"

"OK, it *was* my fault," Dan grunted. "Banbara, I apologize. It was my mistake. Let me make it up to you."

Banbara scowled. "How?"

Dan hesitated. "Uh..."

He bent down and picked up both pairs of scissors, then held them out to her. "There."

Artur snorted. "Ye're a man of grand gestures alright, Deadman," he said.

Dan shot him a look. "Shouldn't you be locked up for the night?"

Artur shrugged. "Banbara gave me a massage. Worked the anger issues right out of me, so it did. She's a miracle worker, that one."

"Oh."

"And ye punched her in the face."

"Right."

"Just square in her face."

"I get it. And I apologize again."

He set the scissors down on the chair Ollie had been sitting on, then puffed out his cheeks. "So, uh, I guess if everyone's OK..."

Dan saw his hat hanging from a hook by the door. He took it down and squashed it roughly into shape, then placed it on his head. "Let's meet in the breakfast hall in the morning and we can figure out our plans. It's back the way we came in. Big place, can't miss it."

Ollie nodded. "OK. Yeah. Let's do that."

"Maybe try and not spangle this poor bastard next time ye see her," Artur said, gesturing down at Banbara. "Just a thought, like."

Dan tapped the brim of his hat. "Uh, sorry again," he told Banbara, then he looked from Ollie to Artur and back again. "Guess I'll see you in the morning," he said, stepping backward through the open door. He started to say more, but the door snapped shut between them, leaving him alone in the corridor.

Raising a hand, he considered knocking again, then realized he had no idea what he'd say if anyone answered. He turned away and started on the trek back to his own pod, instead.

"What a fonking day," he grunted, then he pulled up his collar, pulled down his hat, and pressed on through the shouts, cries and sobs that seeped under the doors lining the corridor.

DAN LAY on the top bunk staring up at the ceiling, idly reading the graffiti etched into the rock. Much of it was about the Stagnates' guards. Some of it was about the Tribunal. One was about someone called 'Korolina' who could apparently be counted on for 'a good fun time'.

A couple of other people had been less complimentary about both Korolina and the services she provided, scratching their misspelled reviews beneath the original statement. Korolina was either too much of a 'dirty bedge' or not enough of one, depending on who you believed. It seemed the poor woman couldn't win.

Dan sympathized.

Gunnak, the smaller of his roommates was lying on the floor at the opposite end of the room from the slop bucket, nestled on a pile of coats like a cat. Tor, the other, much larger guy, took up the bunk below. The frame shook every time he moved, and Dan had spent the first twenty minutes or so convinced the whole thing was going to come crashing down at any moment.

He tucked a hand behind his head and closed his eyes. His skull still ached from the beating he'd taken, but his lack of blood flow meant the bruising hadn't come to much.

After taking off his coat and patting himself down he'd concluded that at least one rib was broken, possibly two. His left arm was dislocated at the elbow, but he'd been able to pop that back in without too much difficulty. It was probably the most positive development of the past twenty-four hours.

Damn, that was a depressing thought.

The memory of the exploding guy in the bathroom stall coughed politely somewhere at the back of his head. With all the stuff about the office, the Stagnates, and the getting the shizz kicked out of him, he'd mostly forgotten that.

Dan had been sure the guy was about to spill his guts, but he'd expected it to happen in a metaphorical sense, not a literal one. He'd been so close to getting information from him, only for... what? Something to come out of the toilet? That was about the only conclusion he could draw. Something had come out of the toilet, explosively murdered him, then dragged what was left down into the sewers.

What a way to go. Still, at least Dan could take comfort in the fact that *someone* was having a worse day than he was.

A blade stabbed through him from below. He heard the *shikt* of it passing through the thin mattress, then saw it emerge through his stomach just a little left of center.

Tor's face appeared as he emerged from the bottom

bunk. His eyes were narrow slits, his mouth twisted into a triumphant grin. The knife twisted in Dan's gut, ruining another perfectly good shirt.

"Not so full of yourself now, are you? Not the big 'I am' now!" Tor hissed. "You see what happens? You see what happens when you come in here and try to throw your weight around, you ugly piece of— Urk."

Dan hooked a finger into Tor's single nostril and jerked him closer. "I suggest you shut the fonk up and go back to bed," he warned. "If you're lucky, I might pretend this was all just a dream, and say no more about it. If you're unlucky, I might not."

Tears rolled down Tor's cheeks as Dan wriggled his finger further into the cavernous nostril. "Do we have an understanding? Have I made myself clear?" Dan asked him. "Nod for yes."

Despite the finger currently probing deep inside his nasal cavity, Tor glanced at the knife sticking out of Dan's guts, then managed a single nod.

"Good call," Dan said, yanking his finger free with a slightly mucusy *pop*. He wiped the fingertip on Tor's cheek, then gave him a pat.

The bed shook as Tor clambered back into the bunk. Dan caught the eye of Gunnak, who had been watching the whole thing. The little man quickly closed his eyes and pretended to be asleep, which Dan fully approved of.

Relaxing onto the pillow, Dan waited.

"You might want to take the knife out," he said.

There was a pause, then a *swishkt* as the knife withdrew.

Dan prodded the hole in his shirt, then the one in his stomach.

Yep. What a fonking day. Still, tomorrow could only be better.

Or so he thought.

FIVE

Ollie and Artur were already in the breakfast hall when Dan arrived, although it was something of a miracle that he was able to find them.

The dining area was a vast cavern with hundreds of long metal tables bolted to the stone floor. A metal walkway ran around the walls halfway up, creating a sort of balcony on which dozens of other tables had been arranged.

Ten food stations had been set up around the room, each one operated by six staff. They all dispensed the same identical-looking yellow slop to the queues of hungry patrons impatiently awaiting their rations.

The room rang out with the clatter of plates, the hubbub of a thousand different conversations, and several accusatory shouts and accusations. Further into the room, near one of its many exits, a big green thing pushed a big blue thing in the chest. The big blue thing retaliated, then they both spasmed violently as taser snipers took them out from the balcony above.

The rest of the queue stepped over their twitching, semi-conscious bodies, acting like this sort of thing happened all the time. Which, Dan reckoned, it probably did.

Ollie had managed to find a space at a table near the door, and waved Dan over when she'd spotted him through the crowds. Banbara sat on Ollie's left. She sported several knuckle-sized bruises on her face, and scowled at Dan when he joined them at the table. Artur took up a chair on Ollie's right, but hopped up onto the tabletop when Dan arrived.

"Been keeping it warm for ye," said Artur. He gestured at a bowl of the yellow mush in front of him. "Unlike the scran, which is feckin' freezing. Ye want some?"

"What is it?" asked Dan, taking the offered seat before any of the circling tray carriers could swoop in and steal it.

"It's yellow," said Artur. "That's pretty much the only thing I can say about it. It's cold and yellow. Oh, and it tastes like shoite."

"I'll pass," said Dan.

"Ye're a wise man," Artur said. He scooped some of the sunshine-colored sludge into his mouth and pulled an exaggerated grimace. "See? Foul stuff."

"And yet you're still eating it," Dan pointed out.

"Well sure, I'm a growing lad," Artur replied, digging in for another helping. "Are ye not going to compliment Peaches on her hair."

Dan looked at Ollie's head. "It's... shorter?" he said, mostly guessing. There was definitely something different, but he couldn't pinpoint what.

"Nice work, Detective. Ye cracked that case, alright," Artur said. "No flies on you. Although quite why that is, I don't know, what with ye being a right smelly dead bastard."

"It looks nice," Dan said, even though he had absolutely no opinion on it either way.

Ollie seemed pleased, though. "Thanks. It was all Banbara."

Dan leaned past Ollie and addressed the multi-limbed woman on Ollie's left. "How's the... Uh..."

"The face? How's my face? Is that what you're asking?" Banbara snapped. "How is my face after you punched it? You tell me. How does it look?"

"It looks... I mean..."

Artur intervened. "I think the phrase ye're searching for is, 'like a well-skelped arse,'" he said. "And sure, it's even worse now with all the bruises. No offense, Ban."

Banbara stood up sharply, rattling the table. "I'm going to the bathroom," she announced.

Ollie slurped some of the yellow goo, then looked up. "Wait? There are bathrooms?"

"Not in the rooms, but in here," Banbara confirmed, gesturing to one of the many doors around the hall. "Why? Do you need to go?"

Ollie closed one eye and concentrated for a moment. The expression quickly changed to one of panic and she leaped to her feet. "Didn't but now I do!" she yelped, crossing her legs. One of Banbara's many limbs caught Ollie by the arm.

"This way. Follow me."

"Hurry!" Ollie urged, and they both scampered off, Banbara shoving her way through the crowds, Ollie hobbling along at her back.

"So," began Artur, once they'd gone. "How was your night?"

Dan tilted his head left to right a little. "Well, I was attacked in my room. I had all my stuff put into quarantine, then was beaten unconscious by security and left for dead. I accidentally punched a hairdresser in the face, then I was stabbed in the back with such force the knife came all the way out through my stomach."

Artur nodded slowly. "The usual, then?"

"Pretty much," Dan conceded. "The sooner we get out of this place the better."

"Hey! Dead guy!"

Dan and Artur both looked round to see a tanned muscular figure sliding into Ollie's chair, a tray balanced expertly in one hand.

"Seat's taken," Dan grunted, but the newcomer just grinned back at him.

"It's me. It's Finn. From last night?"

Artur snorted. "From last night? Ye didn't tell me ye'd had a gentleman caller, Deadman. Ye sly old dog, ye."

"Shut up, Artur," Dan sighed.

"Here, there's no harm in it. Each to their own, ye know. That's what I say."

Dan decided to ignore him.

"I know who you are," he told Finn. "But seat's still taken. Sorry."

"It's fine, brah. I'm a fast eater," Finn said, slurping down an impressive amount of the gunk to prove his point. "See?" he said, then half of the contents of his mouth spilled out over his chin and down onto his vest.

"Fine. Eat up and get going," Dan told him.

Artur strolled along the tabletop, passing between Dan and the cactus-faced creature sitting opposite, who was gazing forlornly into his food as he scooped it resentfully into his mouth.

Stopping by Ollie's bowl, Artur leaned back and looked up at the new arrival. He was dressed like a surf bum. Artur, on the other hand, was dressed in hot pink leggings and a turquoise roll-neck sweater with floppy cuffs that made him think of a wizard's robe. Quite where he'd gotten them from, Dan could only speculate.

"Well now. Who might you be?" Artur asked.

Finn, to his credit, didn't seem the least bit put out by a tiny bearded figure in women's clothing questioning him. "I'm Finn. Finn Cariss."

"Are ye now? Is that a fact?" Artur said, narrowing his eyes. "And how d'ye know old scrotum-face here?"

"I don't. Not really," Finn admitted. "I saw him getting messed up by some goobers last night, and hung off to make sure no one... took advantage."

"Did ye now? Did ye really? Ye saw some lads layin' boots into him, and ye kindly stuck around to play guardian angel, did ye? Just out of the goodness of yer heart?"

Finn slurped up some mush, then nodded. "Yeah."

Artur's face brightened. "Ah well, good on ye, then. Fair play. Any friend o' Deadman's is a friend o' mine," Artur said. "Actually, no, that's not true at all. Sure, some of them are unbelievable arseholes. But I'm prepared to give ye the benefit o' the doubt, and that's the main thing."

Dan cleared his throat. "Art. Two o'clock."

Artur turned his head just enough to look over his left shoulder. "I see them," he said.

An ugly knot of brutish-looking alien types was pulling together over by one of the other tables. Dan's roommate, Tor, was in amongst it all. He and some of the others glanced over at Dan, then muttered quietly between themselves.

"More friends o' yours?"

"Remember I said someone stabbed me?" Dan said. "Big guy sitting on the edge of the table."

"Someone *stabbed* you?" said Finn, his eyes widening.

"Are you OK?"

"Kid, at some point the phrase, 'I'm already dead,' is going to sink in. Why not make that happen now, and save us both some time?"

"Think they're going to try anything?" Artur asked.

Dan nodded, just once. "I guarantee it."

Artur's face split into a beaming smile. "Ye know," he said, cracking his knuckles and slipping his feet out of his plastic stilettos. "I was hoping ye might say that."

OLLIE FINISHED FASTENING her pants and leaned against the cubicle door. "Phew. That's *so* much better," she breathed. "That was close."

The bathroom had been full to bursting when they'd arrived, but Banbara had faked a vomiting episode when one of the stall doors had opened, and hurriedly dragged Ollie inside, brushing off the objections of those standing waiting.

The toilet groaned as Banbara lowered herself onto it, covering her modesty with two of her tentacle arms. "You don't mind if I go quickly, do you?" she asked.

"Hmm? Oh, no," said Ollie. "I'd have peed myself if you hadn't got us in. You go ahead."

"Thanks," said Banbara.

She grunted.

Something heavy splashed into the water beneath her. For some reason, she maintained constant, unwavering eye contact throughout.

Ollie shifted uncomfortably and looked up at the ceiling.

Banbara strained. Her tentacles trembled.

"Ung," she ejected.

There was another splash.

"There it goes," Banbara mumbled. "Two down..."

She braced four of her tentacles on her hefty thighs and groaned like she was in the process of giving birth.

"Here we go for the big finish," she announced in a slightly breathless whisper.

Ollie became fascinated with her own fingers. She studied them with a level of intensity she'd never studied anything in her life before. She wasn't sure why, exactly, but it was preferable to watching anything else that may or may not currently be taking place in the confines of the bathroom stall.

"Hnng. Hoofra."

Ollie whistled quietly.

"Unnnnnk! Nearly there. It's on the cusp..."

Ollie whistled slightly less quietly.

"Here... we... g—!" Banbara cried, then something black and spikey erupted up from the toilet bowl and out through the top of her head, spraying Ollie in blood and innards and substances even more unpleasant.

Somehow, despite the pointy appendage currently skewering her like a kebab, Banbara managed to scream. It was a half-hearted rasping sort of thing, like air escaping from the neck of a balloon, but it was enough to get on the nerves of whatever had spiked her.

Ollie pressed herself flat to the stall door, frozen in terror, as the appendage thrashed left and right, smashing Banbara against both walls.

"Hey, what the fonk? Keep it down in there," barked a female voice from the next cubicle over, then the voice became a gargle as another of the spikes stabbed up from inside the toilet bowl and ripped through her.

A series of choking cries rang out as blood and brain matter splattered against the ceiling above all of the stalls. Ollie started reaching a hand out to Banbara, but she quickly realized it was a pointless gesture. Most of what had been inside Banbara was now in various locations outside her. Her skin was a gelatinous sack flapping limply on the thrashing spike.

Spinning, Ollie struggled frantically with the door lock. By the time she stumbled out of the stall, the bathroom was empty, everyone else having sensibly opted to leg it the moment heads started to go pop.

Stunned, and dripping with assorted bodily fluids, Ollie stumbled for the bathroom door. As she reached it, she glanced back and saw the spiked appendage in her cubicle retreat down into the plumbing, dragging Banbara's now fully empty skin with it.

A moment later, the toilet flushed, but Ollie was already staggering out of the bathroom, and so didn't notice.

She stopped just outside the bathroom door, and stared in horror at the scene before her. A riot had broken out in the dining hall. Fists and feet and flailing figures were flying in all directions. Bowls were being smashed over heads, while trays were doubling as makeshift shields. The tables were bolted down, but at least two of them had been ripped free, and one was now being used to battering-ram a small crowd of stumpy-legged creatures who clearly didn't want to get too involved.

The place was an uproar of shouts, screams and taser fire. Ollie turned, panicked, searching for an exit as heads, bodies and limbs went *whump* and *crunch* and *crack* around her.

Something large and hairy came staggering past her,

grabbing in vain at a tiny figure scrabbling around on its back.

"Ye alright there, Peaches?" Artur asked, screwing a stiletto heel into the spine of the hairy thing and forcing a howl from it. "It's just that, between you and me, like, ye appear to be covered in guts."

"B-Banbara," Ollie stammered.

Artur clambered up onto the hairy thing's back and shoved an arm into its dog-like ear, making it yelp in pain. "Banbara did this? Shoite. Don't tell Deadman or we'll never hear the fecking end of it."

"Dead. She's... Banbara's dead."

"She's dead?" Artur said. The hairy creature grabbed for him, but he bit its finger, making it pull back. "D'ye mind? We're trying to have a fecking conversation here."

He yanked on the thing's hair, dragging its head back. Once he was sure it was going to behave itself, he turned back to Ollie.

"Well, good on ye, Peaches. Don't you stand for any shoite from no one, even if they did make a cracking job of yer hair."

Ollie shook her head. "N-no. Wasn't me. She... she... there was a thing. In the bathroom. It... I don't know what it did. It came out of the toilet. She's dead. Everyone's dead."

Artur threw his weight forward. Considering there wasn't a lot of weight to throw, the effect was impressive. The hairy thing bent double and his forehead hit the table with a solid-sounding *thack*. Artur hopped onto the tabletop just as the creature slid off it and landed unceremoniously on the floor.

"Out of the toilet, eh?" Artur said, glancing from Ollie to the bathroom door and back again. He turned to face the rioting crowd and cupped his hands around his mouth.

"Deadman! Deadman, ye big ugly bag o' spanners, ye'll be wanting to hear this."

He scanned the dining room, but there were too many things throwing too many punches for him to be able to spot Dan. It wasn't until a few seconds later, once Deadman kicked his way free from beneath a pile of Gronnian War Midgets, that Artur set eyes on him.

"Here! This way!" Artur called. "Some shoite is going down in the bathroom. Pun absolutely intended, and a bloody good one it was, too, if I say so meself."

It was only as Dan punched and elbowed his way through the crowd that Artur realized Finn was draped over one of his shoulders, out for the count.

"You have a man on you," Ollie pointed out.

"Yeah. I'm aware," said Dan. He dumped Finn onto the table. A red welt ran up the side of the younger man's neck and face, and a crust of blood was forming around his nostrils.

"Who is that?" Ollie asked.

"It's Deadman's boyfriend," said Artur.

Ollie gasped. "You have a boyfriend?"

"No, I do not have a boyfriend," Dan insisted. "He's just some idiot who got himself slapped by an Igneon. I kind of feel obligated to watch over him until he wakes up."

"Because he's yer boyfriend," Artur concluded.

At the far end of the hall, a thirty-strong Stagnates Riot Dispersion Squad piled in through three different doors.

"We got into a spot of bother with the natives," Artur told Ollie. "And things escalated quite quickly." He gestured to the bathroom door, then at Dan. "Now tell him about Banbara, and how she got sucked down the shizzer."

Dan's brow knotted. "What?"

"In there," Ollie confirmed, tilting her head towards the

bathroom door and wrapping her arms around herself. Both movements made a *squelch*. "It just… There was a thing…"

"Wait out here where it's safe," Dan instructed, sweeping past her, his hand reaching for a gun that, to his annoyance, still wasn't there.

"*Safe?*" snorted Artur. Behind him, a feathery little man in a jumpsuit and goggles was smashed head-first into a bench, while a rhino-headed thing with a lizard tail trampled three guards into a gelatinous paste on the floor. "Ye call this 'safe?'"

His only answer was the *clunk* of the bathroom door as it closed at Deadman's back.

Dan stepped into a bathroom that echoed with the *drip d-drip drip* of falling blood droplets. They drizzled from the ceiling directly above each of the stalls, some of them *plinking* into the toilets below, others spattering on the tiled floor.

One of the stall doors was open, revealing a toilet awash with blood and walls that were pebble-dashed by excrement and gore. The door opened outwards, and Dan could make out a near-perfect humanoid outline in the patina of bloody chunks. It took him a full minute to figure out this was where Ollie had been standing, actual detective skills not exactly being his strong point.

He approached the stall cautiously, regretting once again his lack of gun. He'd clenched his fists, but if some giant spike-monster suddenly came rising out of the John, he wasn't convinced a quick one-two would do all that much to dissuade it.

The water level in the toilet was lower than he'd have expected, although this wasn't the first thing he noticed. The first thing he noticed was that the water was red. Very red. All the way red, in fact, as if all the water had been flushed away and replaced with a couple of quarts of blood.

The second thing he noticed was the beady, marble-sized eyeball floating in the center of the liquid. It seemed to gaze at him slightly accusingly, as if it still hadn't forgiven him for that punch last night.

Then, and only then, did he notice that the water level was lower than usual. All things considered, though, it wasn't something he was going to spend a lot of time thinking about.

He was pretty sure no one was going to answer, but he knocked on the door of the next cubicle over, just in case. If someone in there had survived whatever had happened, the last thing they needed was him walking in on them with their pants around their ankles.

"Open up," he instructed, thumping the door with his fist. He addressed the stalls in general. "Anyone in here? Last warning."

As expected, nobody answered, which Dan took as permission to kick the stall door open. A scene more or less identical to the one next door was unveiled, although this time without the eyeball.

The next couple of stalls were much the same. In the final one, Dan found a large strip of damp scalp stuck to the wall, the long brunette hair spread out like the legs of a squashed spider. The impact of the door being kicked open had shaken it loose, and Dan watched in a sort of mesmerized horror as the scalp *incy-wincied* its way down the wall, the hair clumps slapping through the lacquer of blood and toilet water until it finally flopped down onto the floor.

There was nothing to be done here. There was nobody to save, no monster to fight. There were probably clues, if he knew where to look. The splash patterns on the walls and ceiling might reveal the size of whatever did this, or the speed at which it moved. Analysis of the 'remains' – a word he reckoned had never been quite so appropriate – would tell him who the women all were, and might even reveal some connection between them.

Beyond the obvious one of them all having been skewered through the nether regions and killed, he meant.

But that sort of thing wasn't his area of expertise. Hitting people and making them talk – *that* was where his strengths lay. The problem was, there was no one around to punch, and none of these women were likely to start talking anytime soon. Congealing, maybe, but not talking.

Dan relaxed his fists, took another look around the room in case anything jumped out at him – hopefully literally – then muttered a, "Fonk it," and headed for the door.

Outside, most of the rioting had been replaced by some good old-fashioned police brutality. The crowds had thinned considerably as the rioters realized what way the wind was blowing, and quietly fled through one of the many doors.

"I'm not sayin' it in a pervy kind of way, Peaches," Artur said. "I just think, for health and safety reasons, ye should get out of them clothes. Only, ye know, slowly so ye don't flick brains and shoite all over the place."

Ollie, who appeared to have been considering this, turned away at the sound of the bathroom door closing. She hurried to intercept Dan. "Well?"

"She's dead, all right."

Ollie nodded. Despite her naivety, even she'd been able to figure that one out. Still, she shrunk back a little, like having it confirmed had poured salt in the wound.

"If it's any consolation, she probably didn't suffer," Dan said.

"She was making this sort of squeal. Sort of screaming, but not really able to," Ollie said. "Then it smashed her against the walls."

Dan looked like he was about to offer some counter-argument, but then changed his mind. "Well, in that case, she probably did suffer. Sorry."

"So she was sucked down the bog?" Artur asked.

Dan nodded. "All of them. Five people. Gone. Just like Bonbo."

"Bonbo?"

Finn sat up, one hand clutching his head, the other arm wrapped around his ribs. He winced when his feet touched the floor. "Bonbo Rolan?"

Dan shrugged. "Fonked if I know. Little rat-faced guy. Drank in a bar over by the east docks."

"*Grimster's*," said Finn. "I know that guy."

"*Knew* him," Artur corrected.

Finn's bronzed brow creased. "Huh?"

"He was kebabbed up the arsehole," Artur said, in a tone that suggested this should be a full and frank enough explanation to set the matter to rest.

Clearly, though, it wasn't.

"Wait. He was what?"

"Something came out of the John and killed him," Dan explained.

Finn's frown deepened. He flicked his gaze to the door behind Dan. "Why was he in the ladies?"

"No, not here. Yesterday. At Grimster's."

Finn lowered himself onto the edge of the table. "Bonbo's dead? Aw, brah, that sucks."

"I take it you knew him?"

"Yeah. We used to work together."

"Well, sorry for... Wait, what? Doing what?" Dan

demanded.

Finn shook his head. "Uh... nothing much."

Artur squinted up at him. "Ye worked together doing 'nothing much'? Sure, maybe ye could get me a job with ye, too. Sounds right up my street, that does."

"Artur, take Ollie and get her cleaned up," Dan instructed. "Ollie, if he tells you he has to watch, tell him 'no'. Firmly, like that. 'No.' Got it?"

"Feckin' spoilsport."

Ollie nodded. "Uh, yeah. I got it. Where are you going?"

Dan clamped a hand on Finn's upper arm, his grip tightening like a vice. "Me and the kid here are going to go and have a little talk."

SIX

"Look, brah, I don't know anything about that stuff. I swear!"

Finn was pressed against the wall of Dan's pod, the detective's hand pinning him by the throat. Dan still didn't have his gun, but he had found a pen. It was amazing, he'd explained to Finn, the damage a pen could inflict, if you know what to do with it. He hadn't demonstrated this yet, but the emphasis was definitely on the 'yet' part.

"You said yourself, you worked for Krato," Dan growled. "You must know something."

Finn managed to shake his head, despite Dan's death grip. "N-no, dude. I mean, I heard about the mall thing, but through the TV or whatever. Some bomb or something, right? People died?"

"One-hundred-and-thirty-four people," Dan confirmed. "Thirty-eight of them were kids."

"Shizz. That's harsh," Finn wheezed.

"And it wasn't a bomb. Best anyone can tell it was some kind of frequency resonator."

"I don't know what that is," Finn coughed.

"No, me neither. But I know what it does. I've seen it," Dan said. "It vibrates your insides until they become your outsides. They come out through the eyes first. Down the nose. Out your shizzpipe."

Dan leaned in closer. Finn's attempts to recoil were somewhat hampered by the wall behind him.

"Then your skin splits. Just splits wide open, and whatever's left of you just flops out around your feet. Just flops out onto the floor."

"Whoa. That's... I mean..."

"One-hundred-and-thirty-four people. Thirty-eight children," Dan said, putting emphasis on almost every word. "I think Krato either deployed or sold the weapon. But I want to be sure."

He jerked Finn off the floor. "So, let me ask you again. What do you know?"

"N-nothing," Finn gargled, his face reddening. "Only m-met him once. I swear, brah."

The pod door opened, revealing Gunnak and Tor.

"Fonk off," Dan warned them.

Both men quickly about-turned and left. Dan waited for the door to close again before continuing.

"Maybe I didn't tell you about the pen," he said.

"I s-swear. I don't know anything!" Finn insisted. "I'd tell you if I d-did."

Dan stood motionless for a few moments, watching him gag and splutter. Finally, he released his grip and let the kid crumple to a snot-sputtering heap on the floor.

"If I find out you're lying to me... Well, let's just say I'll be unimpressed," Dan warned. He squatted down. "And you do not want to see my unimpressed face."

Finn quickly shook his head. "I swear, brah. I don't know anything about the guy. I just dealt with Bonbo. The guy had a job for us. Just one job. That's all we ever did for him."

"What was it?" Dan asked.

"He wanted us to..." Finn's voice trailed off. His eyes darted from side to side, as if searching for something. "He wanted us to..."

"To what?"

"I don't remember," Finn said. He flinched when Dan raised the pen and clicked the button on the bottom. "No! I swear, I swear, brah. I met Bonbo out by one of the docks, then we drove to this... I don't know. Office, I guess. There was a guy there. Said he was Krato. Tall and skinny. And red. He was red. Friendly, but kind of creepy at the same time."

"Sounds like him," Dan confirmed. "Then what?"

"Then... I don't know," said Finn. He frowned in concentration. "It's foggy. I think maybe we got drunk, or something. I remember... bright lights. Like headlights, maybe? Or a crazy bright torch."

"What else?"

Finn's eyes darted around again, then he shook his head. "Nothing. There's nothing else," he said, sounding more than a little weirded out. "Next thing I remember is waking up with some cash in my pocket and a hangover that wouldn't quit."

"And when was this?"

"Week ago, maybe? A little less."

"I swear, kid, if you're lying to me..."

"I'm not, brah! I swear on my life."

"I'll hold you to that," Dan said. He clicked his tongue against the back of his teeth a few times. "This office? Could you find it again?"

"Uh, yeah. Yeah. Maybe. I think so."

"Good. You can take me there," Dan said.

"Uh, OK. Yeah. Sure, brah. No problem," Finn said. "Now?"

"No. Later. This afternoon," Dan said.

"I've got work this afternoon."

Dan tutted. "Can you get time off?"

"Maybe. I mean... yeah. I can."

"Good. Write me down the details," Dan said. He stood up, unhooked his hat from the end of the bunk beds, and pulled it on. "Right now, I've got a monster to kill."

ARTUR PEEKED around the doorframe into the room, where an old woman sat behind a semi-transparent barrier screen.

"Sure, I don't know why ye can't just get her told," he whispered. "It's my stuff, give me it back, ye saggy-faced auld bastard. Like that, ye know? Diplomatic, yet firm."

Dan shook his head. "Not going to work. I'll keep her busy, you get what we came for."

"Which is what, exactly?" Artur asked.

Dan tutted. "I told you. We went through this."

Artur grinned. "Ah, just messin' wit' ye, Deadman," he said. "Little round gizmo on a chain. Bottom drawer. Right?"

"Right," Dan confirmed. "You get it, and I'll keep her talking."

"How? Ye're not exactly a sparkling conversationalist," Artur said. "I mean, I'm yer best mate, and I can barely stand talking to ye."

"I'll think of something."

Removing his hat, Dan held it low to the floor. Artur

hopped inside, then braced all four limbs against the material.

"Eurgh. It stinks in here, Deadman, ye smelly-headed bollocks. Ye owe me one for this."

"Yeah, yeah," Dan grunted, then he picked the hat up, strode into the room, and approached the old woman behind the glass. His filing cabinet and boxes were still there, which was one of those rare examples of things actually going his way.

"Well, well, well," said Notty, looking up from where she was idly drawing on the top of her desk. "If it isn't Mr Verbal Abuse. What brings you back?"

"Well—"

"You shizz-flavored fonkwit humper."

"Well," Dan tried again. "One of the guards told me I had to hand in my hat."

Notty's eyes flicked to the fedora in Dan's hands, just briefly. "You call that a hat?"

"I do," said Dan. "And they told me to hand it in. For quarantine."

Notty leaned forward and clasped her hands in front of her on the desktop. "Oh, *did* they now? Is that what they told you?"

"It is," Dan confirmed.

"And so you just did it, did you? You just did what they told you, like a good little boy?"

Dan tried very hard to keep his cool. "Yes. It seemed like the best course of action."

"Oh, *did* it? Did it seem like the best course of action, you gelatinous retard?"

Dan came very close to questioning the insult, but remembered what had happened last time.

"Yes. It did. So, here's the hat."

Notty eyeballed him contemptuously for several long moments, then tapped a button under her desk. Dan braced himself for the alarm, but then a small rectangular opening appeared in the screen, and Notty's hand tore the hat from his grip.

"It stinks," she said, tossing it onto the boxes behind her. "You'll be lucky if we don't just burn it. It's not even a hat."

"Well, it definitely is a hat, so..."

Notty glowered at him. "It's not a hat."

Dan considered arguing, but suspected that's what the old woman was hoping for. Instead, he decided to blindside her.

"Hey look, Notty, we got off on the wrong foot," he said. He held the old woman's gaze, resisting the urge to glance at the movement in the box behind her. "You said some things, I said some things..."

"I had you beaten unconscious..." Notty continued.

"Ha. Yeah. That too," Dan said, forcing something like amusement into his voice. "I mean, kind of unnecessary, I thought, but... My point is, I'd like us to start again. You know, wipe the slate clean. A fresh start."

"It'd be the only clean and fresh thing about you, you manky ball-munching—"

"I'd like to take you out," Dan said, interrupting her. Notty leaned back suddenly, and Dan felt the urge to clarify. He put a finger to his head like it was the barrel of a gun. "Not... take you out. I mean..."

He took a deep and wholly unnecessary breath. "For dinner. Or whatever. Outside. Not here."

It was around this point that Dan realized what he was saying. He'd been aiming to find some way of keeping conversation going between them, but was starting to suspect he'd vastly overshot the target.

"I mean... Now that I say it out loud..."

"Yes."

Dan blinked. "What?"

"Yes, I'll go out with you."

Shizz.

"Uh... OK."

Notty leaned forward eagerly. "When?"

"When what?"

"When are we going out? Tonight? I'm free tonight."

Double-shizz.

"Are you sure?" Dan said. "I mean, I'm not much to look at. And you said yourself, I have a certain... odor."

"Do I look like I'm being inundated with offers?" Notty asked him. "You know when the last good hard fonk I had was?"

Dan found himself taking a step away. "Uh, no. No, can't say I—"

"Tuesday," said Notty. She tapped a chipped fingernail against the desktop. "Here on this desk."

"Um. Well done?"

"Tuesday. Today's *Friday*," Notty said. "So when? Tonight? I can do tonight. We don't even have to go out, I can just darken the screen. Or not, if you're into that sort of thing."

"Out the road, ye mad old bastard!" cried Artur, flicking a switch under the desk as he clambered up on top.

"What the hell?" Notty yelped, shoving herself back from the desk. Her chair rolled back until it hit the open bottom drawer of the filing cabinet, then it toppled over, depositing her on top of the boxes containing Dan's stuff.

Artur scrambled across the desktop, dragging Dan's upside-down hat with him. The rectangular opening appeared again and he and the hat slid through. There was a solid-sounding *thunk* as they both hit the floor.

"Tell me this is it," Artur said, tilting the hat to allow Dan to see inside. An object a lot like a pocket watch lay nestled inside.

"That's it," he confirmed, then he snatched up both Artur and the hat, and hurried for the door.

"Wait, come back!" Notty shouted after him. "What time are you picking me up?"

But the only reply was the fading *clomp* of Dan's heavy, lumbering footsteps, and a palpable sense of relief.

———

DAN HEAVED ASIDE the manhole cover, letting a gaseous green haze bloom briefly into the corridor before dissipating into the air, leaving behind only the distinctive aroma of raw sewage.

"You sure you want to come down here?" he asked. He had left his coat back in his pod, in order to minimize the number of garments he would likely have to incinerate later, revealing the battered waistcoat and shirt he wore underneath. The pocket watch-like device was attached to the front of waistcoat like... well, like a pocket watch.

Ollie nodded at him. "I'm coming," she said. "Banbara was my best friend. Apart from you guys, I mean."

"She was literally the only other person I've ever seen ye even speaking to," Artur pointed out from where he was perched on Dan's shoulder.

"Exactly. So, I'm coming," Ollie said. "You're not talking me out of it."

"I wasn't going to try to talk you out of it," Dan said. "I

don't have a gun. If we find whatever killed those women down there, I might need your help."

"Oh," said Ollie. "Oh. OK, then."

"Everyone OK with the smell?" Dan asked.

Artur shrugged. "Sure, we've lasted this long. Just stand downwind whenever ye can."

"The sewers, I meant," Dan sighed, aware that Artur knew exactly what he meant.

"Oh. That. It'll be a breath of fresh air, to be honest."

"Fine. Let's do this," said Dan.

There was a ladder, of course, but he chose not to take it. Instead, he stepped off into empty space and landed with a *splosh* in the knee-deep sludge below.

Artur immediately vomited down the front of Dan's shirt. "Shoite. I take it back. This place stinks even worse than you."

"I'll take that as a compliment," Dan said.

Artur vomited again. This time, it splashed into Dan's ear.

"Oops. Sorry, Deadman, totally didn't mean to—"

He threw up for a third time, filling the ear all the way.

"No, I can't do this," Artur groaned. "It's the smell that's the problem."

"I guessed that," Dan said.

"Ye be alright without me?"

"I'm sure we'll cope," Dan said.

Artur rubbed his stomach. "Actually... I might be adapting to—"

Vomit erupted from his mouth and down his nose. "No. I tell a lie."

Dan grabbed him and looked up through the manhole entrance. "Ollie. Catch."

Artur yelped as Dan tossed him straight upwards.

There was a moment of panicky flapping, a shouted, "Ya bastard!" then he landed safely in Ollie's cupped hands.

"Got you."

"Cheers, Peaches," he said. He hiccupped, then violently retched. "And sorry about that. I appear to have thrown up in yer hands."

SEVEN

It was not Dan's first trip to the sewers but, just like every time he'd been down here before, he hoped it would be his last.

There were actually half a dozen or so different sewerage networks buried beneath Down Here, but no one could agree on an exact number, or where one ended and the others began. As the city had grown over the centuries, so too had the need to dispose of its growing mountains of waste. Most of the planet was ocean, and Down Here had been pumping their waste out to sea since before the history books started taking note. The method by which it did this had varied quite wildly, and at least three previous sewer networks had collapsed, imploded or, in a surprising development, shifted into an alternate universe in the past hundred years alone.

What was left was a haphazard cobbling together of the old and the new. One minute, Dan and Ollie were trudging through tunnels of crumbling brick, then a couple of corners later they were slipping and sliding on an impossibly smooth frictionless metal floor.

The only constants were the river of murky gray water, and the soft green glow of the lichen that patterned the walls and ceiling like a fungal infection.

Sewer Slugs put in a number of cameo appearances, too. They were a hangover from one of the city's previous attempts at waste disposal - foot-long gelatinous brown blobs with whirlpool-like mouths designed to suck up any liquid they came into contact with. They could have a pretty good go at most solids, too, and released their own waste products as a clear odorless gas.

They would've been the perfect way of dealing with the city's growing sewage problem had it not been for the speed at which they bred. A month after they'd been introduced, the entire sewerage network had become clogged with them.

A week later, they had filled the Stagnates. It took just a couple of days for the streets of Down Here to be heaving with the fonking things.

Their mass-extermination had taken months. No matter how many of the things the city killed, more appeared to take their place. It wasn't until a smorgasbord of genetically engineered Sewer Slug diseases was introduced into their population that the tide began to turn.

The intention had been to wipe them out completely, but a few proved immune to whatever was thrown at them. Beyond the occasional 'acid flush' every day or two to keep numbers down, no one really bothered with them these days.

Except Ollie.

"What is that?!" she yelped, pointing to one of the fat squirming blobs. It wriggled in the water just ahead of them, its shiny back rising out of the murk like the world's least desirable desert island.

"I already told you. It's a Sewer Slug," said Dan. "They're harmless, long as you don't get too close."

Ollie lowered her hand. "Oh. Is that another one of them? It looks different."

"It doesn't look different. It looks identical to the five others we've seen."

Ollie fell into step behind Dan, giving the slug a wide berth. It farted and squelched in the water as they passed.

They walked on for a while, the only sound the sloshing of the sewage around them.

"Have we found a new office yet?" Ollie asked. She gasped. "Wait. It's not down here, is it?"

"No," Dan said.

"To which part?"

"Both parts. No, I haven't found a new office, and no, it won't be down here."

Ollie nodded. "That's good. The second part, I mean." She looked around them. They were in a particularly old section of the network now, and the bricks were crumbling and rotten. It was darker here, too. A large patch of the wall was stained completely black and free of the glowing moss. "This reminds me of home. Except, you know, less torture."

"Right," said Dan. He knew Ollie's origins, of course. She'd been stolen from her own universe and taken to one of the countless Hell-like pocket dimensions collectively known as the Malwhere. They'd never really spoken about what had happened to her growing up there, or what horrors she'd had to endure.

And he wasn't about to start now.

"This is a waste of time," he admitted.

Ollie frowned. "What? Why?"

"There are thousands of miles of pipes down here. We could take a whole army down with us and still never find whatever's down here. If it even *is* still down here. There's no saying where it's moved on to."

"We can't stop!" Ollie urged.

Dan stopped.

"*Can't* stop, I said. Can't."

"Sorry, kid. This was a bad idea," he told her. "If we were going to find anything, we'd have found it by now. That thing could be a hundred miles from here in the opposite direction. We should go back."

"But... Banbara," Ollie said.

"I know. I want to find it just as much as you do, but we need to think it through. It's not like it's going to just appear out of..."

The black stain shifted on the wall at Ollie's back. It was a big stain. Huge, in fact. Dan slowly raised his eyes, watching as it peeled from the ancient brickwork, revealing more of the luminous lichen below.

Spiked tentacles unfurled themselves from its shapeless body. They moved constantly, undulating like underwater weeds on the tide. It had no facial features that Dan could see, yet he got the impression that it was staring right at them, and that it didn't look happy.

It was several times larger than he'd been expecting, although its constant movements and the way the light danced across its shiny exoskeleton made its exact size hard to estimate.

"Appear out of what?" Ollie asked, completely unaware of the thing unfolding itself behind her.

Dan swallowed. "Give me your hand," he told her.

Ollie hesitated, but only for a moment. "Which one?" she asked.

"Either one."

It took her a moment, but Ollie chose a hand – the right

one – and held it out to Dan. He wrapped his fingers around her wrist and began walking back the way they'd come.

"Where are we going?" Ollie asked. "We can't go back."

"I need you to listen carefully," Dan said. "First, keep your voice down. Second, no sudden movements unless I tell you. Third…"

A spiked tentacle stabbed him through the shoulder from behind.

"Aw, fonk it," he grunted. "Run!"

He stumbled on, dragging Ollie as he pulled himself free of the spike with a stomach-churning *schlurp*. Ollie looked back over her shoulder as they ran.

"Is that it? Is that the…? Ooh, it's big. Why's it so big?"

"Because I'm having one of those weeks, that's why," Dan said.

He stopped at a junction leading into another part of the sewer system and shoved her into it. "Wait there," he barked, unhooking the pocket-watch device from his waistcoat.

The shadow-thing had expanded to fill almost the entire diameter of the tunnel now. This was both good news and bad. Bad, because the fonking thing was ludicrously big, and ludicrously big monsters were rarely on anyone's wish-list. Good, because it meant he had a target he couldn't possibly miss.

Holding the end of the pocket watch device's chain, he began to spin it, whirling it around and around at his side like a bolas. As it twirled, lights flickered across the surface, blurring as Dan twirled it faster and faster until they formed a continuous circle of light in the air beside him.

"What are you doing?" Ollie whispered, her eyes twirling in tight circles as she followed the light.

"Sending this thing back to the Malwhere," Dan said. "Stay back there. When this hits, things are going to get crazy."

He narrowed his eyes. "Here goes!"

Dan let fly with the spinning device. It whistled past his ear, ricocheted off the roof, then landed with a *plop* in the water behind him.

"Shizz. Out of practice," he muttered, relieved that Artur hadn't been around to see that. Retreating to where he could just make out the glow of the gadget through the sewage, he fished it out and tried again.

"OK, this time," he announced, building up speed again. The shadow-thing seemed to draw back, as if sensing what was about to happen. Dan could almost sense its panic. It was perhaps the single most enjoyable moment of the past seventy-two hours. "Go back to Hell, you piece of shizz."

This time, the gadget flew straight and true. It rocketed off on an upward trajectory and had only just started to curve downwards when it found its target. Dan held his hands out in front of his face, half-shielding his eyes as he waited for the fireworks.

The circle of metal *thudded* against the monster. Dan followed the device as it bounced off and vanished into the sewage below.

Silence followed.

"Are things getting crazy yet?" Ollie whispered.

"It's not from the Malwhere," Dan said. He clicked his tongue against the back of his teeth. "We may have a problem."

"What kind of problem?" Ollie asked, then she jumped back in fright as one of the black shape's tendrils *whammed* Dan into the wall, cracking the already crumbling brickwork. The limb snaked beneath him as he fell, then flicked him upwards. Dan hissed as he smashed into the curved ceiling, then grimaced as he plopped face-first into the water below.

"Oh. That kind of problem," Ollie said.

Stepping out from the side tunnel, she raised her hands in front of her, taking aim at the enormous dark shape.

"OK. I can do this. I can do this," she told herself.

"Wait, no, don't!" Dan spluttered, but the warning came too late.

Blue fire flickered at Ollie's fingertips. The sewer gas, which had been waiting for its moment to shine, ignited. Ollie screamed as she was blasted backward off her feet and joined Dan in the murky water.

"Close your mouth," Dan warned, then he pulled her all the way under as the air burned and crackled above them. She squirmed and wriggled, but Dan held her down while the fire raged.

It took just a few seconds for the gas to burn itself out, then Dan was up on his feet and heaving the gasping and gagging Ollie onto hers. The explosion had driven the shadow-thing back a little, but not nearly enough for Dan's liking.

He had no weapons, and they daren't risk Ollie triggering another explosion. There was only one option available.

"Let's get the fonk out of here," Dan urged, shoving Ollie back in the direction they'd first come.

Dripping from head to toe with raw, unprocessed effluent, Ollie didn't feel any urge to argue. She speed-waddled ahead of him, Dan's hand on her back to steady her and hurry her on.

The shadow-thing had been hurt. That was good. If it

could be hurt, it could be killed, but it wouldn't be here and it wouldn't be now.

It was pulling itself together too quickly. They'd walked for maybe half an hour. They could run it in twenty minutes, but that assumed they didn't meet any problems and that the other thing couldn't run faster.

"Keep your eyes peeled for an exit," Dan told her, scanning the shadowy ceiling above. He was sure they'd passed a few other ladders during their search, but for the death of him couldn't remember where.

Glancing back, Dan saw that the shape was on the move. It tore along the tunnel behind them, its spiked limbs flapping on the walls, floor and ceiling as it pulled itself along. It wasn't moving with any great speed, so it was closing slowly, but closing all the same.

"Shizz. Come on, kid, we've got to move faster."

Ollie winced as she forced her legs to stop waddling and start running instead. They splashed around a bend and the old brickwork became a slick metal tube rising in a slight incline. Ollie's feet immediately slid out from under her, but Dan managed to keep her from hitting the deck.

"I got you, kid," he said, then his own feet went and they both plunged face-first into the foul water, then slid the foot or so back onto the brick section.

"That's not going to work," Dan realized, heaving the spluttering and wheezing Ollie back onto her feet.

He looked around, searching for an alternative route. On the wall beside them was a semi-circle of slightly different colored bricks, suggesting an old tunnel had run off at a right-angle from this one in the dim and distant past, but was now closed off.

Fonk it. Worth a try.

Running at the wall, Dan threw his weight behind his

shoulder and charged. The impact bounced him back a few steps, but did little, if anything, to the wall. Roaring, he tried again. Again. Again. He slammed himself onto the same spot over and over.

Something went *crick*. At first, Dan assumed he'd broken a bone, but then he saw it – a vague indent in the wall where the bricks had started to loosen.

He charged it again, spurred on by this glimmer of hope. The thing was still closing. It would be on them in thirty seconds, maybe less.

"It's coming!" Ollie said.

"I know it's coming! Why do you think I'm—"

An alarm sounded.

It was quite a relaxed sounding alarm – just a series of unconcerned-sounding *chirps*, really – but it made Dan hesitate.

"What's that?" Ollie whispered, then she yelped as a Sewer Slug slid down the slope behind her and began squirming in the direction of the approaching shadow-thing.

Dan watched as six or seven more of the slugs arrived at the bottom of the slope and followed the first.

From somewhere in the distance, there came the sound of thunder.

"Aw... *fonk!*" he spat, then he threw himself at the wall even more frantically and furiously than before. There was another cracking sound which definitely came from inside him this time. He ignored it and pushed back from the wall, giving himself space for a run up. A dozen more Sewer Slugs slid down the slope beside him. He dodged them as he ran, aiming his full weight at that single indent he'd created in the wall.

"Dan, hurry!" Ollie cried, and there was something inhuman in her panicky squeal. An invisible force hit Dan from behind, launching him towards the wall in a blistering blur of speed. Luckily for those parts of his skeleton that were still intact, the same force hit the wall just as he did, punching a hole through it.

Dan landed in a foot-deep layer of greasy black goo, rolled twice, then slid on for several seconds. Insects rose up in clouds around him, buzzing and whistling angrily.

"Ollie, get in here!" he barked, struggling out of the sludge. The walls of the tunnel were trembling as the roar of thunder grew louder.

Not actually thunder, of course. Not water, either.

Acid. Slug-killing acid. Thousands of gallons of the fonking stuff.

Ollie clambered through the hole in the wall, then frantically flapped her arms as her feet slid in opposite directions. "Wheurk!" she yelped, fighting to keep her balance as clouds of bugs took to the air around her. "What is this stuff?"

"Same as out there. This stuff's just been here longer," Dan said, grabbing her by the arm and pulling her on through the sludge.

They slid and staggered through the swarming insects, dust shaking from the ceiling as the roar of the acid flush swept down the main pipe. Dan caught a glimpse of movement back by the hole in the wall – the shifting of some immense black shape – and then a torrent of green-tinted liquid crashed into it. Big and powerful as the thing was, there was no way it could stand its ground against the force of all that acid.

It tried, though. Its tendrils gripped the broken brickwork and managed to hold on for a good few seconds before the weight became too much for the wall to withstand. The bricks broke. The shadow-thing spluttered.

And then there was no sound but the thunder of the acid flush, the buzzing of flies, and the faint rasping of Ollie's breath.

"Is it... is it dead?" she asked, as the sound of thunder began to fade.

Dan shook his head. "Unlikely. The acid's strong enough to dissolve Sewer Slugs, but not a whole lot else. It'll be flushed out to sea."

"So... it's gone? Everyone's safe?"

Dan swatted away a particularly large and irritating bug. "More or less."

"What do you mean?" Ollie asked.

"Well, if you're sitting on the toilet, you're probably more safe than you were. If you live near the docks, probably less."

Ollie gasped. This made her inhale a fly, and she spent several seconds coughing it back out.

"You mean it might climb out of the water?!"

Dan shrugged. "It might. There's no way of knowing. Unless it does, I mean. Then we'll know about it."

The acid flush had died away to a trickle now, so Dan started plodding back in the direction of the broken wall. Now that they weren't being chased by a murderous shadow creature, maybe they could find a way back up the slippery incline.

"We have to do something," Ollie said. "Or tell someone."

"What we need is to get you clean before you catch every disease in the city," Dan said. He looked her up and down. "I hate to say it, kid, but you smell even worse than I do."

Ollie frowned. "How? You're covered in the same stuff, and you already smelled bad."

"I guess so," Dan conceded. "But it's part of my charm. You don't carry it off like I do."

He leaned out through the gap in the wall, checked that the coast was clear, then stepped through. The knee-deep slurry of shizz had been replaced with a thin trickle of acid. It was, he reckoned, a fair trade.

"Now come on," he urged, beckoning her through. "If we're lucky, we might get back before anyone flushes..."

ARTUR STOOD with his hands on his hips, looking up at first Dan, then Ollie. Two expanding puddles of lightly-smoking bodily fluids had merged to become one larger one around them, and Artur retreated a couple of steps to avoid getting any on his shoes.

Ollie's hair was plastered to her face. At least, Artur guessed it was her face, but the mask of blackish-brown goo made it difficult to make out any actual features.

Dan hadn't had a lot going for him visually before they'd gone down the manhole, yet he managed to look considerably worse coming out.

The brim of his hat was weighed down by... Actually, Artur didn't care to know precisely what it was weighed down with, but it was weighed down with something. It sagged down around Dan's ears as if it were suffering from depression, and yellow-brown liquid dripped from it like tears.

"So," he asked them, making no effort to hide the smirk on his face. "How did it go? Did ye have fun?"

"Does it look like we had fun?" Dan asked.

Artur looked them over again and puffed out his cheeks.

"Some people are into that sort of thing, I hear," he said. "And who are we to judge? So, I don't know. Maybe."

"Not fun," Ollie said, shivering. "Definitely not fun."

"Did ye kill the big monster thing, at least?" Artur asked. "Or did ye both just go take a shoite bath for an hour for no real reason?"

"It's gone," Dan said.

"*Gone* gone or just gone?" Artur asked.

"Gone. Maybe gone gone, but I doubt it."

"Ye useless pair of bastards," Artur said, but he sounded good-natured about it. "Ye know what else needs gone? That fecking smell."

He jabbed a thumb back along the corridor behind him. "Come on, I'm sure I spotted some shower rooms this way," he said, then he winked at Ollie. "If ye're lucky, Peaches, I might even scrub yer back."

EIGHT

THEY STOPPED by Dan's pod first, so he could grab his coat. If it came to it, he could shower off the shizz, dispose of his clothes, and then use the coat to cover himself until he could find replacements. Ollie reckoned she could 'borrow' some of Banbara's clothes, although as Banbara had been several dress sizes larger than Ollie, and had twice as many limbs, Dan couldn't quite fathom how this was going to work.

To his surprise, when he returned to his pod his filing cabinet and boxes were standing in the corner beside the slop bucket. With some difficulty, he wrenched open the second drawer of the cabinet, revealing a tangle of stained shirts and patched pants. Fishing inside, he pulled out a set, then opened the drawer below so Ollie could get to her own clothes.

She took out a t-shirt with a green blob on the front. The blob had two big round eyes that seemed to gaze hopefully at her as she considered it.

But no. Returning it to the drawer, she chose something else and held it up. The text on this one announced that you didn't have to be crazy to wear it, but went on to suggest that it probably helped.

No. She returned it and reached for something else.

Dan grabbed the first available shirt from the drawer and thrust it into her arms. "Here. It isn't a damn fashion show. Now grab some pants and let's go get showered."

Artur rubbed his hands together. "Now ye're talking," he said, but Dan had bad news for him.

"Artur, stay here and guard this stuff. I don't want those shizznod roommates coming back and helping themselves."

"What?" Artur glanced at Ollie, then back to Dan. "Aw, come on there, Deadman. Don't ye be acting the maggot on me."

"I mean it," Dan insisted. "If they get their hands on some of the gear in that bottom drawer, there's no saying what they might let loose. Stay here. Keep it safe."

"Why can't ye do it yerself?"

Dan gestured to himself, and the layer of fecal matter currently air drying on his clothes and skin.

Artur groaned. "Fine. But ye owe me big time for this."

"Fair enough," Dan said. He looked to Ollie. "You ready?"

Ollie nodded. "Ready," she said. "No, wait!"

She quickly swapped the t-shirt for a different one, then nodded again. "Ready."

It wasn't far to the shower room, but they had to pass quite a few people to get there. Fortunately, even in the busiest corridors a path would magically open ahead of them as anything with a nose hastily pressed itself against the walls and turned their faces away.

The soundtrack to their walk was a chorus of gagging, retching and derogatory remarks, but at least no one tried to get in their way or challenge them.

Behind the shower room door were three identical cubicles. Each one had a drain in the floor, and cracked, grotty tiles on the walls. The only other feature was a rectangular storage chest that stood against the back wall and doubled as a bench.

"What do I do?" Ollie asked, looking the stalls up and down.

Dan pointed to the first. "Go in there. Get undressed. Put both sets of clothes in the locker, but keep them well apart so the new set doesn't get dirty."

"Then what?"

"Then wait. I'll be right next door."

Ollie took a deep breath. Considering the state of them, and how confined a space they were in, she regretted it immediately, but she tried not to let on.

"OK. Let's do it!" she announced, visibly steeling herself.

"It's just a shower," Dan said. "Just water. Nothing dangerous."

"Got it!" said Ollie. She took a step forward.

She took a step back.

"What if I drown?"

Dan sighed. "It doesn't *fill* with water. It'll just pour down on you and wash everything away."

"OK, then!" Ollie said. She took a step forward.

She took a step back.

"What if it washes me away?"

"Just get in the damn shower," Dan said, pointing into the cubicle.

He waited until she had stepped inside before entering the next stall along and closing the door behind him.

Opening the lid of the storage chest, he placed his clean clothes inside, tucking them all the way over on the left.

Technically, they were now merely clean*ish*. While he'd wiped his hands as best he could before picking them up, the fact he'd wiped them on his current filthy attire meant his fingers were pretty much still as shizz-sodden as the rest of him.

That done, he began peeling off his waistcoat and shirt. They were stuck to his back and under his arms with toxic moisture, and it took him several seconds of wrestling until he successfully pulled his way free.

"On second thought, don't put your old clothes in the box," Dan said, watching the liquid dribble out of his. "Toss them on the floor or put them on top of the box. We'll leave them here."

Ollie's voice came out muffled as she wrestled her shirt over her head. "Mmkay."

Dan kicked off his boots. As one toppled over, yet more liquid spilled out. His feet left blackish-brown prints on the tiled floor as he took off his pants and tossed them onto the floor in the corner.

From outside, he heard the main shower room door open, and a man's voice let out a cheep of surprise and delight.

"Oh, *man*..." the guy said.

"Hello," said Ollie.

"Hell-*lo!*"

Dan groaned. "Ollie, tell me you closed the damn cubicle door?"

"There's a cubicle door?"

Dan wrenched open his own door, revealing his fully naked body in all its hideous, stitched-together glory. A scrawny man with a beard, a sponge-stick and a visible erection stood framed in the shower room doorway. His face fell when he saw Dan. It wasn't the only thing that drooped.

"Fonk off," Dan warned him, as the man stumbled back in horror. "Ollie. Close the door."

Both doors clunked shut pretty much simultaneously. Dan hung off a second to make sure the man wasn't going to come back in, then closed his, too.

"OK. I'm naked," Ollie announced.

"Good for you," said Dan.

Once upon a time, his head would have been filling with some fairly vivid mental images right about now, but his lack of blood flow and hormones meant the thought didn't even occur to him.

"What happens now?" Ollie asked.

Dan looked up at the ceiling, expecting to see water jets there. Instead, he saw a few patches of damp, a peeling strip of paint, and a hand-written price-list for some quite specific sexual services, along with the number of a pod to visit if interested in making further inquiries.

"Uh, there should be water," Dan said.

"OK," said Ollie. She waited. "When?"

"I don't know," Dan admitted, then the floor vibrated beneath them as the cubicle began to move.

Of course.

"What's happening?" Ollie yelped.

"It's nothing to worry about," Dan said. "We used to use these back in some of the older Tribunal stations. It's a conveyor system."

"Aha! Right," said Ollie. Then: "What does that mean?"

"It means..." Dan began, then a jet sprayed and Ollie screamed in the next stall over. Despite the last couple of days he'd had, Dan couldn't help but smile. "...you're about to get wet."

The water blasted down on him from above as the conveyor system carried the cubicles on. The first burst was cold enough for even his mostly lifeless nerve-endings to pick up on, which explained Ollie's reaction.

The second burst was less cold, but only marginally. It had a detergent sort of smell to it, and formed a thin layer of bubbles where it hit Dan's skin. The bubbles foamed and fizzed as they consumed the dirt, and by the time the third – and coldest – water blast had hit him, Dan was as clean as he was ever likely to get.

"You OK?" he called.

"F-freezing!" Ollie replied through chattering teeth.

"Almost done," Dan said.

Ollie chirped in panic. "*Almost?*"

She needn't have worried. No more icy downpours lashed her bare skin. Instead, two cushions of warm air rose from the floor and rolled down from the ceiling, meeting somewhere around her stomach. It felt like slipping into socks that had been warmed in front of the fire, only the sock wasn't just for her foot, but her whole body.

"Aah. That's better," she said.

Dan nodded. "When it stops, get your clothes on," he said, then he made a point of clarifying. "The new ones. Leave the old ones."

"You mean this is going to stop?" Ollie groaned, wriggling in the warm air as she tried to wring every last moment of enjoyment out of it.

And then, to her immense disappointment, the warm air became just regular air, and goosebumps prickled on her purple-pink skin.

Dan lifted the lid of the chest and took out his mostly clean clothes. He leaned against the wall as he pulled on his pants.

"I've been thinking," said Ollie.

"How did that go?" Dan asked.

"Remember the monster thing? In the sewers?"

"It was forty minutes ago," Dan said. His buttons locked themselves together, then the pants tightened around his waist. "Yes, I remember it. Why?"

"Did you get the feeling that it was suffering?"

"You ask me, it wasn't suffering enough," Dan said.

"No, it's just... Did you get a sort of feeling from it?"

"I got a spike through the fonking shoulder from it," Dan said, pulling on his shirt. "Does that count?"

"It's just..."

Dan pulled the front of his shirt together and waited until it had fastened. "Just what?"

"I kind of got the feeling that it was in pain, or sad, or something," Ollie said. "I can't really explain more than that."

Dan shrugged and reached for his waistcoat. "I'm not sending it a card, if that's where this is going."

The shower cubicles rumbled to a stop, almost throwing them both off balance. The doors opened all on their own, and Dan was just wrestling his feet into his surprisingly dry boots when Ollie appeared around the door frame, fully dressed and perfectly clean.

The slogan on the front of her t-shirt read: *My Other Ships a Nebucore 6000!*

It bothered Dan for a couple of reasons. Firstly, it was missing an apostrophe. Secondly, it didn't make any fonking sense. He chose to rise above both issues, though, and kept them to himself.

"Ready?" she asked.

Dan pulled on his hat, curved down the front of the brim a little, then nodded. "All set."

THEY RETURNED to the pod to find Artur sitting on top of the filing cabinet, and Dan's roommates unconscious on the floor. Technically, Tor – the larger of the two – only had the back of his head and top of his shoulders on the floor, the rest of him being wedged between the wall and the bunk beds, but the result was much the same.

"What happened?" Dan asked. "Did they try to get into the filing cabinet?"

"They did," Artur confirmed. "Well, they didn't *try* exactly, but they were going to. I could tell."

Dan nudged Gunnak with his foot to check if he was alive. The little guy whimpered beneath his breath, which was proof enough.

"How could you tell?" Ollie asked.

"They just... they had that sort of look about them, ye know, Peaches? Like, I could tell by their faces they were thinking about opening one of the drawers and taking a look-see. Sure, it was written all over them."

"So you beat them unconscious?"

"So I beat them unconscious," Artur confirmed. He pointed to Tor. "Twice, in the big lad's case. He woke up. Near frightened the life out of me."

Dan bent over and slapped Tor around the face a few times until he grunted awake. "Hey. You listening?" Dan asked.

Tor's eyes widened when he got an up-close eyeful of Dan's scarred, decaying features. He tried to back away, but there was nowhere for him to go.

"That's mine," Dan said, pointing to the filing cabinet. "Is that clear? Everything in there, and everything in those boxes is mine. It's also rigged, so I'll know if you've touched anything. And so help me, if you touch anything, I will not be responsible for my actions."

He gestured to Artur. "And I'll be even less responsible for his. Is that clear?"

Tor didn't hesitate. He nodded frantically. "Clear. It's clear. I've got it."

Dan straightened. "Good. Because I'm making you responsible for it. Anyone touches it – anyone – and the buck stops with you." He smiled, showing off his surprisingly good teeth. "Got it?"

"Got it. G-got it," Tor confirmed, still nodding. It wasn't clear, in fact, if he was ever going to stop nodding. "I'll make sure no one touches it."

"I appreciate that," Dan said. He eyeballed him for a while, then turned to Artur and Ollie. "Now, what time is it?"

"Half past *how-the-feck-should-I-know*?" Artur replied. "Why?"

"Because I have an appointment," Dan said. He made for the door. "But first, I'm getting my gun back."

THE HATCH in the mirror closed, but Dan barely noticed. Instead, he focused on the weight of Mindy in his hand, and spent an enjoyable few seconds kneading her butt between his fingers.

Man, he'd missed this weapon.

Artur stood inside the breast pocket of Dan's coat, his head and shoulders visible, his arms hanging out over the front. Ollie stood on Dan's right, taking in her own reflection. She fiddled with the front of her hair. "I miss Banbara," she said.

"We all miss Barbara," Dan lied.

"Banbara," Ollie corrected.

"Hmm?" Dan looked up from the gun. "Oh. Yeah. Her, too."

"I just wish—"

"Yeah, yeah, she's gone, no point dwelling on it," Dan said, taking Ollie by the arm and ushering her toward the ladder. "Let's get moving. We've got some business to take care of."

"Where are we headed, exactly?" asked Artur.

"*Loopy Lou's*."

Artur craned his neck to look up at Dan, but from that angle could only make out the bottom of his chin. "*Loopy Lou's?*" he asked, his eyebrows rising in surprise and consternation. But mostly consternation.

"Yup," Dan confirmed, and Artur felt a faint shudder ripple through the detective. "We're going to *Loopy Lou's*."

NINE

LOOPY LOU'S billed itself as the premier children's entertainment, soft play and food venue chain in all of Down Here. It was correct in none of these assertions. Even the vaguest scrutiny of any one of its thirty-seven establishments would reveal that it wasn't even the premier children's entertainment venue on any given street.

In the case of this particular branch, that title instead belonged to *House of Faces* two doors down – a museum whose exhibits consisted entirely of painstakingly recreated waxwork faces of once-famous Down Here 'celebrities', only a handful of which even faintly resembled their owners. It was a testament to just how terrible *Loopy Lou's* was that in terms of its ability to keep children amused and entertained, it came second to some largely unrecognizable model faces. And not even a close second, at that.

The street outside both buildings was mostly deserted. Dan parked the Exodus as close as he could to *Loopy Lou's* entrance, in the hope the sheer awfulness of the building would make the car look better by comparison.

Years ago, the place must've been a real assault on the

eyeballs, but now the colorful murals had faded to pastel shades, and the neon awnings were dirty and torn. The large windows, designed to show how much fun the kids were having inside, were now crusted with dust and grime, making it almost impossible to see through them. Metal spikes had been bolted to the long flat windowsills, either to discourage people from sitting on them or to ensure that the only people who did were either perverts or psychopaths.

The name of the place had been painted above the door in swirly, swooping script, but time had taken its toll on that, too, and anyone seeing the place for the first time would be forgiven for thinking it was called *Loop Lo*.

There was a sandwich board style sign outside that promised 'Fun! Food! Fun!' Dan wasn't sure if the second 'Fun' was deliberate, or if the person who'd written it had some sort of short-term memory problems. Either way, he was sure they could be brought to trial for false advertising.

Like everywhere Down Here, throngs of pedestrians bustled by. Unlike other places, though, practically nobody stopped here, and Dan didn't see a single person step inside as he and the others watched from the car.

"God, we don't have to go in, do we?" Artur asked.

"I hope not," Dan said, watching the building's front door.

"What is this place?" Ollie asked.

"It's where Deadman's man works," Artur said. "Ye know, the tanned fella wi' the big muscles?"

"No, I know. But what is it?"

"It's a horrible place," Dan informed her. "That's all you need to know."

Ollie pointed past him. "But it says it's fun."

"It's lying," Artur assured her. "Trust me, I've been inside."

"Me too," said Dan.

Artur drew in a slow breath. "My condolences."

"Thanks. You too."

They waited and watched as thousands of Down Here citizens ebbed along the sidewalk like a river. No one spoke. No one smiled. They just flowed, endlessly flowed, from one end of the street to the next.

Eventually, Dan sighed through his nose. "He's not coming out."

"Give him a blast o' the horn," Artur suggested.

Dan shook his head and pressed the car horn. It emitted a single disappointing *parp* that barely registered as audible. "No use," he said. He opened the door. "I'm going in."

"Ye're not!" Artur gasped. "Are ye?"

"Got to. If he isn't coming out, I'm going in," Dan said. "You coming?"

"Shoite, no. Not if ye paid me," Artur said. "Well, I mean, it would depend how much, I suppose. How much are ye offering?"

"I'm not," said Dan.

"Ah well, feck ye, then," Artur replied, folding his arms across his chest. "Ye're on yer own."

"I'll come," said Ollie.

"No, you won't," replied Dan. He caught the look of disappointment on her face. "Trust me, I'm doing you a favor."

THE MOMENT DAN opened the door, a spring-loaded Loopy Lou puppet *twoinged* at him, its arms jiggling, its plastic mouth twisted up into a grin. Electric motors inside it *whirred* gently as its jaw flapped up and down.

It was... what? Dan had no idea. Some sort of anthropo-morphic animal? A member of some off-world species he'd never seen before? A half-assed attempt at a mascot kids would love, but which had inadvertently gone on to haunt their nightmares instead?

Probably that last one, he thought. He'd never known kids to actually *like* the character, but they would gener-ally sit there in a transfixed stupor as he paraded around for their – and Dan used the word very loosely – amusement.

"W-w-w-welcome to Loopy Lou's!" the puppet cried in a loud deliberate stutter. A few notes of utterly tuneless music blasted from some sort of speaker hidden beneath its colorful satin clothing and it began to sing. "Loopy-Loopy-Loopy-Loopy-Loo-pee Lou's, it's fun for me, and it's fun for—"

"Shut the fonk up," Dan muttered, pushing past and leaving the thing singing at the empty doorway.

Loopy Lou's was even more depressing than he remem-bered, and he'd remembered it being practically suicide inducing. It was made up of three distinct sections – a soft play area where children could jump and climb without fear of smashing their heads open on the floor, a café where parents could sit and watch them, and a little stage where Loopy Lou himself would occasionally come out and 'enter-tain' the audience.

It wasn't the real Loopy Lou, of course – there was no such person. Instead, it was someone wearing a genuinely unsettling full-body costume and carrying an assortment of tediously predictable props.

Hidden panels in the floor *parped*, *honked*, *tinkled* and made assorted other annoying sounds as Dan trudged across the scuffed vinyl floor to the café counter. A single individual sat behind it, bent double so their forehead rested on the glass countertop, not moving.

Despite the fanfare of farts and whistles that had accompanied Dan's arrival, the shriveled prune-faced man sat up with a start when Dan rapped his knuckles on the glass.

"Whootcha?" he yelped, kung-fuing the air in front of him.

There was a crash as he fell backward off his stool and disappeared out of sight. Dan flicked his eyes around the place while waiting for the guy to reappear.

It was hard to pinpoint what, precisely, was the problem with any given branch of *Loopy Lou*'s. It wasn't that there was one single thing that made the places so bleak, but rather a multitude of little things, from the cracked mirrors on the café walls to the cordoned off sections of the soft play area where Tribunal 'Do Not Cross' tape delineated the boundaries of various major incidents.

Generally speaking, patches of damp would have been painted over multiple times, before eventually being left to do their worst. Half the lights wouldn't be working, and those that were would emit an annoying *buzz* that was loud enough to hear, but quiet enough to make you doubt if it was all in your imagination.

Music was piped in constantly through tinny speakers that vibrated unpleasantly on all the bass notes – the same tune looped over and over and over again.

And then there were the characters.

Loopy Lou was the main one, of course – a grinning, goggle-eyed *whatever-the-fonk* who wore a vibrantly yellow t-shirt on his top half, and nothing whatsoever on his bottom half. This, in itself, wasn't unusual. Dan had seen plenty of cartoon characters who wore a similar get-up. The difference was, someone somewhere had decided that Loopy Lou should be anatomically correct. And generously anatomically correct, at that.

Given the age of the clientele, this was a mistake, Dan reckoned. He also noted that none of the other characters had any genitals to speak of, but chose not to get bogged down in the psychology of it.

Limp, glassy-eyed mannequins of them all were tied high on the walls around the place, displayed like the contents of a serial killer's trophy cabinet.

Dan faced front as the prune-faced man clambered to his feet. Despite the wrinkles, his voice suggested he was young. It also suggested he was terrified.

"W-welcome to... to..."

"*Loopy Lou's,*" Dan finished for him.

"Huh? Right! Welcome to *L-Loopy Lou's,*" he said in a high-pitched nasal whine. "Um... What do...? How can...?"

He sort of gave up at that point and just shrugged. "There's no money in the register," he said. He raised his hands. "Please d-don't kill me."

"I ain't here to rob you, kid," Dan said. "I'm looking for Finn."

Prune-face kept his hands up. "Finn?"

"Tall guy. Tanned. Says 'brah' a lot, though I have no idea why."

"Are... are you going to hurt him?"

"Not deliberately," Dan said. "Is he here?"

"I... I don't... I mean..."

"Hey! Dead dude!"

"Guess he is," said Dan, not yet turning. "Put your hands down, kid."

Prune-face looked at his hands as if only now realizing they were raised. He let them flop to his sides and sat down as Finn shambled over to join them. He wore four-fifths of a *Loopy Lou* costume – legs, body, arms and furry genitalia – and carried a head under one arm. He grinned at Dan as if seeing a long-lost friend for the first time in years.

"Hey, brah! Good to see you. What brings you here?"

A frown briefly troubled Dan's brow. "We were going to do that thing."

Finn saw Dan's frown and raised it. "What thing?"

"You know. You were going to take me to see your boss."

Finn pointed to the floor with a fluffy finger. "Of this place?" he asked, then the memory popped back in there. "Oh! You mean Krato."

Dan glanced back at Prune-face, but the kid had obviously concluded none of this was anything to do with him and had returned to his forehead-on-counter position.

"Not so loud," Dan warned Finn. "But yes."

Finn shook his head. "Sorry, brah, I can't. Got a show."

Dan looked around at the empty space. "A show? For who?"

"Got a birthday party coming in."

"Here?" said Dan. "There's a birthday party coming *here?*"

"I know, brah. Crazy, right?" Finn said, breaking into that easy grin of his. "It's for a family of, like, Noogins or Snoobins or whatever. Puffy white guys. Heavy into irony. They can't get enough of this place."

"Damn it," Dan muttered. He knew asking the kid to skip out on work would be signing his death warrant. The Tribunal didn't mess around when it came to the city's workforce taking unauthorized time off. And since holidays and sick days were outlawed, all time off was unauthorized.

"Fine. Then just give me the address," Dan said.

"No can do, brah," Finn said. "I never had it. I've only

seen the place once, so I can't even draw you a map. But I know how to get to it." He shrugged, although it was hard to see it beneath the padded shoulders. If it hadn't been for the suddenly penduluming penis, Dan wouldn't even have been aware of the movement. "I can take you when I'm done."

Dan sighed. "And how long will that be?"

"Maybe, I don't know... Two hours?"

It was not the news Dan had wanted to hear. Now the toilet monster had been taken care of, Krato was next on his list of priorities. He had been itching to get his hands on the mass-murdering fonk for days, and any delay was an unwelcome one.

"Well, I guess I'll just have to..." Dan began, then he stopped. "Wait. What do you have to do, exactly? For the show, I mean."

"Just, you know, sort of dance around," Finn said, kicking one foot out a little and waving a hand at his side. "The head's got, like, motors or robot parts or whatever. It's synced up to the rest of the show, so it does most of the work for me."

Dan nodded slowly. He pointed to the suit. "And is it adjustable? Could it fit someone a foot smaller, say?"

"Yeah. Oh yeah, totally, brah. There's an adjustable dial inside that—"

"OK, OK, I don't need you to read me the instruction manual," said Dan. "Take it off."

Finn looked down at himself. "But... the show?"

"Don't worry about it," said Dan. A smile tugged at one corner of his mouth. "I'm going to get you a stand-in."

OLLIE STOOD in the headless Loopy Lou suit, idly flapping her big fluffy penis.

"So, you know what to do?" Dan asked her.

"Not really, no," she admitted.

Dan sighed. "Like Finn says, all you have to... Will you stop doing that?"

"Doing what?"

"Fiddling with that thing," Dan said.

"It's fun," Ollie said. "I've never had one of these before. What's it for?"

"Doesn't matter."

"Is it a bell? The end bit looks like a bell."

Artur wheezed. He had been curled up on the floor wheezing for a while now, his beard sodden with laughter tears, his arms wrapped around himself as he attempted to stop his sides from splitting.

"A *bell!*" he shrieked, barely able to breathe. "A feckin' bell!"

"No, it's not a..." Dan began, then he slapped Ollie's hand away. "It's not a bell. The point is, don't touch it."

"It's hard not to, brah," Finn pointed out.

"I know, right?!" laughed Ollie. She waggled the furry penis and made a sort of *blimminy-blimminy-blim* sound which almost killed Artur stone dead. Dan slapped her hand away again.

"Cut it out!" he warned, then he shot a look to Finn. "Tell her what she has to do."

Finn stepped up in front of Ollie and smiled at her. As he did, several different expressions passed fleetingly across her face.

"You're tall," she said.

"Thanks. We haven't really met properly. I'm Finn."

"Right. Yes. Finn. Good. Finn. Yes."

Ollie blushed slightly, cleared her throat a couple of times, then briefly went *blimminy-blimminy-blim* with her artificial penis, before concluding that it possibly wasn't the right time.

"Ha! Yeah, I do that all the time," Finn said.

Ollie looked pleased by this. "Isn't it great? I mean, it's just right there!"

"Yeah! Great," said Finn. He gazed at Ollie for a while. "*Totally* great," he sighed, then he realized he'd said that part out loud and quickly glanced down.

Dan's eyes narrowed a little as he looked between Ollie and Finn. Even with his limited detective skills, he couldn't miss the goofy grins on both their faces.

"Oh great. That's all we need," he grunted. "Just tell her what she has to do so we can get going."

Finn thought for a moment, then let his arms sag limply to his sides. His whole body flopped a little, like all tension had left it. "Just, like, do this."

Ollie sagged as best as she could inside the suit. "Like this?"

"Beautiful!" Finn said, which made Ollie blush again. He picked the head up from the floor. "Just do that and you'll be fine."

"What about the dancing?" Dan asked. "I thought she had to dance?"

"Don't worry about it," Finn said, easing the Loopy Loud headpiece over Ollie's own head. "The electric shocks do that for you."

Ollie's voice came muffled from beneath the mask. "Wait, what?" she asked, then a jolt of electricity surged through her, making her arms and legs flap, and spinning her into a twirl.

"See?" said Finn. "Takes care of itself. The kids love it.

Well, they don't *love* it, but they can't stop watching. It's... what do you call it?"

"Horrifying?" Dan guessed.

"Hypnotic," said Finn.

Ollie spasmed and Artur erupted into laughter again. "Oh... Oh, shoite. That's priceless," he said, watching Ollie jerk around helplessly. "That's the greatest thing I have ever seen in me life."

"Does it hurt?" Dan asked.

Finn shook his head. "No, brah. I mean, not really. It's unpleasant, but that's all. Although one time it did make me wet myself. But only, like, a cupful."

Dan lifted the headpiece off a little and Ollie's jerking stopped. "You OK in there?"

"Are you kidding?" she asked. "That was *awesome*! Put the head back on."

Dan glanced back at Finn, and both men shrugged. "Fair enough."

"Once the kids arrive, you can't take it off, OK? Don't want to spoil the magic for them," Finn said. "They all love it."

"Magic my arse," Artur snorted. "Ye mean ye don't want anyone reporting to yer boss that it's not you in the suit, or ye'll get fired."

"That, too," Finn confirmed.

The headpiece clicked into place at the neck. There was a muffled, "Whoa!" as Ollie flapped and flailed around again.

"Looks like she'll be fine," Dan said. He motioned in the direction of the door. "Now, lead the way. With any luck, I can get this scumbag put down by lunchtime."

"Aye, and if there's one thing we're renowned for, it's our luck. Right, Deadman?" asked Artur, wiping away his laughter tears on the billowing sleeve of his cream satin blouse.

Dan grunted. "Got to be a first time for everything," he said. Then, with Ollie flapping and twirling behind him, he honked, *brrringed* and *whooped* his way to the door.

TEN

DAN AND FINN stood on a rooftop in one of the more upmarket sectors of Down Here, peering into a window of what appeared to be a bog-standard apartment block standing on the opposite side of the pedestrianized street.

They were eight stories up, which afforded Dan a decent view of the streets immediately surrounding the apartments. From this height it was also possible to watch dozens of cargo ships ascending and descending between Down Here and the floating cities of Up There. That was where the real wealth was. Even relatively decadent Down Here areas like this one, where the cars were all under six years old and the walls were mostly free of obscenities, were considered ghetto-like by those living above.

Dan had left the Exodus parked a few blocks away so as not to draw too much attention. The car wasn't quite old and broken down enough to be noteworthy in most of the other sectors, but it'd stand out like a sore thumb here. A sore diseased thumb. With failing brakes and a shizzy engine.

Finn looked the building up and down, then gazed

along the street in both directions. "I think... I think that's it," he said.

"That's it," Dan confirmed.

Artur, who was nestled in Dan's breast coat pocket, frowned. "How d'ye know that?"

"There are bars on the windows of the first three floors," Dan pointed out. "And it's the only building on this street with a guard stationed out front."

"Well, I never," said Artur, almost sounding impressed. "Would ye look at that? Maybe ye're not such a useless big bollocks, after all."

"I appreciate that."

"I said 'maybe.' Let's not get too excited," Artur said, then he puffed out his cheeks. "So, what's the plan? Sneaking in the back door? Shimmying up the drainpipe and smashing through a window?"

Dan reached into his coat and took Mindy from her holster. "Thought we might go noisy," he said.

Artur nodded appreciatively. "I like yer style, Dead-man. But won't that mean he knows we're coming?"

"Yeah, well." Dan nodded. "Maybe I want him to know I'm coming."

"Whoa. So, you're going to, like, kill him?" Finn asked.

"Here's hoping," said Dan. "But first, I have to be sure he's responsible."

"Yeah should probably just shoot him and be done with it, either way," Artur suggested. "I mean, we know he's a wrong 'un, don't we?"

"I need to know I've got the person who killed all those people," Dan said. "If it wasn't him, it was someone else, and they're not getting away with it."

Artur nodded. "This one really got to ye, didn't it?"

"Thirty-eight kids," Dan said, not taking his eyes off the

building across the street. "Twelve of them were in a damn toy shop."

"Oh wow, brah. That's horrible."

"That's your boss," Dan said.

"I told you, he's not my boss! I did one..." Finn's smooth forehead crinkled as he tried to recall precisely what he'd done. "I don't know. Whatever it was. I don't remember seeing any weapons, though, brah. Although, for some reason, I don't actually remember very much."

"Hey, Deadman!" Artur said. "I think we've been made."

Dan's head snapped down and saw the guard looking up. He was barking orders, presumably into some hidden microphone. There was a series of *clangs* from the upper floor of the apartment block as metal shutters slammed closed across the windows.

"Fonk. They're going into lockdown," Dan realized. "Wait here, kid, and stay back from the edge. Artur, hold onto something."

"What? Why?" Artur asked, then he gasped as Dan stepped up onto the ledge. "Don't ye fecking dare step off this—"

The rest of the sentence was lost as it became a gurgled scream at the back of Artur's throat. Dan plunged straight down the side of the building, his gun in his hand, his coat billowing out around him. It all looked very impressive, right up until the point he crunched against the ground, when it immediately became far less so.

Bones compacted in his legs and spine. Muscles tore. The remains of his last meal ejected themselves through both nostrils, then his face met the road surface and he lay there as a crumpled, motionless heap on the ground.

Across the road, the guard had been backing towards

the door, but he hesitated now with his gun drawn. There was a look of absolute bewilderment on his face as he raised his eyes to the rooftop, then down at the lifeless figure on the street.

"Uh, hold the door," he instructed whoever was on the receiving end of his microphone. "The guy just jumped. Off the roof, yeah."

He listened for a moment. "Well, he sure fonking looks that way. I'm going to go check it out. Stand by."

Keeping his gun ready, the guard approached the unmoving mound. He was large and heavy-set – real night-club doorman material – and moved with all the grace of a beached sea cow.

A small knot of people had begun forming around Dan, but they quickly dispersed when the guard waved his gun in their general direction. "Go on, get out of here. I'll take care of this," he instructed. Because they knew who he worked for, everyone was quick to oblige.

Sticking out a foot, he gave Dan a tentative prod.

Nothing.

He kicked him harder, but still got no reaction.

"Yeah, he's paste," the guard said, turning away. "Must've just been a jumper. Cancel the lockdown and call a cleaning crew or something to get this shizz off the street."

A slowdown round hit him in the back, grinding him into five percent movement speed.

By the time he'd figured out something was wrong, Dan had got to his feet, dusted himself down, taken the guy's earpiece, then smashed him in the face with the butt of his gun.

The nose exploded in breathtaking slow motion, glob-ules of blood floating away from it as if they were in zero gravity. Dan watched the blood wobble off through the air while he clicked his bones back into place and retrieved his hat.

"Ye're a fecking maniac!" Artur yelped from his coat pocket. "I mean... Ye almost squished me!"

"But I didn't," Dan pointed out, turning his back on the guard and limping in the direction of the building's front door. His right leg needed some serious adjustments, but now wasn't the time. Someone would figure out the guard was gone, soon, and the lockdown would start again. He had to be inside before that happened.

As he slipped the earpiece into his ear, he caught the tail end of someone's sentence. "...Down are up here. He wants to know everything's clear. Confirm."

Dan hobbled across the pedestrianized street, closing on the door. "Confirm," he said, doing his best to replicate the guard's dulcet tones.

"Who the fonk is this?" the voice in the earpiece demanded.

The shutters on the upper windows snapped closed. A metal barricade began to drop down over the building's front door, but another slowdown round reduced its rate of descent to a leisurely creep, allowing Dan to duck beneath it and into the hallway beyond.

A spray of blaster fire screamed toward him. He dodged, but heard the sizzle as one of the bolts took a chunk out of his thigh.

"Mindy, stun shot," he instructed. He squeezed the trigger a fraction of a second before the round chamber had finished spinning, and the gun's lights illuminated in red to indicate a jam.

"Shizz," Dan grunted. He fished into his coat pocket. "Art, you're up," he said, tossing Artur overarm toward the gorilla-like gunman at the other end of the hall.

Artur roared as he flew through the air between the blaster bolts, his blouse and crisp white slacks flapping around him.

He landed on the guy's face, then simultaneously bit his nose, kicked a tooth out, and forced three fingers into one of his eyeballs. The gorilla dropped the gun and grabbed at the multiple pain points on his face, but Artur quickly scrambled up onto his head, took hold of some strands of hair, then flipped down the back of the guy's head.

Tugging with a surprising amount of force, he yanked the gorilla's head back so sharply the guy was pulled off his feet. The head *clonked* against the floor. Artur waited a moment to make sure the gunman was unconscious, then wiped his hands on his thighs.

"Greasy-haired bastard," he observed, then he raised his arms above his head, and Dan picked him up on the way to the stairs.

Mindy's chamber clicked and the lights around the weapon's barrel turned blue. "Looks like we won't have to kill everyone," Dan said, slipping Artur back into his pocket.

"We won't *have* to," said Artur. "But, sure, wouldn't it be more fun if we did?"

A heavily built figure with two robotic arms appeared at the top of the first staircase. He had some sort of grenade in one hand, the trigger mechanism still fully depressed. Dan shot him between the eyes and the weight of his limbs toppled him forward down the steps. He slid to a stop at Dan's feet, twitching a little and foaming gently at the mouth, the grenade still clutched in his hand.

With some difficulty, Dan prized the explosive from the cocoon of metal fingers, keeping the trigger held in. He flicked the lock switch on top of the device, then gave it a cursory examination. He was hoping it would be some highly-illegal or experimental explosive that would confirm Krato was still in the arms trade. Annoyingly, it was just a *Disorientator* – a confusion grenade readily available at any Down Here gun store – and so it proved nothing.

Still, it might come in handy, so he slipped it into one of his pockets, stepped over Robo-arms, and continued up the stairs.

There were light scatterings of guards on the next two floors. Dan disposed of them without too much difficulty, and only a minor stab wound to the thigh. He kept the knife. Again, it might come in handy.

The fourth floor was a different matter. Dan heard the humming of blaster rifles from the bottom of the steps, and the conspicuous silence that came from a lot of people all holding their breath.

So, Krato was on this floor. Either that, or this was just a cover and he was actually on one of the floors above. Either way, Dan would have to get through the miniature army of henchmen first.

He flicked the switch, released the trigger, then tossed the grenade. The silence became a panicky thunder of footsteps and shouts, then a blinding flash illuminated the rectangle of ceiling that Dan could see.

"Three, two, one..." Artur counted. Just as he reached zero, several rifles began firing erratically.

Dan took a moment to adjust his collar and reposition his hat while he waited for the shooting to stop.

"Ye think Peaches is having a better or worse time than us?" Artur asked him.

Dan considered this. Upstairs, someone screamed.

"Worse," Dan said. "Definitely worse."

"Agreed. Poor cow," said Artur. He gestured up the stairs to where the blaster fire had fallen silent. "Shall we?"

Dan trudged up the stairs into a scene of chaos and carnage. As expected, there had been several people waiting up there. About eight, he thought, if he extrapolated numbers from the remains.

A good few of them had been shot repeatedly at point blank range with high-powered fully-automatic blaster rifles, and their charred remains now decorated the scorched and blackened corridor walls.

Three had avoided being shot. One of them was attempting to run away but was fleeing directly into a wall, and so going nowhere. Another spun in tight circles, his eyes wide and staring at nothing. The third seemed intent on doing a handstand but was having difficulty finding his center of balance. He also didn't seem to know where his hands were, which wasn't making things any easier.

None of them acknowledged Dan as he proceeded down the corridor to a grand set of double doors at the far end.

"So, we find out if he did yer shopping mall thing, then we shoot him either way on account of him being a scumbag?" Artur asked. "Is that the plan?"

"Pretty much," Dan confirmed.

"I mean, it's only fair. Sure, look at all these people he had trying to shoot us. That's just impolite."

Reaching the end of the corridor, Dan kicked the doors where they met in the middle. The damage he'd sustained in the fall from the roof stole some of the usual force away, and it took several attempts before the lock splintered and the doors flew open.

"Don't hurt them! Don't hurt the kids!"

Dan paused, Mindy raised in front of him. A red-skinned figure with a sharp suit and a ludicrous quasi-beard that grew like an extension from the end of his chin stood at the far end of a quietly opulent room. Krato, Dan assumed. He fit the description at least.

Six wide-eyed child-sized figures were huddled behind him, tears cutting tracks down their faces. They were of a species Dan couldn't identify, but there was definitely something *aquatic* about them, he thought. Their blue-green skin glistened like scales in the overhead lights, and there were semi-transparent webs between each of their long, slender fingers.

Music played from a speaker on Krato's desk. It was a soft and sleepy sort of tune that made Dan think of warm pajamas and hot milk. A lullaby. Why the fonk was an arms dealer playing a lullaby?

"What the fonk is this?" Dan muttered.

"I'll give you whatever you want," Krato said. "Just don't hurt the children."

"Deadman, yer left," Artur barked.

Dan brought an elbow up, crunching it into the face of another blue-green figure. This one was bigger than the others, and presumably an adult. He was dressed in a gold-colored armored bodice and a pair of shiny silver trunks that left very little to the imagination.

"Ooh, those must chafe like a bastard," Artur remarked.

Dan pointed the gun at the man's face, although the way he was sobbing and clutching his broken nose suggested he wasn't about to try anything.

"Get over there," Dan instructed, ushering him toward Krato and the rest of the group.

Krato beckoned the man over, then guided him into the group of children. "Seriously, there's a safe. I have money," Krato pleaded. "Just let them go."

Dan adjusted his grip on the gun, buying himself a second or two to consider his answer. He'd been expecting one of two things when he kicked open the door. Either it was going to be a trap, or Krato would already have left. He knew it would be unlikely that the arms dealer would just hang around while all that shooting was going on.

The kids, though. He hadn't been expecting the kids.

"You're Krato, right?" Dan grunted.

"Yes. Yes, I am. I'm Krato. You've heard of me. Then you know I'm telling the truth. I can pay you a lot of money just to walk away."

"I don't want your money," Dan said. "I'm here for you."

Krato's pointed eyebrows arched. "Me?" he said, then he nodded quickly. "OK. OK, yes, that's fine. Take me. Do what you want. Just don't hurt the kids."

"I'll level wit' ye, Deadman. This is not what I was expecting," Artur whispered.

"What are they? Hostages?" Dan demanded. "You going to use them for target practice?"

Krato shook his head. "What? No! They're just kids. They're just here for a visit. They have nothing to do with... whatever this is about. OK? Just kids."

"Like the kids in that mall, you mean?"

"Mall?" Krato's expression became mostly blank. "I don't... what mall?"

"On Eighteenth," Dan said. "One-hundred-and-thirty-four people killed."

Krato's face paled. "Oh... N-no. That was you?"

"It was *you!*" Dan spat.

"Are ye sure about this, Deadman?" Artur whispered.

"Me?! What are you talking about? I'm a businessman not a... a... *terrorist.*"

Dan advanced a pace. The children and their bloody-nosed adult supervisor all shrunk back. Krato raised his arms at his sides, like he could somehow shield them all.

"No, but you supply weapons to terrorists, don't you?" Dan said. "And I hear you supplied whatever was used to kill those people."

"Then you heard wrong!"

Dan's grip tightened on his gun. Krato raised his hands in a calming gesture.

"OK, OK. Let's talk about this. Take me wherever you want. I'll go with you, no complaints." He gestured back to the children behind him, all sobs and snot now. "Just let them go. They have nothing to do with anything."

"Might be for the best," Artur suggested. "Sure, ye don't want to be blowing him to pieces in front of the skiddlers now, do ye?"

"Fine," Dan grunted. He beckoned Krato over, then forcibly shoved him toward the door. He turned to the kids. "You can go," he said, then he remembered the carnage in the hallway outside. "But, uh, I'd probably close your eyes until you get down a floor or two."

"Just be careful on the stairs," Artur suggested. "We take no responsibility for any accidents or mishaps ye may or may not have."

Dan jabbed the gun into Krato's back and urged him on.

"Oh gods. What happened?" he gasped, eyes flitting around the carnage. "Did you do this?"

"They did it to themselves," Dan said.

"Although, technically, we did give them a nudge in the right direction," added Artur.

Krato stepped over a twitching severed arm and made for the steps leading down. Dan caught him by the shoulder and steered him in a different direction. "Uh-uh. We're going up."

"Up? Why, what's up?" Krato asked.

"The roof," said Dan. "We're going to the roof."

"N-NO, please! Please! Don't let go, don't let go!"

Dan adjusted his grip on Krato's ankle and gave a non-committal grunt. "Then I suggest you stop wriggling."

Krato continued to flap for a few seconds, before letting himself go limp. His red skin had initially gone completely pale when Dan had shoved him over the roof's edge, but was now darkening again as all the blood ran to his head.

"Please, don't kill me," he whimpered. "I've done nothing wrong."

"Ninety-six adults. Thirty-eight children," Dan growled.

"It wasn't me! I don't know what you're talking about! I had nothing to do with that!"

"My sources say otherwise," Dan replied.

"Then they're wrong!" Krato sobbed. "I had nothing to do with any mall!"

Dan shook the man's leg, making him squeal and whimper.

"You provided the weapons. You deal in guns."

"What? No!" Krato spluttered. "I'm not an arms dealer, I'm a drug dealer! *Legal drugs*, I mean! Pharmaceuticals!"

"You're lying," Dan spat.

Artur, who had been sitting on the ledge and flicking through Krato's wallet, looked up. "Uh, I hate to say it, Deadman, but I don't think he's talking' shoite."

He held up Krato's ID card. This required two arms. "Says here he's the boss of some big drugs company. 'Karma-Pharma.'"

"That's it!" Krato yelped. "That's it!"

Artur dug out a Karma-Pharma business card and read

it. "If ye believe this, they're a drugs company 'with a conscience,'" he said.

"We're developing a cure for acute Ingospasmonsis," Krato said.

"What the fonk is Ingospasmonsis?"

"It's a genetic condition. Those children downstairs, that's why they're here. They're our first patients!" His voice cracked into a throaty croak. "We're trying to save them. They're here for their treatment."

Dan looked down at Artur, who shrugged. "Don't ask me."

"You're an arms dealer," Dan growled.

Krato shook his head. "OK, listen. One of my old companies did deal in weaponry," he began, then he screamed as Dan dropped him a foot before tightening his grip again. "Legal, government contract planetary defense stuff! When Krone started moving his task forces into the sector, the bottom fell out of the market. I sold all my shares months ago and plowed the money into Karma. It's the truth, I swear." His words descended into a mess of sobs and wails. "I *swear*."

"Call me a sentimental old wanker, but I kind of believe him," Artur said.

"Why the guards?" Dan demanded.

Artur peeked over the edge. "I think he may have passed out."

Dan scowled. "Seriously?" He jiggled Krato around a little, but got no response.

"Either that or he's just decided now's the perfect time to get some shut-eye." Artur shrugged. "Or he might be dead, I suppose."

Dan heaved the motionless figure back up over the edge and dropped him onto the rooftop. Artur licked his own hand until it was good and wet, then shoved it in Krato's ear, startling him awake.

"Wha—?" Krato's dark eyes darted around as he remembered where he was and what was happening.

"Why the guards?" Dan asked. "If you're curing kids of whatever it was you said, why the armed guards?"

"Because we're offering free medication. Free treatment," Krato said. He rubbed the hip of the leg Dan had been holding and winced with the pain it brought. "Do you know how many drugs companies operate Down Here? Not to mention those Up There. They don't like us. They don't like what we're doing. We need to protect ourselves. We used to rent an office downtown, but it wasn't safe, so we moved up here."

"That does make sense," Artur said. "Ye reckon, Deadman? That does make sense."

Dan gave another non-committal sort of grunt. "I'm not buying it," he said, raising Mindy until she was pointed between Krato's eyes.

"No, look, stop!" Krato protested. "You want the truth? OK, OK, the truth!" He took a deep breath. "Am I an angel? No. I've been successful in business for twenty years. You know how difficult that is Down Here? You know how much it costs to bribe the Tribunal? You know how many minor but terrible things you have to do on a daily basis? The lines you have to cross?"

He saw Dan's jaw tightening and held both hands out in front of him. "But that's not me anymore! I'm trying to do good now. I'm trying to make up for it. To make a difference. What happened at the mall? I know nothing about that. Nothing. I swear to you. I swear."

His eyes flitted to the gun and he swallowed. "But if you

have to shoot me, go ahead and shoot me. Just leave those kids alone. Their only crime is being ill."

Dan ground his teeth together, chewing this over.

"Nope, still not buying it," he decided, then he tightened his grip on the hand cannon and—

"Hey, brah!"

Finn's voice drifted across from the opposite rooftop. Dan kept the gun trained on Krato, but looked up.

"That's the Krato guy, right?"

"It is," Dan shouted back.

"Thought so. When I saw him, it all started to, like, come back. I remembered what the dude hired me to do!"

Dan felt a spark of hope. "You did?"

"Yeah, brah!"

Dan waited.

"*Well?* What was it?" he called over, quietly hoping the answer would be, 'Transport a lot of guns to a shopping mall.'

"Some, like, clinical trial thing," came the answer. "Like a drug test. He paid us a hundred each."

"Yes! That's right! I did!" Krato babbled. "Listen to him, he knows who I am!"

"Pretty generous if you ask me, brah."

Dan's spark of hope flickered, then went out. He brought the gun down to his side. "Fonk," he muttered.

He puffed out his cheeks, then looked down into Artur's eyes just as the little man winced.

"Well. This is a bit awkward, ain't it?" Artur said.

Dan cleared his throat, holstered his gun, then tapped the brim of his hat. "Uh, sorry for the inconvenience," he said. "It seems we—"

"*I*," Artur corrected. "The word ye're lookin' for is 'I.'"

"It seems *I* may have made a mistake," Dan said.

Krato looked between them. "You mean... you're not going to kill me?"

"No. Not going to kill you," Dan said. He shifted awkwardly, cleared his throat again, then picked Artur up. "Apologies again for the inconvenience," he said, then he turned and headed for the door leading down from the roof.

Halfway there, he stopped and turned back.

"Wait, did you say you used to rent an office downtown?"

Krato blinked slowly, like he couldn't quite process what was going on. "Huh? Oh, yes. Yes, we did."

Dan nodded. "Don't suppose you'd happen to know if it's still on the market?"

ELEVEN

THEY FOUND Ollie collapsed in the *Loopy Lou's* depressingly gray staff room, twitching occasionally as the costume shocked her. Finn hurried to her side and removed the headpiece, letting a wave of warm air roll up out of the neck. Her purple-pink face was now all the way red, and shiny all over with sweat. She gasped as the cooler air rushed in, like a drowning swimmer breaking the surface for the last time.

"You OK? Why are you still in the suit?" Finn asked.

"Um. Hi!" Ollie said, giving a little wave of her big furry hand. "You told me I couldn't take it off."

"When the kids were here," said Finn. "They're gone."

Ollie's eyes widened. "Oh! I didn't... I thought... I just didn't want you to get into trouble."

Finn smiled and brushed back his tousled blond locks. "You didn't? Aw! That's so sweet of you."

"Oh, for fonk's sake," Dan muttered.

"Were they into it? The kids, I mean?" Finn asked.

"So much!" Ollie cheeped. "I mean, at first I thought they were kind of scared and, you know, kind of horrified?

But then they just sat there smiling at me the whole time. Like totally silent and just smiling."

"I'd have shoite meself if that happened," Artur said. "Creepy little bastards."

Dan grunted. "Just ditch the suit and let's get out of here."

Finn looked Ollie up and down. "Want me to help?"

"She can get it," Dan told him.

"It's just, the catch at the back can be—"

Dan caught Finn by the back of the neck and steered him toward the door. Artur scowled at Finn from inside Dan's top pocket. "Ye heard what the man said. She can get it."

"We'll go wait out front. Come out when you're ready," Dan told Ollie.

"OK. See you soon!" said Ollie, trying to reach the fastener on the back of the suit with very little success. "I'll just be... This won't take..."

She fell over, rolled on her 'comically' large padded belly, then flopped sideways out of sight behind a coffee table.

"I'm fine. I'm OK," she called. "I've totally got this, guys."

Her head raised from behind the coffee table. "Guys?"

But the guys were gone.

OLLIE SLID into the front seat of the Exodus and, after three attempts, closed the door. Dan sat in the driver's seat, his hands impatiently gripping the wheel. Artur was slouched in his usual indent in the dash, turned so he could keep a close eye on the annoyingly handsome fecker in the back.

"Hey! You're here," said Ollie, turning in her chair. Finn beamed back at her, showing off some *very* nice teeth.

"Yeah! I asked Dan if I could—"

Dan cleared his throat and fixed his rear-view mirror with a cold stare.

"Sorry. I asked *Mr Deadman* if I could bum a ride back to the Stagnates with you guys."

Ollie appeared equal parts delighted and surprised. "And he said 'yes?'" she asked, turning to Dan.

"Couldn't think of an excuse fast enough," Dan admitted, then he turned over the ignition and eventually teased the engine into a spluttering and wheezing form of life.

"Your car doesn't sound too healthy," Finn pointed out.

"I know."

"I could take a look for you, if you like? I mean, I'm not officially trained or whatever, but I know a thing or two about engines, brah."

"It's fine. It's under control. I like it like this," Dan said, guiding the Exodus out into traffic. "And don't call me 'brah.'"

"Sorry, dude."

Dan rolled his eyes, but said nothing.

Ollie faced front and crossed her arms. "So, back to that underground place?" she asked, and her voice conveyed her feelings about the prospect of returning to the Stagnates.

"Afraid so," said Dan.

A horn blared as he cut in front of a mag-lev truck. Artur extended the middle fingers of both hands in the truck's direction.

"Get it up ye! Are ye feckin' blind?" he roared, then he

lowered his voice to a low mutter. "Ye know that was totally your fault, right?"

Dan chose not to pass comment on the matter and merged the car onto a slipway leading up onto the main route downtown.

"Uh, I don't think this is the quickest way to the Stagnates," Finn told him.

"I'm aware of that," Dan said, fighting the suddenly all-too-tempting urge to reverse into a wall. "We have to quickly swing by somewhere else first."

Ollie frowned across at him. "Where?"

Dan didn't take his eyes off the road ahead with its stop-start streams of traffic. "I think I might have found us a new office."

DAN AND OLLIE stood in the office suite's main reception area, quietly taking it all in. Finn had been instructed to wait in the car, and while Dan had asked Artur to keep an eye on him, Artur had announced he could, "bugger that for a game of soldiers,' and had tagged along with Dan and Ollie, instead.

A largely apathetic letting agent leaned against the doorframe, flicking idly through a stack of printed pages he had fastened to his clipboard.

"So, as you can see, it needs some work."

"That's a feckin' understatement," Artur said.

"The last tenants got involved in, I don't know, some sort of altercation," the agent explained.

"Is that why there's no wall?" asked Ollie, gesturing to a big, mostly empty space where one of the building's outer walls should definitely have been.

The agent flicked through his notes. "Yes. Yes, that's right. Also, the ceiling is at risk of collapse and the plumbing has all been completely destroyed."

Dan nodded. "Right, but—"

"And the entire floor is structurally unsound."

Dan and Ollie both looked down. The floorboards groaned beneath them.

"But you'd fix that, right?" asked Dan. "If we took the place, I mean."

"Repairs are the tenant's responsibility," the agent was quick to point out. "So you'd have to deal with it yourself."

"What?" Artur spluttered. "Why don't we build ye a feckin' extension at the same time? Sure, we could maybe add another story on top with a roof garden and a landin' pad. How would that suit ye?"

"That would be fine," the agent confirmed.

"Well tough shoite. 'Tenant's responsibility,' he says. Do we look like we sailed up the street in a handkerchief?"

"Do you look like what?"

"Shut the feck up and answer the question," Artur said. "No, we don't," he continued, answering it for him before he had the chance. "If ye think we'll be footing the bill for making this shoitehole habitable, ye've another thing coming."

The agent shrugged and flipped his pad closed. "Fine. That's not a problem. Sorry you wasted our time," he said, taking care to emphasize the "our" part.

"Hey, wait a minute, hold on," said Dan. He huffed out a sigh and looked around the place. "We do need somewhere to go. So... what's the estimate? For the repairs, I mean. What's it likely to cost?"

The agent flipped open his pad again. "Around two-hundred-and-seventy-thousand credits."

Dan choked on nothing but air. "*How much?* What the fonk are you building it out of? Ultrium?"

"I don't know what that is, sir," said the agent. "So, no. That's just a standard finish."

"It's daylight feckin' robbery is what it is!" Artur argued. "I swear, Deadman, if ye give this thieving bastard so much as a single credit, I'll... I'll... Well, I don't know what I'll do, but no one will enjoy it, that's for sure."

"I have a couple of questions," Dan said. He ran a finger along a buckled window frame in one of the room's three remaining walls. "What actually happened here? This must've been some 'altercation.'"

The agent shrugged. "That's all I know. Some business competitor pulled up outside and shot the place to pieces, or something."

Dan nodded slowly. "That would make sense," he said. "Except this window is bent outwards."

The agent regarded it with forced interest. "So?"

"So someone shooting from the outside wouldn't have done that," Dan explained.

"Presumably they shot back."

"Must've been one big gun," said Dan. He jabbed a thumb in the direction of the missing wall. "Looks like that fell out the way, too. Which makes me wonder, what exactly were they trading in here? Guns? Could it have been guns?"

"I'm afraid I can't give you that information, sir," the agent said. "Client confidentiality."

Dan hoisted him off his feet with one hand. With the other, he pushed back his hat so the agent got a full, uninterrupted up-close view of his face.

"Drugs!" the man gargled. "They were a drugs

company! But above board. I mean... I think. They had all the paperwork, that's all I know!"

Dan tutted. That wasn't the answer he'd been hoping for, but he didn't think the agent had any reason to lie.

"P-please don't hurt me!"

Dan let the man drop. He landed on his feet, but his legs gave way, collapsing him to the floor. Bending, Dan plucked the clipboard from the agent's hand, pulled the pages out, then shoved them, folded, into his inside coat pocket.

"Sorry," he said, returning the now empty clipboard. "It's a little outside our budget."

"And ye're an arsehole," Artur added.

"Yeah," agreed Dan. "That, too."

"Nice to meet you, though," said Ollie, then she scuttled after Dan as he strode out through the missing wall and into the little car park beyond.

Dan marched quickly towards the Exodus, forcing Ollie to jog to keep up. "So, we're not taking the office?"

"What office?" asked Dan. "It doesn't have a wall."

"No, I know," said Ollie. She groaned. "I just really don't want to go back down into the thingummy."

"The Stagnates."

"Them. Yes. I don't want to go back down there."

"No one does, kid," Dan told her.

Pulling open the driver's door, he slumped into the front seat of the Exodus, then deposited Artur into the indent in the dash. He started trying to goad the engine awake before Ollie had made it around to the passenger side.

"It's just... after what happened to Banbara," Ollie said, seamlessly picking up the thread of the conversation again.

"And what if it's still around somewhere? The monster thing?"

Finn leaned forward from the back seat. "Wait, didn't you say you were going to kill that thing, brah?"

"Don't call me brah," Dan said. "And yes, that's what I said, but it was harder than expected. We flushed it out to sea."

"Oh," said Finn, slouching back. He let this sink in for a moment. "So, it's still alive? Even after what it did to those people? To Bonbo?"

Dan met his eye in the rear-view mirror. "Hey, you want to go take it on? Be my guest."

Finn straightened. "Yeah, well... maybe I will."

Dan snorted. "Right."

"I'll come," said Ollie.

Finn's smile returned. "Cool!"

"Wait, what? No," said Dan. "It was a joke. You can't take it on."

"Why not?" asked Ollie.

"Uh, because it murders people and leaves them as just skin, it's probably way out somewhere in the ocean by now, and – oh – it's a giant unkillable monster," Dan said. "And those are just off the top of my head."

"Nothing's unkillable, Deadman," Artur pointed out.

"Whose side are you on?"

"And I can get my hands on a boat," Finn added.

"Fine. *You* go ahead," Dan said. He stabbed a finger in Ollie's direction. "But you're not going."

"Why not? That's not fair!" Ollie protested.

"Yeah, well sometimes life isn't fair," Dan muttered. "It's too dangerous."

Artur raised a hand. "Uh, point of information. Ye are

remembering that she's got, like, magic powers or whatever?"

"That's what I'm worried about," Dan said. "All that power, and she doesn't have the first clue how to use it."

Artur shrugged. "Fair enough. Then show her."

Dan frowned. "What?"

"Show her. Teach her what to do. Sure, it's either that or she winds up accidentally killing us all, and half the city with us."

Dan hesitated. For a moment, it almost looked like he was going to go for it, but then he shook his head. "How am I supposed to teach her? What do I know?"

"Ye know a damn sight more than most about all that mumbo jumbo bollocks," Artur said. "I'm sure ye could give the girl a few pointers, at least. Steer her in the right direction."

Ollie's head had been tick-tocking between Dan and Artur as they'd discussed her. It stopped on Dan now, and she looked worried as she waited for him to give his verdict.

"I suppose we could head south past the outskirts. Well away from people," he conceded.

"We could at that," Artur said. "I like yer thinking, Deadman. Ye might have a face on ye like a burst hemorrhoid, but ye've still got it going on upstairs where it counts."

Dan grunted and steered the Exodus out of the car park. "We'll drop the kid off back at the Stagnates first," he said, but Artur had other ideas.

"Not at all! I think we should bring yer man with us. Sure, I think it'd be good for him to see our Ollie here in all her full glory, don't ye agree? Her full *terrifying* glory."

Dan clocked the expression on Artur's face, and caught the little man's wink.

"Yeah," he said, a smile tugging at the corners of his dry, cracked lips. "That might not be such a bad idea, after all."

IT TOOK an hour for them to reach the southernmost city limits, then they drove on over the dirt and debris for half that again to make sure nobody would accidentally chance upon them. Ideally, they'd have gone further, but the ground had gone from 'uneven plain' to 'no fonking way are we getting past this,' and Dan had decided they'd gone far enough.

After stopping the car, Dan and Ollie had picked their way through the scrub until they'd reached a suitably-sized flatter area a short distance away. Finn had moved to follow, but Artur had suggested – quite firmly – that they should both hang back and leave the other two to it.

They had taken up positions on the hood of the Exodus – Finn sitting cross-legged, Artur standing on the top of the grille to give himself a better view. Planting themselves there had been Artur's idea, and Finn was worried that Dan might not be best pleased.

"Quit worrying," Artur told him. "Sure, he might look mean – and, ye know, completely horrifying – but he's a big softie at heart."

"He is?"

"Oh aye. Soft as a baby's shoite," Artur beamed. The smile eroded, just a fraction. "I mean, unless ye mess with his friends, like. Ye know. Like me. Or young Ollie there even more so. Then it's a different story. He don't like that." Artur sucked air in through his teeth. "He don't like that one little bit."

"Uh... OK," Finn said.

"Ye understand what I'm sayin' there, boyo?" Artur asked, squinting up at him. "Both Deadman and I... well, we've grown awfully fond of our Oledol, so we have. He'll never admit that to ye, but it's true. She's a lovely girl. Too good for the likes o' this city, that's for sure."

He advanced up the hood a little, closing the gap between them. "And, well, if anything should happen to her – if someone was to, say, hurt her or make her upset or what have ye – well, we would have something of a problem with that person, Deadman and me."

"Right," said Finn.

"By which I mean, I'd personally rip their eyeballs out through their arse," Artur said. "Then he'd reinsert them the wrong way round." He smiled. "D'ye hear what I'm saying'?"

Finn nodded, but looked a little blank. "Yeah, brah. But who'd want to hurt her?"

"Well, let's hope we never find out, shall we?" said Artur. He eyeballed Finn for a while, then shrugged. "Now, forget all that 'kind and innocent' shoite, and cast yer eyes in that direction. Ye're about to witness a whole other side to our Ollie, so ye are."

Out on the clearing in the scrub, Dan stopped walking. "This'll do," he declared, shoving his hands deep down into his pockets. He didn't physically feel the cold these days, but the stark emptiness of the place and the way the wind whistled around them made him shiver, all the same.

Ollie looked around them. "Why here?"

"Why not?" Dan grunted.

Ollie didn't really have any answer to that. She danced slowly on the spot, swinging her arms. "So... What do we do?"

"Fonked if I know," Dan told her. He exhaled. "But

134

Artur's right. You've got power, but you've got no idea how to control it. We need to work on that. I mean, we don't even know what you can do. Not really."

Ollie's head dipped, like she was in trouble somehow. "Sorry."

"Not, that's not... You've got nothing to be sorry for kid. And don't let anyone make you think you have. Least of all me," Dan told her.

"Sorry. I mean, not sorry!" she said, then she stood to an awkward attention. "How do you want to start? What should I do?"

"You tell me," he said, but her blank expression told him that was unlikely to happen anytime soon. "Let's start with the sewers. When you almost blew us up. What did you do then?"

Ollie blushed a little, then looked down at her hands. "Just sort of... whoosh. You know?"

"No. I don't know," said Dan. "Show me."

Ollie pointed her hands at him. He quickly knocked them aside so they were aiming elsewhere. "Not at me! Over there. See that rock?"

"There are lots of rocks," Ollie pointed out.

"The big one. Kind of looks like someone lying down."

"I see it," Ollie said. She raised her hands again, only for Dan to push them down.

"Wait. That is someone lying down. Hey, buddy!"

The rock didn't move. Dan drew his gun, switched to explosive rounds, and detonated a spot on the ground twenty or so feet away. It went up like a bomb blast, spraying soil and stones and sediment into the air.

The person-shaped rock suddenly shifted. A hulking Igneon sat up, then groaned like he immediately regretted it. He wore a tiny party hat at a jaunty angle on his boulder-like head, and someone had written some pretty unpleasant things about him in lipstick on his craggy forehead.

"Ow. Fonk," the Igneon groaned. He blinked several times, then looked around and tried to get his bearings. "Where am I? What time is it?"

"Late afternoon," said Dan. "And you're a few miles south of the city."

The Igneon jumped to his feet, displaying a surprising amount of dexterity. "What? Oh, fonk! Oh fonk, no! Afternoon? I'm late for work!"

The ground trembled as he began to run, then he stopped when he spotted the car. "Hey! Can you give me a lift?"

Dan looked the figure up and down. Like most Igneons, he resembled a landslide on legs, albeit with a funny hat on.

Dan looked to the Exodus with its low roof and cramped seats.

"No," he said. "No, I cannot."

"Oh well thanks a *bunch*!" the Igneon spat, and then he was thundering off in the direction of the city's tall spires, the world shaking beneath his feet.

"OK, let's try that again," said Dan. He picked another rock. This one wasn't in the shape of anything, and was almost certainly just a bog-standard big boulder. "Try that one."

Ollie raised her hands. Her tongue poked out of the side of her mouth as she concentrated.

"In your own time," said Dan.

Ollie waggled her fingers. "Right. Here goes," she said, then she glanced across to where Artur and Finn were sitting on the car.

"Don't look at them, look at the rock," Dan instructed.

"I am," said Ollie, despite the fact she very clearly wasn't.

Dan side-stepped to his left and blocked her view of the car. "Forget them. Just shoot the damn rock."

"Right. Yes. OK," said Ollie. She took a deep breath and thrust her hands forward.

Nothing happened.

"I know I said 'in your own time,' but if you could make that time at some point today, I'd appreciate it," Dan told her.

Ollie let out a little squeak as she thrust both hands forward again. The rock remained unshot.

"What are you waiting for?" Dan demanded. "Just shoot the fonking thing."

"I'm trying!" Ollie protested. "I just... it's only a rock."

"Exactly. It's a rock. It doesn't have feelings. It's not going to be upset if you blow it up."

Ollie lowered her hands. "No, I mean... When it's happened before we've been in danger. We've been attacked, or... or... I don't know. But it sort of happens automatically and it's just like I'm, I don't know, guiding it. Does that make sense?"

"Not particularly," Dan admitted. He ground his teeth together, deep in thought. "I could throw it at you."

"Huh?"

"The rock. I could throw it at you."

Ollie considered this.

"That might work," she said.

"OK, wait there," Dan said.

He trudged over to the boulder and got into a lifting position. Artur's voice drifted over to him on the wind.

"Lift wi' the knees, ye daft bollocks, not the back. How many times?"

Dan ignored him. He heaved the rock up until it was almost at chest height, then the weight proved too much and he staggered as he was thrown off-balance. "Fonk. No, forget that," he grunted, letting the boulder fall.

"Well, that was embarrassing," Artur hollered. "Sure, I'm cringing over here on yer behalf."

"Shut the fonk up," Dan muttered, then he saw that Ollie was laughing.

Shizz. That was the final straw.

"Something funny?" he demanded, marching back to her. "You got something to laugh about?"

Ollie's eyebrows raised in surprise and her smile took a dent. "What? No, I just—"

Dan jabbed a finger at her as he closed the gap. "You almost wiped out this city once. You almost killed yourself today. Maybe even me, too. And you think this is funny?"

"No. No, I... I don't..."

"We don't know what you are or what you can do. We don't know anything about your power levels, and you're standing there *laughing*?" Dan spat. "You might be the most dangerous fonking thing on this planet, and you can't even control yourself enough to shoot one damn—"

The rock exploded. Or imploded. Possibly both. Where there had just a moment ago been a lump of stone there was now a distinct absence of one. More than that, though, a circular patch of ground around where the rock had been was now shiny and smooth like polished glass. Tiny fragments of dust flitted in the air like microscopic insects, before being carried off on the wind.

Dan, to his surprise, was lying on the ground some twenty or thirty feet away from where he'd been standing, and mostly upside-down. His coat flopped up over his head as he clumsily attempted to get back to his feet.

Once he was upright, he brushed himself down, nodded like he'd totally meant everything that had just happened, then returned to Ollie. Her arm was still raised and shaking slightly. He placed a hand on it and gently guided it down.

"So ends your first lesson," he said, then he ducked as the sound of another explosion roared through the air, knocking his hat off and shattering one of the Exodus's windows.

"What the fonk?" he grimaced, turning in the direction of the sound. A mushroom of flame rolled up from the distant Down Here, a heaving mass of black smoke moving beneath it

"That wasn't me!" Ollie said, tucking her hands behind her back. "I didn't do that." She bit her lip. "Did I?"

Dan shook his head. "Don't think so, kid," he said, squinting into the smoke. If he used his imagination a little, he could see a shape moving in there. A big black shape, he thought. With pointy tentacles.

"I think we just found our sewer monster."

TWELVE

By the time they made it back to the city, the sewer-thing was gone. Its trail of damage remained, though, and once the Tribunal had done their usual half-assed clean-up job, Dan had taken a look to see what he could find out.

That didn't, however, amount to very much.

It had come out of the water by one of the ports where fishermen landed their catches. It had destroyed a few boats, killed half a dozen people, then wandered further into the city. Soon after, it had discovered a power plant. Soon after *that*, it had discovered that water and electricity didn't really mix.

Dan couldn't tell if the initial short-out had caused the explosion, or if the thing had gone on a post-shock destructive rampage. Whatever the cause, the plant was now an indent in the ground, and thirty blocks in all directions were in complete darkness as the evening drew in around them.

"From what I can make of the tracks it left, it looks like it went back into the water," Dan said, gazing off in the direction of the harbor.

"You mean the Tribunal wasn't able to stop it?" Finn asked.

Dan snorted. "The Tribunal wouldn't have even tried to stop it. Uptown, maybe. Down this end, it's a miracle they even bothered to show face."

"But people died," Ollie said. "When it came out of the water, you said it killed people, right?"

"Unless those six corpses we saw all butchered and beheaded themselves, I'd say it's a safe bet."

"Then someone needs to do something! It killed all those people. It killed Banbara!"

"And Bonbo," Finn added.

"Nobody gives a shoite about Bonbo. Sure, I don't even know who Bonbo is," said Artur. He was on the ground, peering into a deep gouge mark in the road that the monster had presumably left behind. "No offense, like. I mean, we only just *barely* care about Banbara, and two of us fecking lived with her."

"*I* care about her!" Ollie insisted. "She was my third-best friend."

"Out of the three people who you knew at the time," Artur clarified.

"People die in this city every day," Dan pointed out.

"Mind you, they don't all die with a monstrous great spike up their arse," said Artur. He held up his hands. "Not that I'm siding with anyone in this here debate, I'm only stating the facts as I see them."

"What if it comes back?" asked Ollie. "What if it comes back and... and... it kills a hundred more people. A thousand more!"

"What, is it going for a record?" asked Dan. "It might never come back."

"But it might!" Ollie insisted.

"She's right, brah."

"Shut the fonk up and stop calling me 'brah'," Dan warned. He sighed. "Look, what do you want me to do? I'm a detective. People pay me to take cases. That's what I do."

"And yet ye went roaming around in the sewers trying to find the thing," said Artur. "Not to mention when ye saved those kiddies from that mind-controlling whatever-the-feck-it-was. No one was paying ye then."

Artur's eyes narrowed. "Or were they? Are ye holding out on me, ye hatchet-faced robbing bastard?"

"No, Artur, no one was paying me for that. But this is different," Dan said. "That was from the Malwhere. This isn't. Also, that was in a school. This thing's out in the ocean."

"It might be in a school next time," said Ollie. "Or... or..."

"Two schools," said Finn.

"Right!" Ollie agreed. Their eyes met for a moment, then they both quickly looked away.

"Well, if that happens we can worry about it at the time."

Artur shook his head. "It's no use. He isn't going to go for it, kids." He squinted up at Finn. "Ye said ye could get a boat, right?"

"Sure thing, brah."

"OK. Then if ye want my opinion – and I've no doubt that ye do, on account of me being a very clever man – then I suggest ye go out in the morning and see if ye can find anything." Artur nodded to Ollie. "The two of ye, I mean. Together."

"Wait, what?" said Dan. "That's a bad idea."

"Ye think? I don't see the harm in it, meself."

"The two of them together? Alone out on the ocean?"

Dan said, speaking about them like they weren't there. "Uh-uh. Not happening."

"Why not?" Ollie demanded.

"Because it's dangerous," Dan said. He pointed to Finn. "And you know nothing about this guy."

"Well... neither do you!" Ollie protested.

"Exactly! But I know guys in general, and I know that a young girl going out on a boat with one she's just met – monster or no fonking monster swimming around the place – is a bad idea. It's a terrible idea."

"Actually, now I think about it, I have to agree, Peaches," said Artur. He raised a hand to stop her before she could reply. "I know, I know, ye're old enough to make yer own decisions, and ye're right, we can't actually stop ye."

"The hell we can't," Dan muttered.

"Come on, ye shouted at the girl about a rock and she blew ye thirty feet through the air," Artur reminded him. "Ye really think ye're going to be able to ground her? Look at the pair o' them. They've made their minds up. They're going, whether we like it or not. There'll be no getting in their way."

"Fine. Then I'll go, too," said Dan, crossing his arms across his chest.

Artur rubbed his beard as he mulled this over. "Hmm. Ye know, ye might just have stumbled upon a solution to this whole problem there, Deadman," he said. "Aye, ye know what? I reckon ye've cracked it. Me and you can tag along to make sure there are no untoward shenanigans going on. Great idea."

Dan looked pleased with himself, but it didn't last long before he realized what had just happened.

"Fonk," he sighed. "Fine. We'll go out and take a look."

Ollie clapped her hands excitedly. "Yay!"

"But not for long," Dan said. He pointed to both Ollie and Finn. "And you two are sitting at opposite ends."

NEXT MORNING, following a night which had seen him stabbed, clubbed, and repeatedly propositioned by Notty from property storage, Dan stood on a jetty listening to the water lapping around him, and wondering what the fonk that thing floating on it was.

"That's it?" he asked.

Finn, who was standing in the thing, looked down at it. His feet sloshed in the ankle-deep water as he stepped back to make room for Ollie to jump aboard. "Yeah, brah. It's my cousin's."

"It's your cousin's what?"

"Boat."

Dan blinked. "That's a boat?"

"It's his pride and joy!" Finn beamed. "Well, it was."

"Why 'was'?" asked Artur. "Did he get his eyes fixed?"

"He died," said Finn.

"Oh. I'm sorry," said Ollie. She rested her hand on his arm as he helped her into the boat, and let it linger for a moment.

"Thanks."

"What happened?" Dan asked.

"He drowned."

"OK, out of the boat," Dan said, beckoning her back. "Come on. You're not going anywhere in that thing. Hell, I don't want to go in that thing, and I'm already dead."

"But you said we'd go out and look," Ollie objected.

"That may be, but we're not going anywhere in that," Dan said.

He looked around them at the other jetties jutting out from the harbor. Most of the boats were battered old fishing vessels, but a small yacht with far more style and far less rust was tied to a little pier at the far end.

It sat on the water rather than in it, a faint blue light glowing around the bottom of the hull and extending like a knife blade into the ocean below. The yacht's bow was pointed like the nose of a missile and rose into a smooth canopy that covered the whole front half of the deck.

It was, Dan realized, the *exact opposite* of the deathtrap Finn was currently standing in.

"Let's go in that one."

"SO, WE STOLE IT?" Ollie asked, raising her voice so Artur could hear her above the wind.

"No. We didn't steal it, Peaches, don't worry. We took it without permission. That's a very different thing."

Ollie frowned. "Is it? I thought it was the same thing."

"Only technically," Artur assured her. He pointed up to the floating cities overhead. The blue engine glow of the vast island directly above them cast a supernatural glow over the water. "Deadman reckons it probably belongs to someone Up There."

Ollie raised her eyes to the Heavens. "But they don't have any water."

"Exactly. Which is why they tied it up Down Here, so they could pop down and have themselves a little sail, or whatever."

"It's not a sailboat," said Finn from up front.

"What?" asked Artur.

Finn, who had been offering his help to Dan, but had

been consistently ignored, looked back over his shoulder. "It's not a sailboat."

"How do you know?" Ollie asked.

Finn shrugged. "I picked up a few things from my cousin," he said, then he pointed to something that wasn't there. "Also, there's no sail."

Ollie regarded the empty space, then smiled at him. "Right," she said, her pink skin reddening at the cheeks. "That's... You're so clever."

Finn beamed back at her. "Thanks. So are you."

Artur rolled his eyes. "Oh for feck's... A little sail *or whatever*, I think you'll find I said," he retorted, then he turned back to Ollie. "Anyway, the point is it's not technically stealing on account of that lot all being insufferable arseholes and deserving whatever the feck they get. D'ye understand?"

Ollie looked at the boat. She regarded the cities above her. "Not really," she admitted.

"We're borrowing it. How about that, then?" Artur asked. "Does that make ye feel better, if we say we'll take it back?"

"Uh, maybe. Yeah. I guess," said Ollie.

"OK, then!" said Artur. He leaned over to where Ollie's hand was resting on the bench beside him and patted her on the finger. "You just tell yerself that."

Up front, Dan stood behind the yacht's controls, trying to act like he knew what he was doing. He'd been on a few boats before, mostly back in his Tribunal days, but he'd never driven one, and those he'd been on hadn't been anything like this.

The controls seemed to be motion-guided. Move your hands a certain way and the yacht moved forward. Shift them just a fraction and it changed direction. After a few false starts, some creative swearing, and twenty minutes with the instruction manual, he felt like he might finally be starting to get the hang of the basics. He also felt like he might capsize them at any moment, which was less encouraging.

Glowing green spots clung to the tips of his fingers, growing brighter or fainter depending on how he moved his hands. Pushing them forward made the boat move faster and the lights more vibrant. Easing back slowed them down and dimmed the lights to a dim glow.

That was easy enough to grasp. But what happened if he moved his hands suddenly sideways? Or pushed one forward and one back? Or raised them above his head? The fear of suddenly flipping the whole fonking yacht into the air was almost paralyzing, and if Dan could sweat, his shirt would've been sticking to his back by now.

The bewildering array of dials and readouts weren't helping. They were mostly green, but occasionally one would flash red for reasons not made clear. When that happened, Dan made some imperceptible movements with various fingers until whatever had turned red turned green again.

The yacht plowed on over the waves – 'over' being the operative word. Unlike the other vessels they'd seen at the dock, this one hovered just above the surface on a cushion of light. The lazy hum the light gave off was the only sound from the boat itself, although the whistling wind was more than making up for that.

"You sure you don't want me to drive?" Finn asked.

"No. I got it," said Dan. "We're not going far."

"Because I could, if you wanted," Finn said. "I know a lot about boats."

Dan shot him a glare. Even this little movement shifted

the boat's direction a fraction and made three different displays flash angrily, so he faced front again.

"I got it. It's fine."

Finn nodded and gazed out through the transparent canopy at the unending ocean ahead. "You don't trust me, do you, brah?"

"I don't trust anyone, kid," Dan told him. "But yeah, you're way down the list. And I might trust you more if you stop calling me 'brah.'"

"And I might stop calling you 'brah' if you stop calling me 'kid,' brah."

Dan's eyes darted sideways, briefly regarded Finn, then flicked back to the front. "I'll consider it."

Finn puffed out his cheeks, clicked his fingers a few times, then shrugged. "OK, well if you don't need me, I might go and sit with Ollie."

Dan stiffened.

"That's OK with you, right? If I go sit back there?"

"Actually, you know what?" Dan said. "You *can* take a turn at the... lights."

Finn managed to look both pleased and utterly crushed at the same time. "Oh. Really?"

"Sure," said Dan. "Why not? It pretty much drives itself. What's the worst that could..."

Roughly fifty percent of the yacht's readouts turned red. Several of them began to flash. The words 'PROX-IMITY ALERT' scrolled across the transparent canopy like a news ticker.

"What's that all about?" Dan wondered, then a shout from Artur shone some light on the situation.

"What in the name of all that is fecking holy is *that*?" he cried, pointing out at the ocean on the ship's starboard side.

No, not at the ocean, Dan realized, at the thing *in* the ocean.

Its mouth was a vast sphincter of a thing, lined all around with spear-like teeth, and big enough to swallow the boat whole. A series of interlocking armored frills ran from the top of its head and down its snake-like back, and three gelatinous yellow eyes glinted demonically at either side of its face, roughly where its ears might reasonably have been expected to be.

The occupants of the yacht had just a moment or two to take in all these details before the thing slid beneath the waves again without so much as a splash.

"Was that it? Was that yer toilet monster?" asked Artur.

"No. That wasn't it," Dan said. "That's something else."

The vast majority of the planet Parloo was covered by ocean, only a fraction of which had ever been explored. While the land-dwelling Parloo natives – the Parlooqs – were a tediously slow-moving and dim-witted species who had positively welcomed centuries of invasion and oppression, the water-dwelling locals were far less passive.

Nobody really knew what lurked out there beneath Parloo's oceans but based on countless reports from fishermen – not to mention the lack of reports from those who never returned to dock – most of it was either A) huge, B) fonking horrible, or C) both.

Whatever had just buzzed the yacht was definitely A, and despite no real evidence Dan was prepared to guess it would tick off B and C, too.

"What was it?" Ollie whispered.

"Nothing to worry about," Dan said.

"Ye what? Have ye lost yer fecking mind or something? Did ye see the size of the bastard? And the teeth on it? Holy shoite, the teeth!"

Dan sighed. "I was trying to reassure the kid."

"Oh," said Artur. He cleared his throat, then patted Ollie on the hand again. "I mean, I'm sure it's nothing to worry about."

"Should we go back?" Finn asked.

"Before that thing swallows the whole fecking boat with us on it, ye mean?" said Artur. He smiled up at Ollie. "Again, Peaches, nothing to worry about. That was just a figure of speech."

There was a *thud* beneath the boat, shuddering everyone on board.

"We're all going to die," Artur whimpered.

"Maybe we should cut the engines?" Finn suggested.

"And leave us stuck out here?" Dan scowled.

"Just until it goes away. Maybe the light's attracting it."

Dan didn't like to admit that the kid had a point, but the kid had a point.

But still.

"We can outrun it," Dan said. "This thing practically flies. No way it can keep up."

The yacht rocked again, more violently this time. Artur rolled along the bench, bounced once, and was only saved from being flung overboard by a frantic grab from Ollie that almost made his eyes pop out.

"For feck's sake, Deadman, whatever ye're doing, ye'd better do it fast!" he wheezed. "Oh, and thanks, Peaches," he added, kissing her on her thumb. "I mean, ye squeezed me 'til I explosively shoited meself, but it's still appreciated."

The ocean frothed behind the boat. Ollie screamed and Artur cursed as two slimy green feelers snaked up over the stern, wriggling and squirming as they explored.

"Deaaaaadmaaaaan!" Artur hollered. "Get us the feck out of here!"

Dan thrust both hands all the way forward until green light encased them all the way to the wrists. The boat's response was almost instantaneous. It shot through the water like a torpedo, the sudden burst of acceleration almost catapulting everyone backward into the water.

Flailing his arms out to steady himself, Dan sent the yacht into a surprisingly graceful spin. On the third or fourth rotation they all caught a glimpse of that tooth-filled sphincter mouth rising from the water, then Dan bellowed at everyone to "Hold on," and shoved his hands forward again, albeit a little more gradually than last time.

The humming of the yacht rose in pitch and volume as it streaked across the waves, heading straight for the horizon. The city was still clearly visible in the distance behind them. Dan knew if he didn't keep it in sight they might never find it again. But, on the other hand, they were being chased by a huge fonking sea monster, and charging straight on at full speed gave them their best shot at outrunning it.

He hoped.

"Is it still there? Can you see it?" Dan hollered.

"It's gone back under," Ollie said, scanning the surface behind them.

"No sign," Artur confirmed. He was still clutched in Ollie's hand, and while he still appreciated the save, it'd be nice if she stopped squeezing him whenever she was startled. The cleaning bill for these cream slacks was already going to be through the roof, and every ounce of pressure around his midsection was only making it worse.

"Get up here," Dan told her. "Both of you. Get up to the front."

"On a boat it's called 'the bow,'" Finn told him.

"Well, on this one it's called 'the front'. Now shut the fonk up and give them a hand."

Finn shuffled back along the deck. It was sloping downward, the front of the boat raised a little as it powered on across the waves.

Reaching the end of the covered area, Finn took hold of the edge of the canopy and steadied himself. Stretching, he held a hand out to Ollie. "Grab on," he instructed.

The ship's speed fought against Ollie as she tried to stand, shoving her back toward the lowered stern. She flopped back onto the bench and yelped as the air was knocked out of her. Artur grimaced and concluded that, on balance, his pants were probably now ruined.

Dropping to her knees, Ollie crawled up the incline until she could reach Finn's hand. He caught her by the arm, his powerful fingers wrapping all the way around her wrist. He pulled while she clambered, and Artur sighed with relief when they were safely under the canopy.

"Are you OK?" Finn asked, gazing into Ollie's wide and frantic eyes.

"She's fine," Dan said.

"Can ye seal us in here?" Artur asked. "Is there, ye know, like a magic door ye can close, or something?"

"Don't know. Check the manual, kid," Dan instructed.

"Sure thing, brah."

Before Finn could reach for the doorstep-sized instruction book, the warning on the canopy display blinked out. Several of the red displays turned amber, fluctuated between the two for a few seconds, then became a soft, soothing green.

"That's good, right?" said Ollie. "Does that mean it's gone?"

Finn turned and searched the ocean on all sides. "I can't

see anything," he said. He exhaled and broke into a wide smile, then patted Dan on the shoulder. "It's gone. Looks like you lost it, brah."

Dan's neck *creaked* as he turned to look at the hand on his shoulder. He let his stare linger there for a while, before raising his gaze in Finn's direction. "Let's not get cocky, kid," he warned.

The yacht slowed as Dan eased his hands back.

"Why are we slowing down? Should we be slowing down?" Ollie asked. "I don't think we should be slowing down."

"We need to turn around," Dan explained. "If we lose sight of the city we could be stuck out here forever. We've got no food or water."

"And I've shoite meself," Artur added.

Dan opened his mouth as if about to ask for an explanation, but then shook his head as he concluded he probably didn't want to know.

"I reckon we head over that way for a few miles," he said, nodding to the boat's starboard side. "Then, assuming nothing else tries to eat us, we head back to land."

There was a general murmuring of agreement from everyone but Ollie. She bit her lip and looked out to sea. "But what about the thing that killed Banbara? That's the whole point of us being out here."

"Look at it. Look at the size of this ocean," Dan said. "No way we're finding anything out here."

"And sure, ye saw what the neighbors are like, Peaches," Artur said. "Spikes or no spikes, yer toilet monster won't stand a chance out here with things like that swimming around. Sure, I bet it's already been eaten by something big and ugly. And no, I wasn't talking about ye there, Deadman, I meant a fish."

Ollie smiled, relaxing a little. "I guess you're probably right."

"Of course I'm right. I'm always right," Artur said. "Now let's turn around, get back to land, smash this boat to pieces out of sheer bloody-minded spite, and – dare I say it? – all go have ourselves a drink in the closest available pub." He raised his bushy eyebrows at everyone in general. "Any objections?"

A single display flickered amber. It lasted just a moment, but the atmosphere aboard the yacht, which had been creeping in the direction of 'almost jovial' changed instantly. Breath was held. Lips were bitten. Bowels were evacuated.

"Too tight. Too tight," Artur wheezed.

All readouts were green again, but Dan lowered his voice to a whisper, just in case. "I'm going to start us moving again," he said.

And then the boat was buffeted on a sudden wave and the console ignited in a wave of flashing red warning lights.

The thing rose straight up out of the water ahead of them, its shizzhole-like maw opening and closing, its elongated teeth turning outward and gnashing at the air.

"Oh... fonk," Dan groaned, leaning back to take in the monster's full height. It towered thirty or forty feet above the surface, revealing that its snake-like body was merely a snake-like neck. Only a suggestion of its torso was visible through the churning ocean foam, but it was enough to give the impression of something hugely, stupidly, *impossibly* big.

Dan stared. Ollie screamed. Artur soiled himself, only without any external pressure this time.

Finn fell suddenly forward, throwing up his hands and grunting as he was slammed against the boat's deck. "What the fonk? Get it off!" he cried, kicking out at a slimy tendril that had wriggled up over the port side and ensnared him by the ankle.

He grabbed for the deck, fingers splayed, nails digging into the rough flooring. Ollie moved to help him, but too late. A sudden yank flicked him into the air. An animal-like squeal burst from his lips as he was swung up and over the side of the boat. He grasped at nothing but empty space as he hurtled backward.

For a brief, all-too-fleeting moment, his eyes met Ollie's, and then he smashed into the ocean and vanished into its watery depths.

THIRTEEN

"*FINN!*"

Ollie's cry carried across the rippling waves, but only the sloshing of the water and the humming of the boat replied.

Up front, Dan had some more pressing concerns – namely the huge fonking sea monster looming above them. Its head and part of its neck were silhouetted against the blue glow of the Up There engines, making it look even more menacing than it already did. Which was really saying something.

"Maybe if we stay *very* still," Artur suggested, but then the monster's head came crashing down toward them, its teeth spinning like the blade of a circular saw. "No, feck. Move, move, move!"

Dan pushed and pulled simultaneously, and the yacht careened into a frantic spin. It powered forward just as the thing's head smashed into the water's surface, violently rocking the boat and knocking everyone aboard off their feet. Especially Artur, who rocketed upwards, smacked against the canopy, then thudded against with floor with a "Ye bastard!"

The monster's yellow eyes swiveled and pulsated as its spinning teeth churned the sea into foam. It took it just a second or two to locate the boat again. Its vast neck *creaked* as it swung its head in the yacht's direction.

"Mindy, explosive rounds!" Dan barked, tearing his gun from its holster. "Everyone down!" he commanded as the chamber spun and illuminated.

"We're already down! Just shoot the fecking thing!" Artur hollered, but the last few words were drowned out by the scream of gunfire and the squelchy *boom* of an eyeball exploding.

A spray of a yellow mucus-like gunge splattered across Ollie, but she barely noticed. Her gaze was fixed on the water, on the spot where Finn had vanished.

"Come on, come on," she whispered. "Where are you?"

Dan opened fire again. This time, two rounds exploded against the monster's teeth as it raised its head from the water. It squealed or roared, or some combination of the two. It sounded like a ship's foghorn and the sheer volume of it flattened the squally ocean surface for a second.

"Yeah, didn't like that, did you?" Dan growled, opening fire again. This time, the shot rebounded off the creature's neck, arced through the air, then hit the ocean with a *hiss*.

"Don't hit that bit," Artur suggested. "That bit didn't work."

"I noticed," Dan snapped.

"Aim for the eyes or the teeth."

"I know!" Dan said. He fired again. The monster thrashed, deflecting the shot. It hit the ocean just a few feet from the yacht's starboard side, spraying the deck with hot water.

"Ye weren't aiming for the eyes and teeth!"

"I *was* aiming for the eyes and teeth!" Dan insisted. "It moved."

"*Of course, it fecking moved!*" Artur roared. "Ye're trying to shoot its face off, it's *bound* to move! Ye should've anticipated where it was going to go. Call yerself a marksman?"

"I've never called myself a marksman," Dan replied.

"Well now we know why, because ye're a useless bastard who can't aim for shoite."

Ollie turned away from the ocean and raised her hands. "I'll get it," she said, but Dan and Artur quickly shouted her down.

"Peaches, no!"

"Don't do it!"

Keeping her hands raised, Ollie looked back over her shoulder at them. "Why not?"

"Because ye're not exactly renowned for yer levels of control," Artur said. "And we're in a tiny fecking boat in a big fecking ocean that's positively hoachin' with monsters. Like it or not, we're in the hands of Hopeless Joe here."

Dan jabbed a finger at Artur, then at Ollie. "You. Shut up. You. Drive. Get us out of here."

"What? No!" Ollie spluttered. "What about Finn?"

"What about him? He's dead," said Dan. He winced a little as he said the words, but there was no time to soften the blow. "We aren't. Not yet."

"Well, technically some of us—" Artur began, but a flurry of sudden movement from all around the boat silenced him.

Eight long, probing tendrils like the one that had snatched Finn away snaked up over the sides and squirmed along the deck. Ollie screamed and jumped clear as one brushed against the back of her thigh. Dan stamped on it and tried to keep it pinned beneath his boot, but it wriggled free and grabbed for his ankle.

"Deadman! Shoot them!" Artur yelped, smashing a small but surprisingly powerful right hook into the side of one of the snake-like appendages.

"If I shoot them, we'll sink!" Dan barked, stamping down on the tendril trying to grab his ankle.

"Stun them, ye daft bollocks!"

"Shizz. Right. Mindy, Stun Shot," Dan commanded. The gun's chamber began to spin, but then a tendril snared him around the wrist and yanked sharply, sending the weapon clattering across the deck.

Dan pulled against his fleshy bonds, but they tightened sharply, cutting into his wrist and ankle. He hit the deck hard, both tendrils fighting to pull him in opposite directions, and both winning. He felt old sutures in his back and stomach pop. The fonking things were literally going to tear him apart.

With a roar, he heaved against the one wrapped around his wrist and heard the sickening *krick* of snapping bone. Congealed black blood *flobbed* out of the opening wound and spattered on the deck, then the hand landed in it with a stomach-churning splat.

Bending, Dan grabbed the thing around his ankle with his one remaining hand and heaved it into what he hoped was the right position.

"Mindy, fire!"

Mindy kicked and slid further along the deck. The stun shot screamed through the air and hit the tendril close to where Dan had grabbed it. He felt the jolt of the impact through his mostly lifeless nerves, but the monster took the worst of it. It roared that foghorn roar again, and the snake-

159

like appendages all released their various grips and thrashed around as if they were on fire.

The creature itself thrashed beneath the yacht, rocking it up into the air. "Ah, *fonk!*" Dan groaned as he watched Mindy flip up over the edge, then heard the *splosh* of the gun hitting the churning waters below.

"Great. Now what?" Artur cried.

Dan puffed out his cheeks. "All I've got is 'I told you this was a bad idea,'" he said. "And that feels kind of petty."

Ollie looked up at the monster.

She looked at her hands.

"Now?" she asked.

Artur and Dan exchanged a look. They both shrugged. "At this point, Peaches, I don't see what harm it could possibly—"

The sea-monster screamed. It was a piercing, high-pitched drone that was quite unlike the foghorn sound. That sound had been an angry one. This sound was made up of desperation and terror and pain.

Its head swung wildly atop its long neck. A previously unseen tail curled up from the ocean a few hundred feet ahead of the boat, then slapped against the water with an ear-splitting *thack*.

Dan and Ollie staggered toward the listing edge of the ship, but caught the railing before they could be flipped overboard.

From there, they were staring almost straight down into the ocean beneath them. They could make out the curved belly of the beast, but there was something else moving around down there, too. Something much smaller, but with substantially more pointy bits.

"Is that...? Is that the toilet thing?" Ollie whispered.

"I think so. Yeah, maybe," Dan replied. "Although, I don't know. Does it look different to you?"

"Not really."

"Smaller? I think it's smaller?" He shrugged. "Or maybe not, I don't know."

Bubbles of blood broke on the surface, obscuring the view of what was happening below. From the way the monster was screaming, though, it clearly wasn't having a very good time.

"Wait, what's happening?" asked Artur.

"The thing from the sewers. I think it's down there," Dan said. "I think it's fighting the big guy."

"So... what are ye saying? It's helping us?"

"I doubt it's deliberate. Wasn't exactly acting like it wanted to be friends last time."

"How the feck did it find us? I mean, in an ocean this size, what are the chances of it just turning up? Ye think it was following us the whole time?"

Dan contemplated this. It was not a comforting thought. "I don't know. Maybe."

The sea-creature's wailing stopped abruptly. The head flopped limply back and slapped against the ocean surface.

It bobbed there for a while like flotsam, then the neck sank out of sight, pulling the rest of the thing down with it.

Silence followed. The boat's engines had cut out at some point, and the yacht now rested in the water rather than hovering atop it, waves lapping at the hull. The whole scene felt disconcertingly peaceful, considering what had come before.

"Is it gone?" Ollie whispered.

"It is," Dan confirmed. "Don't know about the thing from the sewers."

"Holy shoite, Deadman, if that pointy bastard can

murder a giant sea monster in thirty seconds, there's no saying what else it can do. We can't let it back into the city. I mean, I hate pretty much everyone living there, but even I reckon we need to put a stop to its nonsense."

Something broke the surface on the other side of the boat before Dan could respond. Yelping, Ollie raised both her hands, then she quickly lowered them again when she saw the head bobbing there, blond-hair plastered to its face.

"Finn!"

"Well I'll be. Would ye look at that," said Artur. "Deadman, ye'd best give the lad a hand. Not literally, mind. Ye don't exactly have them to spare at the moment."

Dan and Ollie both reached down and helped drag Finn up and into the boat. He slipped down onto the deck, coughing and wheezing and, nobody could help but notice, completely naked.

"He's got no clothes on," Artur pointed out, on the off-chance that anyone had missed this. Finn's whole body was crisscrossed with scratches and cuts, and bruises were beginning to form on his... well, everywhere, really. However he'd gotten free, it hadn't been easy.

"Hey, look!" said Ollie, gazing at him in wonder. "He's got one of those things, too!"

She reached for Finn's crotch. *"Blimminy-blimminy—"*

Dan caught her by the wrist and eased her hand away. "Uh, let's not do that," he told her.

"Oh," said Ollie, looking disappointed. "But it's fun."

"I'm sure ye'll have plenty of opportunities for fun later, Peaches," Artur told her. "But for now..." He looked around at the ocean, then back at the skyscrapers of Down Here in the distance. "...how about we feck the feck off out of here before anything else rears its ugly head?"

"Good call," said Dan. He held up one hand and one rotten stump. "But someone else is going to have to drive."

COMMISSIONER USAKT POLANI entered his office, locked the door, then slumped into his chair and grimaced in the general direction of the ceiling.

He took a moment to appreciate the cool cocoon of darkness. His window had been broken recently and had been temporarily barricaded until it could be repaired.

At least, that was the theory, but the darkness it had brought had been so soothing, so welcoming, that Polani had decided to keep the shutter in place. He didn't need to see the city to know what a cesspool it was, and the constant glow of those damn Up There engines had been annoying him for years.

He pushed all other thoughts away and let the darkness envelop him. For the first time that day, no one was asking him questions, boring him with protocol, or requesting additional resources. The Tribunal was stretched to the point of transparency, and with Krone establishing an outpost here, he didn't like the way the wind was blowing.

The Tribunal ruled Down Here, and he ruled the Tribunal. On the ground, at least. He had a boss, of course – everyone had a boss – but to all intents and purposes the buck stopped with him. If Krone was going to station troops here, then that might all be about to change.

The worst of it was, the cretins living here would probably celebrate the Tribunal's demise. They'd see Krone's army as the cavalry swooping in to deliver them all from evil.

Fonk, were they in for a surprise.

"On," Polani commanded, leaning closer to his desk.

Nothing happened. He raised his eyes to the ceiling. "Lights on."

The darkness remained. It felt different now. Less cocooning, more smothering.

It was then that he noticed the odor. Years of chain-smoking had dampened his sense of smell to the point of it being pretty much non-existent, but this stench had such a kick to it that it somehow found its way through.

Wrenching open his desk drawer, Polani grabbed for his gun. A boot was driven hard against the drawer's front, and Polani cried out as it slammed on his hand, crushing his fingers.

"Ow! *Kroysh*! What the fonk?"

A rough hand clamped over his mouth from behind. A voice like crunching gravel spoke quietly in his ear.

"Shout like that again and this time it'll be you going through the window, not me. Do you understand?"

Polani nodded. "Mm-hm."

Dan withdrew his hand and stepped around to the other side of the desk. His night vision was significantly better than most people's, and he could see Polani gawping blindly into the darkness.

"Ripley..." the commissioner began.

"Ripley's dead. You killed him, remember?" Dan grunted. "Name's Deadman now."

"Deadman. Right. Right," said Polani. Despite the fact his hand was now twice the size it should be and he couldn't see a thing, he was doing his best to appear in control of the situation. Impressive, given how shizz-scared he must be.

"You hacked my lighting system," he said. "Impressive. The whole system's protected or encrypted or, or... *fire-*

walled, or whatever it is the nerds downstairs do. It's supposed to be tamper-proof."

"Nothing's tamper proof," Dan said. He deposited something on the desk with a soft *clunk*. It took Polani several seconds to make out the shape in the darkness. He flinched, mistaking it for a hand-grenade, then he realized what it really was.

It was a light bulb.

"You have got to be kidding me," Polani said. "All that tech and you can just pull the bulb? Oh, man, we need you back working with us!"

"Stop talking," Dan warned. His tone made it clear that this wasn't a request, and while the commissioner wasn't accustomed to taking orders, he took this one. "That thing that came out of the water yesterday. What are you doing about it?"

Polani looked blankly in the direction of Dan's voice. "What thing?"

"Big, black and pointy," Dan said. "Killed some people at a dock in one of the eastern sectors. Smashed up some property."

The commissioner shrugged. "Doesn't ring a bell."

Dan's one remaining fist clenched. "Then maybe I can jog your memory."

"Cut the shizz, Ripley," Polani said. "You know what it's like out there. You know what we have to deal with every fonking day."

"What about the mall massacre? Any more on that yet? Or haven't you heard about that one, either?" Dan asked. "I mean, all that oppression and subjugation must keep you busy."

"Oh, fonk you, you self-righteous shizznod!" Polani spat. "You might not remember, but we keep this city safe!

Is it necessary to sometimes cross lines to do so? Yes. Yes, it fonking is. But if we don't, then the job doesn't get done."

"The job isn't getting done," Dan pointed out. "A monster came out of the ocean, slaughtered a whole bunch of people, and you know nothing about it."

"Someone will! It's not my job to know every last little detail about what's going on in the city, it's my job to make sure it all keeps running, whatever that takes," Polani argued. "But will there be a report somewhere about it? Sure. Filed alongside the reports on the hundred thousand other things that happened in the past twenty-six hours."

His eyes were growing more accustomed to the lack of light now, and he leaned in Deadman's direction. "We broke up a people trafficking ring bringing sex workers in from the void systems. Eighty kids went missing city-wide. We found forty-three of them, thirty-two of them still alive. We caught an arsonist trying to burn down a hospital, executed sixteen suspected rapists, and got an old lady's pet coosk down from a tree. So, don't you sneak in here and try to tell me the job isn't getting done!"

For a moment, everything was silent but the rasping of Polani's breathing.

"I thought coosks were illegal within the city limits?" Dan muttered.

"They are," Polani said. "We shot it."

"Right. Of course you did. And the old lady?"

"I'm not at liberty to discuss the details of specific individual cases," the commissioner replied, stiffening slightly. "But she was a criminal. She had it coming."

"You know who didn't have it coming? Those people by the docks," Dan said. "And that thing that killed them? It could come back and kill a whole lot more."

"We don't operate on 'could.' We haven't got the

manpower to worry about 'might do' or 'maybe' or even 'there's a very good fonking chance.'" Polani explained. "We are stretched, Ripley. We are paper thin out there. I've got enough to worry about without adding sea-monsters to the mix."

"It's not a sea-monster. It's something else. Some off-world entity. A hunter, maybe. Whatever it is, it's built for killing. And I think it might be testing itself. Finding out what it can do."

"Well, since you seem to know so much about it, why don't you deal with it?" the commissioner retorted. "I mean, that's what you do now, right? Help freaks. Fight monsters or demons or whatever the fonk we're calling them this week. That's what you've been doing with your-self since..."

He made an up-and-down gesture in Dan's direction. "Whatever this is. You're so concerned about the son-of-a-bedge, *you* deal with it."

Lunging, Dan caught Polani by the back of his fleshy neck. His grip tightened as he prepared to smash the commissioner's face against the desktop, but he wrestled with his rage and managed to bring it under control.

"OK," he said, his hand still clutching Polani's neck, the pressure making it clear he could cause him tremendous discomfort at any moment.

"OK what?" Polani whispered.

"I'll deal with it. I'll stop it before it can kill anyone else."

Dan leaned in a little closer, his smell making the commissioner flinch visibly. "But I'm going to need some resources."

"What? What are you talking about? I can't give you—"

His head met the desk. Once. Twice. Dan pinned it

167

there, his fingers splayed against the side of the commissioner's face like the legs of some giant spider.

"An office. Not here, one of the old safehouses will do. Doesn't have to be fancy."

"But—"

Dan leaned his weight on Polani's head until either the desk or the commissioner's skull gave out a worrying *creak*. "I'll need some kind of boat. Preferably armored. And guns. I want guns."

"F-fine. OK, fine. I'll authorize it. I'll authorize it."

"Good," said Dan, releasing his grip. "Also..." He held up the blackened stump of his wrist. "I'm going to need you to let me into the morgue."

FOURTEEN

"FINALLY!" cried Artur as Dan slumped into the driver's seat of the Exodus. "I thought ye were never coming back out."

"Took a little longer than I expected," Dan said, firing up the car's engine.

"A little longer? Sure, me fecking beard has a beard, I've been waiting here so long. Still, at least ye came out the front door this time and didn't just plunge from the top floor window. That's an improvement." Artur peered at Dan's hip. "By the way, is that a severed hand in yer pocket?"

"Yeah."

"Or are ye just pleased to see me?"

"I already said yes, so that joke doesn't work."

"I'll be the fecking judge o' that, thanks very much," said Artur.

"I got us an office. We can go there now, and Ollie can stitch on the..."

His voice trailed off as he noticed for the first time the empty chair beside him. Behind him, too.

"Where's Ollie? Where did they go?"

"I wondered how long it'd take yer keen detective instincts to kick in there," Artur said. "It's fine. They've just gone for a walk, that's all."

"A walk? What do you mean 'a walk'?"

Artur mimed with his fingers. "I mean a walk. Ye know. Like that." He brought up the other hand and copied the finger-movements of the first. "Only there's two of them, so like that. And then I suppose they'll be all..."

He smooshed his fingers together in various positions and began a series of increasingly high-pitched moans. "Oh baby! Oh yes, just like that! Just like that! Now faster! Don't—"

"Stop," Dan snapped. "You didn't stop them? Why the fonk didn't you stop them?"

Artur shrugged. "Because she's a curious young woman with, I assume, a healthy developing interest in the old you-know-what."

"Which is exactly why you should've stopped her!" Dan barked. He crunched the Exodus into gear. "There's no saying what that son-of-a-bedge might be doing to her."

"Me arse. He's OK. He's a good kid."

"Yeah? I'll believe it when I see it."

Dan pulled away from the curb, then immediately slammed on the brakes so hard that Artur *crunched* against the inside of the windshield.

"Ow."

Ollie and Finn stood very close together in front of the car, both grinning broadly and looking a little flushed. Finn was wearing a wetsuit they'd found for him in a storage trunk on the yacht. It clung to his muscles in a way that even Dan had to admit was annoyingly impressive.

"You'll never *believe* what Finn and I just did!" said Ollie, practically frothing at the mouth with excitement.

"Don't want to know," Dan said.

"*Spit nipples!*"

There was a *thump* as Artur peeled off the windshield and landed on the dash.

"Spit *nibbles*," Finn corrected.

"Right! Spit nibbles! We got spit nibbles!"

Dan blinked. "Spit nibbles? What the fonk are spit nibbles?"

Ollie nodded enthusiastically, then held up a greasy paper bag and gave it a shake. "They're delicious, that's what!"

"They're the sugared kind," Finn explained. He hurried around to the driver's side window and held the bag out to the glass. "Want one, brah?"

Dan peered into the bag.

He peered up at Finn.

He wound the window down a fraction. "Just get in the damn car. I'll drop you off."

"What? Where? Why?" asked Ollie, appearing beside him. Her mouth was full of spit nibble, so her words came out as a half-intelligible spray of crumbs.

"I got us somewhere to stay."

Ollie gasped, making a partially chewed spit nibble fall out of her mouth. "You did? So we don't have to go back to that hole in the ground place? That's great!"

Dan nodded. He looked quite pleased with himself. "Exactly, so we'll go drop Finn off, pick up our stuff, and—"

"What? No. What?" Ollie said, her purple brow furrowing. "He should come with us. Right? I think you should come with us."

Finn met her imploring gaze. "I mean, I'd like to."

"You would?"

"Of course!"

"Yay!" Ollie beamed down at Dan. "He said he'll come, too! Isn't that amazing?"

Dan exhaled very slowly through his nose. "No, but—"

"It's *totally* amazing, Peaches. We're both very much delighted about it," said Artur. He hopped down onto the window control button and rolled the glass back into place before Dan could chime in. "Now, best ye hop in before old gonad-features here starts wi' the whinging and the whining."

DAN FLEXED HIS FINGERS.

"No."

Ollie paused, mid-stitch. "What do you mean 'no'?"

"I mean no. It's wrong. You've hooked up the wrong fingers." He waggled his middle digit. "That's my index finger."

Ollie watched it fold in and out. "No, it isn't. It's your middle one."

"I mean it *should* be my index finger."

Ollie stared at him blankly.

"I mean *in my head* I'm moving my index finger, but my middle finger is the one that's bending. So you've hooked them up wrong."

"Oh," Ollie said. She watched his hand, in case it did anything else. "Are you sure?"

"Yes, I'm sure. They're my fingers."

"Well they weren't an hour ago," Artur called over to him. "Could they maybe just be, ye know, wonky?"

"They're definitely wonky," Dan confirmed. "But I'd like them to be unwonky."

He nodded down at his wrist and stared at Ollie until she began unpicking the last few stitches.

They were gathered in the kitchen of the Tribunal safehouse as Ollie worked to stitch Dan's new hand back on. The safehouse wasn't actually a 'house' at all, but a small apartment in an undesirable block in one of the shizzier parts of town. Polani had given him the worst place they had, but it was several steps up from the Stagnates – and not just in a literal physical sense – so Dan wasn't about to start complaining.

Finn straddled a chair, watching on with a mixture of horror, fascination, and a bit more horror. "So... like... that doesn't hurt?"

Dan sighed. He had grudged answering the question the first time. Four times later, it was really becoming a grind.

"No. Like I said, it doesn't hurt."

"Like... not even a little?"

"It doesn't hurt. At all," Dan said.

"So *not* even a little bit?"

One of the stitches Ollie was unpicking tore through Dan's skin. A wad of gelatinous black blood ejected from the wound and spattered onto the rag Dan had placed on the table for moments just like that one.

"Oh, brah! That *must've* hurt!"

"Can we find a way to keep him occupied?" Dan asked Artur. "Like a ball of string or something shiny?"

"Ah, quit yer fecking moaning," Artur told him. He had climbed inside a wall-mounted cabinet and was rummaging inside. "Ye did good here, Deadman. They've got food and all sorts. It's like a home away from home. Only better, on account of the last place being shoite."

"How long can we stay here?" Ollie asked, pulling out

another stitch. The wound in Dan's wrist opened, revealing bone, tendons, and gristle.

"I didn't ask. Until we deal with our monster friend, at least."

"Great! So no rush on that front, then," said Artur. "We'll just bide our time here, and if it turns up then we'll deal with it. And if it doesn't show face, bingo! We've scored a free house."

Dan's fingers all twitched as Ollie dug around in the stump, trying to figure out what went where. He cut Finn off before he could speak.

"Still doesn't hurt," Dan said, then he leaned back in his chair a little. "Tell me what happened. In the water, I mean. Did you see where it came from?"

Finn tore his eyes away from Dan's wound. "Where the water came from?"

Inside the cabinet, Artur snorted.

"No. Where the... thing came from."

"Oh, the toilet monster? No. I didn't see it."

Dan frowned. "You didn't see it?"

"Nah, brah. Didn't see it," Finn said. He shrugged. "It's all kind of a blur. One minute I was on the boat with you guys. Then, like, *sploosh*. I'm in the water. You know? Like *in the water*."

"I understand what being in the water means, yes," Dan said. "Then what?"

"Then... I don't know," Finn said. "I closed my eyes, I think. Something tore my clothes, but I didn't see where it came from."

He frowned in concentration. "There was screaming, I think. Don't reckon it was me, because I was still underwater." His frown deepened. "Can you scream underwater?"

"Not if you want to live," Dan said. "It was the sea-monster. The big one. That's what was screaming."

"Right. Right," said Finn, nodding. "Anyway, after that, next thing I know I'm lying on the deck of the ship, buck naked. What happened in-between? I have no clue, brah."

"Well, that was enlightening," Dan said. "I'm glad now we let you stick around."

Finn's face brightened.

"Yeah, I was being sarcastic, kid. You were no help whatsoever."

"They've got booze!" Artur boomed from inside the cabinet. "They've got beautiful, beautiful... Ah. No. Wait. It's fish sauce. My mistake."

There was the sound of a cap being unscrewed, followed by a series of gulps and an *aaah*.

"Hits the spot, mind you." He burped. "Bit of a salty aftertaste, and it's sixteen months out of date, but beggars can't be choosers, can we?"

His head appeared from inside the cabinet. "Although, just so we're clear, this is *mine*, and if anyone tries to drink it, I'll scratch their fecking eyes out."

"Finished," said Ollie, tying off the suture. "You're all fixed."

Dan flexed his fingers in turn. "Much better," he said. "Not bad at all."

He lifted his hand. The rag it had been resting on lifted, too. Turning it over, Dan saw six stitches crisscrossing through the thin material. Sighing, he placed his hand back on the table. "Still, full marks for trying."

Ollie set to work again.

"Assuming ye're not going to go with my brilliant scheme of just lounging around here drinking fish sauce until we can't see, I take it ye have a plan?"

"You three are going to go to the Stagnates and pick up our stuff. There's an entrance not far from here," Dan said. "We need clothes. Especially Artur. I can't believe you haven't changed those pants."

Artur looked down at the rainbow of browns coating the back of his legs. "That's the beauty of hanging out with yerself, Deadman. No matter how bad I look, or how awful I might smell, it all just pales in comparison."

"Good to know. Thanks," Dan grunted. "But get new pants. Get everything and bring it back here."

"What about me, brah?"

Dan grimaced. "What about you?"

"Should... should I get my stuff, too."

Dan glowered at him for a while, then flicked his gaze across to Ollie. She still had her head down, pretending all her attention was focused on her stitching. Even at this angle, though, Dan could tell she was blushing.

"Fine," he sighed.

Ollie's head snapped up, her face positively glowing. "We can keep him?"

"No, we can't 'keep him.' He's not a pet," Dan said. "But fine. He can stay. For a while. Not permanently."

"Thanks, brah!" Finn said. "You won't regret it."

"For your sake, *kid*, I hope you're right."

Artur gave a brief yelp as he plunged out of the cabinet, bounced off the worktop below, then face-planted onto the floor. He lay quite still for a while, and Dan was just wondering if he should do something when Artur groaned.

"Ooh, me guts," he said, clutching his stomach. "I'm not sure that fish sauce entirely agreed with me."

With some effort, he pulled himself upright. The gurgling of his stomach echoed around the small kitchen.

"Before we go anywhere, I should probably go use the jacks," he announced. "Ye know, for a big old shoite."

"We get it," Dan said. "I'll be gone by the time you're out."

"Gone? Why? Where ye going?"

"I'm going to get us some equipment," Dan said. He felt the weight of the holster inside his coat. Or, more accurately, the lack of weight.

Damn, he was going to miss that gun.

"And we're going to need weapons," Dan explained. "A *lot* of weapons."

POLANI SMELLED Dan before he saw him. He turned sharply, then ejected a short sharp, "Fonk!" when he found the detective looming in the shadows behind him.

"Will you please stop doing that?" the commissioner asked.

Dan shook his head. "No."

He nodded up at the building whose doorway Polani had been lurking in. They were in a large storage yard around the back, out of sight of passers-by. A couple of flatbed cargo trucks stood silently over by the high fences.

"This isn't the armory."

"Of course it isn't the armory. What, you think I can just waltz in and sign you out some military grade weaponry without it drawing attention?" Polani scoffed. "I might be the boss, but I'm still answerable to the people above me. And I do *not* want them asking questions."

"We had a deal," Dan reminded him.

"And I'm keeping my end of it," Polani said, quickly

raising his hands. "Kroysh. Calm down, Ripley. It's in hand."

"I told you, I'm not Ripley. If I was, you'd already be dead."

"Bullshizz. If you were, we'd be working together," Polani said.

Dan shoved his hands deep in his pockets to prevent him ripping the son-of-a-bedge's head off. "I thought we were working together?" he said, then he nodded to the door. "Get us in."

Glancing around at the high-fenced yard, Polani approached a retina scanner fixed to the wall beside the door. He had a small satchel slung over his shoulder, and fished in it as he flicked the scanner's power switch.

"Please look straight ahead into scanner," an electronic voice instructed.

Polani removed a clear plastic bag from his satchel and raised it to the scanner. An eyeball inside the bag stared blankly ahead as the scanner light swept across it, then the heavy door swung open and a series of lights *clunked* on in a warehouse beyond.

"What?" said Polani, stuffing the bag back in his satchel. "You don't think I'd use my own eye, do you? I don't want to be connected to this."

"What about the cameras?" Dan asked.

"All off. We've got an hour," the commissioner said. "I suggest we don't waste it."

Dan peered into the warehouse. Fifty or so racks of shelves ran from floor to ceiling in rows, each one groaning under the weight of the items crammed onto them. They took up around half the space, with several large, bulky tarp-covered objects filling the rest.

"If this is a trap..." Dan warned.

"No trap," said Polani. He sighed. "Now, d'you want this stuff or not?"

Dan stepped past him and into the warehouse. He knew of this place from his time on the force. *Evidence Storage.* It was laughable, really. The Tribunal generally never let themselves get bogged down in the whole 'evidence' thing. Much better to execute the wrong man and send an auto-generated apology to his next of kin later than to waste time worrying about things like proof or motive or due process.

None of the stuff here was ever used as actual evidence, but it was never disposed of, either. It was confiscated, logged, then sent to this place to be stored indefinitely. Dan knew of at least two other Evidence Storage warehouses in Down Here, but this one was the mother lode.

"You have less than an hour. Clock's ticking."

Dan left the commissioner and started to browse the shelves. The first stack was filled with drug paraphernalia – pipes, pore plungers, rectal pumps. That sort of thing. No actual drugs, though, Dan noted. If those had ever reached storage they would've been whisked away by some enterprising Tribunal officer pretty sharpish.

None of the objects on the shelves were bagged, and very few of them were even labeled. A set of industrial scales had a reference number scrawled on the side, but there was no saying the Tribunal had written it there.

The next rack along was mostly old TVs and computers. They were probably old tech when they were brought in, but having sat here rotting ever since, they were now pretty much obsolete.

He found the weapons two racks down, past a few false limbs, a lot of fake watches, and a decommissioned robot with its head missing.

They were piled up on shelves all the way to the ceiling, crammed in in no particular order. The shelf at Dan's eye-height held at least a dozen blaster pistols, several rifles and some kind of plasma launcher. There was a flamethrower, too, but those things were a real pain to pump and prime. Also, they didn't tend to work underwater.

He was disappointed, though not in the least surprised, not to see another Mindy in there. He'd taken the gun from a Xandrie enforcer a while back, and had never seen a gun like it before or since.

Cranking the handle on the side of the rack, Dan wound the next shelf down. This one was just as haphazardly filled as the first. There were a few grenades and mines nestled in between the firearms on this one, and Dan felt a flutter of excitement in his otherwise lifeless belly.

"Yeah. These'll do," he said.

Putting his fingers in his mouth, Dan whistled. He rummaged through the weapons and waited as the rumble of wheels approached through the warehouse.

An unmanned trolley pulled up beside him, the lid of its storage tub unfolding to reveal a space that practically cried out to be filled.

"OK," said Dan, dragging a scoped rifle out of the pile. "Let's go shopping."

THE TROLLEY'S wheels creaked under the weight of the weaponry as it trundled along behind Dan like a dog at its master's heel. Polani stood by one of the tarp-covered mounds, making a very deliberate show of checking the time.

"You understand what 'one hour' means, yes?" the commissioner asked.

Dan's only response was a cold *don't-make-me-kill-you* stare.

"We still have to get this out of here," he said, gesturing to the covered object beside them. "I've backed one of the trucks up to the shutters."

Dan regarded the bulky shape curiously. It was maybe three or four times the length of the Exodus, and a couple of times wider and taller, too. "What is it?"

"You said you needed a boat, right? Well, we don't have any. Not here. But we do have this."

He whistled two short notes and another trolley approached. In place of a storage container, this one had several long metal arms with a variety of attachments fastened to the ends. As Dan watched, it caught the edge of the tarp and pulled it clear, revealing a trailer

Dan's jaw dropped. "Holy fonk," he muttered.

"I assume, from your reaction, you're happy?"

Dan nodded slowly, like he wasn't sure if the question were some kind of trick. "Yeah. I'm happy."

"Thought you would be," Polani said. He whistled out a couple of other notes and a couple of other trollies set to work pulling the thing on the trailer over to the loading shutters. "I'll have it taken to the docks by the safehouse. I already locked it to your voiceprint."

Dan's eyes narrowed. "Why so helpful all of a sudden?"

"Let's call it... nostalgia," said Polani. "You know, for old time's sake."

Dan studied the commissioner's face. "No. No, that's not it. There's something else."

"Kroysh. You always did know me too well," he said. He sucked in his bottom lip and let it scrape across his teeth on the way back out. "I looked into it. The harbor, I mean. Like I said, there was a report on it. I saw what happened. If that thing comes back, a lot of people could die."

"Right," Dan agreed.

"Next time, they might even be someone important."

Dan sighed. "You were actually doing pretty well there for a second," he said. "But you had to go and blow it."

"You know what I mean," Polani said. He looked down at the floor, one hand holding the strap of his satchel.

"There's something else," Dan realized. "What aren't you telling me?"

"Freeze," said a male voice from over by the door, although with none of the urgency the word might suggest. "Nobody... move."

Polani's whole body seemed to become rigid. He raised his hands to either side of his head, but otherwise complied.

"Who is it?" he whispered.

Dan leaned past him to where a saucer-eyed furry creature in a Tribunal Admin Corps uniform stood trembling, a blaster pistol clutched in both hands.

"It's a Parlooq," Dan said, recognizing the officer as a member of Parloo's native species. Even if he hadn't seen him, he'd have known it was a Parlooq just from its slow, drawn-out way of speaking.

"One of mine?"

Dan nodded.

"Damn it." Polani hissed. "OK."

He turned, lowering his hands and cranking up his smile. "At ease, officer."

The Parlooq's wide eyes widened further. "Comm... iss... ion... er...?"

"That's right."

"Pol... ani?"

"Ha. Yes. That's me," Polani said. He waited several seconds for the Parlooq to begin lowering his gun, then strode over to him. "You're probably wondering what I'm doing here – don't answer that, it's a rhetorical question," the commissioner said. Sadly, he said it too late.

"I was... wondering..."

"OK, well—"

"...that... actually."

"OK, well, the thing is..." the commissioner began, putting an arm around the young officer's shoulders. Dan saw Polani's other hand slipping inside his satchel.

"No, don't!" Dan barked.

The Parlooq gargled as the knife was buried in his neck. It wasn't a particularly large blade, but then it didn't have to be. Polani gave it a sharp sideways yank, tearing the officer's throat, then stepped back to avoid the spray of blood.

Released from the commissioner's grip, the Parlooq slumped to the floor, air wheezing from the ragged wound that opened like a grinning mouth in his throat.

"You didn't have to do that," Dan said.

"I did. You know I did," Polani insisted. He wiped the blade of the knife on the officer's uniform, then returned it to his bag. "Like I told you, I can't afford any questions. That means no loose ends."

"You could've talked to him. You could've given him some excuse."

"Maybe. But I wasn't willing to bet my life on it," Polani said. He turned to Dan and pulled something else from his bag. Instinctively, Dan caught his hand and bent it back at the wrist. "Ow! Ow! What the fonk are you doing?" Polani hissed.

Where Dan had expected to see a weapon he instead

saw a data drive. It was a compact silver cylinder with a projection lens on one end and an audio input at the other.

"What's this?"

"You said I had another reason for helping you," said Polani, gritting his teeth against the pain. "You're right. This is it."

"Again, what is it?"

"Just take it. Just watch it," Polani told him. He tried to pull his hand free, but Dan forced it further backward, dropping the commissioner to his knees. "Argh. Cut it out. We don't have time for this! Just take it and let me tidy up."

Dan kept the pressure on for several enjoyable seconds, then released his grip and plucked the data drive from Polani's trembling fingers. He slipped it in his pocket without even looking at it, and shot the dead Parlooq a pitying look. With a shove, he pushed the commissioner to the floor, and then led his faithful trolley of firearms toward the exit.

"Ripley."

Dan kept walking. Polani muttered something less than complimentary below his breath.

"Deadman."

Dan stopped and turned. "What?"

"The data drive," the commissioner said. He breathed in slowly, like he was steadying his nerve. "When you watch it... you're going to want to be sitting down."

FIFTEEN

AFTER CHECKING and double-checking that the trunk of the Exodus was locked and wasn't going to unexpectedly spring open and reveal an arsenal of high-powered weaponry to passers-by, Dan slipped in through the back door of the apartment block and trudged up the stairs to the safe house.

Artur and Ollie weren't back yet. No sign of *what's his name*, either. Dan glanced out of the window. The evening was drawing in, but he told himself there was no reason to get worried yet.

The data drive felt heavy, like the information it held was somehow adding to its weight. He turned it over in his hands, fumbling it a little with his new fingers. There was always a certain amount of clumsiness that came with new appendages, although he was learning to adapt more quickly.

Despite the occasional hiccup, Ollie was getting better, too. She had nowhere near his old friend Nedran's levels of skill, but – on the other hand – she was alive and Nedran wasn't, so it more than balanced out.

Dan raised an imaginary glass in Nedran's memory, then he closed the blinds, plunging the room into a half-assed sort of darkness.

"Open," he said into the end of the data drive, then he set it on the coffee table and watched as several holographic screens appeared around the room. Four of them showed video feeds, while a couple more displayed text and images. Their light danced across the walls, giving the room a strangely ethereal sort of feel.

Dan checked out the screen closest to him. It looked like security camera footage taken from high up. Hundreds of people crisscrossed on a busy... what was it? Street? City square? There were no vehicles, so probably neither of those.

He turned to one of the other video feeds. There was a time stamp on this one that told him the footage wasn't live. Something about the date and time dredged up a half-forgotten memory, but he couldn't quite place it.

Not yet.

This screen was just a reverse of the first, showing the same sea of people from a different angle, with nothing to tell him where it was.

When he saw the third screen, he realized why the date and time seemed so familiar.

Dan sat down.

It was the mall. The mall on Eighteenth.

And one-hundred-and-thirty-four people were about to die.

Dan pointed to the screens in turn and arranged them in the air so all four video feeds were set out like the panes of a window in front of him. The two he'd looked at first – the general mass of people and the reverse angle on the same – were at the top. Below them, side by side, were the feeds from two other cameras. One showed part of the mall's food court and part of a clothes store frontage. The fourth screen focused on a row of doors – three bathrooms, and another door leading out to the parking lot. There wasn't much happening on this screen right now, so Dan gave the others his attention.

The bottom left screen looked to be where the action started, although there was nothing specific to see yet. It was more the reactions of the people in the food court that had caught Dan's attention. The sudden head turns. The looks of confusion, then concern, then the explosion of movement as everyone got to their feet more or less as one and became a stampeding panicky herd. Something off screen had terrified them.

"Pause all," said Dan. He took a moment to examine the other screens for anything unusual, but so far, so normal. "Resume."

The crowd in the bottom left went back to tumbling over one another in their rush to get away. There was no sound on the feed, but Dan didn't need it to imagine the screaming and hollering. The faces of the people in the video told him what he needed to know.

A kid, no more than five or six, tripped and went down hard. Nobody came back for him. Nobody stopped.

The stampeding crowd infiltrated the screen above. They'd been fleeing left in the bottom screen, but ran in from the right on the uppermost feed. Panic rippled through the crowd and spread like a fast-acting virus, quickly infecting the reverse angle image on the right. The whole mall was in a state of terrified upheaval, and Dan still had no idea...

Wait.

Hold up.

"Pause all."

The screens froze.

"Track back three seconds."

There was a blip as the images quickly rewound.

"Play all, quarter speed."

Dan leaned in and studied the screen showing the food court. He watched a straggler at the edge of the screen running in slow motion, her head turned so she could look back over her shoulder. He saw her visibly brace herself, her body tensing as she screwed up her eyes.

Even in slow motion, the elongated black shape that killed her moved almost too quickly to see. It speared her through the back, exploded through her chest in the next frame, then was gone again.

It took Dan seven attempts at trying to pause on that specific image before he remembered he could advance frame by frame through the video. He zoomed in on the woman at the point of impact, but the image lost a lot of resolution and so didn't make things much clearer. He could see she was a Parlooq, though, which explained her inability to get the fonk out of there in time.

She was young, a little overweight, and dressed in the colorful server's uniform of one of the food court stands. She was also impaled on a pointy black spike that could easily have been mistaken for a weapon of some kind. Dan knew better, though. He'd been impaled by one himself down in the sewers, and it was still pretty fresh in his memory.

The toilet monster. The toilet monster had done this.

He sat back, feeling quite pleased with himself for spotting such a relatively subtle clue amidst all the panic and chaos. If he hadn't caught that fleeting glimpse of the thing on the lower left screen, he might never have figured out what happened.

Hell, maybe he *was* a real detective, after all.

"Play all," he said. "Regular speed."

The video resumed. A truck-sized black monster immediately rolled onto the food court screen, thrashing and snapping its pointed limbs as if waving to the camera, and stabbing at anyone within reach.

Fonk. So much for subtle clues.

Dan watched, hypnotized, as the thing tore through the crowd, skewering, slicing and decapitating men, women and...

He looked away. "Pause all."

The images froze. They hung there, suspended in thin air, daring him to keep watching. The thing was visible on the top two screens now, but too far from the camera on both for Dan to be able to make out much detail beyond 'big, black and pointy.'

He pulled one of the text displays toward him and skimmed through it. Witness statements, mostly just describing what he'd already seen, although a few provided a little more detail.

There seemed to be some disagreement about where the monster had come from. Some – correctly – said it had appeared near the food court, but a few insisted it came from the opposite side of the mall's central plaza.

Dan wasn't particularly surprised. People were idiots at the best of times, let alone when an angry ball of limbs had just cut someone in half lengthways right beside them. He could forgive them some lapses in memory.

The apartment's front door flew open and smacked against the wall. Dan jumped up, his hand instinctively grasping for a gun that wasn't there. Finn staggered inside, bent double by the weight of the filing cabinet on his back. Artur perched on top of it, offering advice and criticism, although not in that order.

"Put yer back into it, lad. Ye're making a real meal of this, if ye don't mind me saying. It's light as a feather."

"It... really... isn't," Finn gasped.

"Where would ye be wanting it, Deadman?" Artur asked. "And what's with all the screens?"

"It's footage from the mall," Dan explained.

"The mall? Ye mean the massacre mall? With all the dead kiddies and whatnot?"

Dan nodded.

"Sure, what do ye want to go watching the likes of that for?" Artur asked.

"The Tribunal gave it to me. It's..." He glanced back at the screens. "It's pretty eye opening."

"Uh, brah?" Finn groaned.

"Huh? Oh. Put it anywhere."

Finn started to squat.

"Not in the middle of the fonking floor," Dan snapped. "Against the wall or in the corner."

"Oh. Sure. No... problem."

"'No problem,' he says," Artur muttered. "That's not what ye've been saying for the past forty fecking minutes." He looked back at Dan as Finn shuffled toward the corner. "And ye should've heard him on the stairs. Moaning like an old woman, so he was. I don't know how I coped."

Ollie entered, only her legs visible behind a teetering stack of battered cardboard boxes. The uppermost box wobbled unsteadily as she kicked the door closed behind her and staggered blindly into the room.

"That's more than we had," Dan observed.

"Huh?" Ollie turned sideways to look at him, which

immediately made the top box fall off. A pile of colorful shorts and vests tumbled out and onto the floor.

"That's my stuff," said Finn, putting his hands on his lower back and clicking his spine back into place.

"One box? That's it?"

Finn nodded, but blushed a little. "I travel light."

Ollie dropped the other boxes on the floor, then collapsed into a chair. "Wow, that was a long walk," she wheezed.

"Ye think you had it bad? I had to listen to ye both complaining every step o' the way," Artur pointed out. "Ye ask me, I deserve some kind of award."

Finn regarded the screens in front of Dan. "Huh," he said. "I know that place. Where is that?"

"It's a mall," Dan said. "Over on Eighteenth."

"That's it," said Finn. "Yeah, brah, that's it. I've been there before."

He pointed to the black shape on the top left screen. "And is that... what is that?"

Ollie appeared at his side. "That's it, isn't it? That's the toilet monster."

"It is," said Dan. "That's it. Looks like Krato was telling the truth. This wasn't done with weapons. This thing killed those people."

Finn squinted at the screens. "Thing? Are you sure?"

"I just watched it," Dan said. "I'm sure."

"No, I mean..." Finn stepped closer to the screens. "I mean, you sure it's only one thing, brah?"

Dan sighed. "Yes, *kid*. I'm sure. Look at it."

He indicated the top two screens. "Camera one, camera two. They're at reverse angles."

"OK... but the thing - the monster, or whatever - it's not the same in both pictures."

Dan frowned. "What?"

"It's at the back of the room in both pictures."

"So?"

"So, if it's a reverse angle, it should be far away in one, then closer in the other. I mean... right? Unless it was right in the middle, but it isn't. It's at the far end in both of these."

Dan snorted, but leaned in for a closer look.

"He's right," said Ollie. "And look, in this one it's stabbing that man through the face, but in this one it's cutting a woman's leg off."

Dan's eyes flicked between the two images like they were panels in a Spot the Difference puzzle. Sure enough, the spiky black shape was behaving differently on both screens.

The general theme - violence, maiming and agonizing death - was the same, but the actual specifics of it were different.

"Sync all feeds," Dan said. Maybe there was just a time discrepancy, although the timestamp didn't seem to think so.

The videos all flickered briefly, then returned showing the exact same images they had been a moment before.

"It's a different monster," Dan muttered. He pushed back his hat and scraped his rough hand across the top of his forehead. "Damn it, there are two of them."

"That's unfortunate," said Artur. "And, I mean, if there are two of them, I suppose ye can't rule out there being three of them. Or four."

"No," Dan agreed.

"Or five. Or six."

"We get the point, Artur."

"Or a hundred."

Dan slumped down into the chair. "You might not want

to watch this," he warned Ollie. "I need to see what happens next."

"Oh. Oh, OK," said Ollie. She glanced from him to the screen and back again. "Is it bad?"

"It's bad," Dan confirmed.

"I've probably seen worse," Ollie pointed out. "Where I come from, I used to see some pretty horrible things. I saw someone get turned inside-out, I saw someone be eaten by these sort of bird things with, like, faces. You know, people faces? Little people faces, all scrunched up and mean-looking. And then, this one time someone literally just burst open and—"

"Shizz. OK, fine, you can feel free to watch," said Dan. "Just don't say I didn't warn you."

Finn raised a hand. "Uh, do I have to watch, too?" he asked. "It's just, I'm not big into, you know... whatever's going to happen."

"I don't care," Dan said. He gestured vaguely into the hallway. "Go find somewhere to put your stuff."

Finn smiled with relief. "OK. Shout me if you need me."

"We won't need you," Dan assured him.

He waited until Finn had picked up his box of clothes and left the room before turning to Ollie. "Seriously? Him?"

Ollie's eyebrows dipped. "Him what? What him?" she asked, stumbling over her tongue. "I don't know what you mean," she insisted, but the rising inflection in her voice and the reddening of her cheeks suggested otherwise.

Dan tutted and turned his attention back to the screens. "Play all," he instructed, and all four images became alive with movement. And death. Lots and lots of death.

"Holy father," Artur whispered. These were the only

words anyone spoke until a second black shape appeared on both top screens, confirming the 'two monsters' theory.

The screens all flickered, then went dark. At first, Dan thought there was a problem with the feed, but then realized he could see some light spilling in through the parking lot door in the lower right image. The cameras hadn't been cut, but the lights had. The whole mall was in darkness, and it was impossible to make out anything but the vague sense of movement.

And then the footage stopped. The lights returned as the feeds looped back to the start, ready to play again.

The three of them sat in silence for a while, taking in what they'd seen. As usual, it was Artur who couldn't keep his mouth shut for long.

"So," he said. He reached for a few possible follow-up options, but none of them was particularly inspiring. "There's two o' the bastards."

"Looks like it," Dan said.

"That we know of," Artur continued. "There might be—"

"More. Yes. We established that," said Dan. "For now, let's assume two."

Although the images had stopped moving, Ollie continued to watch the screens. "Look at all those people," she said, whispering in case she somehow startled them all away. The footage was pre-attack, and everyone looked... happy. Happier than they'd look in a few seconds time, at least.

She reached a hand out and tried to brush her fingertips against the face of a girl down near the front of the crowd. The girl had a soft toy tucked under one arm, and a look of awe on her face as she gazed around at the busy mall. The image rippled and distorted as Ollie's fingers passed through it, making the girl look as if she were standing in a Hall of Mirrors.

"Did everyone die?"

"Not everyone," said Dan. "But enough. Still think that thing was suffering?"

Ollie bit her lip. "Maybe," she said. Her voice cracked a little, but Dan and Artur both pretended they hadn't noticed. "But it should suffer more."

"My thoughts exactly, Peaches," said Artur. "Now what's the news, ye smelly bastard? Did ye get us some weapons?"

"I did," Dan confirmed. "Not sure how much good they'll do, but I got them."

"And did ye get us a boat?"

"Not exactly."

"Ah, bollocks. Why not? There's not a whole lot we can do without one. Unless ye plan on swimming, like. In which case, fair play."

"No, not swimming. We have something. You'll see it tomorrow. We'll load up and go out then."

"Tomorrow?" said Ollie. She tried to touch the girl with the soft toy again, then shook her head. "No. Let's go tonight."

Artur and Dan exchanged a glance. "I understand yer enthusiasm, Peaches, and it's a credit to ye. But don't ye think it's getting a little, ye know, dark for us to be out there roaming the ocean waves?"

Dan rubbed his chin, considering this. "Except... It won't matter."

"What won't matter?" asked Artur.

"The dark. It won't matter."

"Why won't it matter? How can we look for them if we can't see feck all?"

Ollie clicked her fingers. "A torch!"

"No, not a torch. Not exactly." Dan stood up. "Ah, what the Hell? Let's do it"

"Yes!" cried Ollie, jumping up.

"Have ye both lost yer minds?" said Artur. "Ye can't seriously be thinking about heading out on the ocean at this time o' day. Ye remember what happened last time? And that was in full daylight."

"We're not going out on the ocean," Dan said. He smiled grimly. "We're going under it."

SIXTEEN

Dan, Ollie and Finn stood on a floating jetty, gazing down into the water as it shimmered and sparkled in the glow from the Up There engines. The only sound – assuming you discounted the distant wailing of sirens, the hubbub of traffic and the occasional gunshot – was the lapping of the waves against the jetty's sides, and the faint *creaking* of an older boat moored somewhere over on the right.

Artur leaned out of Dan's breast coat pocket and joined the others in gazing into the depths.

"I don't follow," he said. "I thought we had a boat? I don't see it."

"I told you, not a boat," Dan replied. He leaned forward and addressed the ocean. "Voice imprint authorization."

Dan straightened again, and they all watched as lights illuminated deep in the darkness and bubbles rolled up to burst on the surface.

"We've got a submarine."

"Whoa!" said Finn, his eyes widening as a smooth, sleek, but unmistakably *bright fonking yellow* submarine rose up from beneath the waves and bobbed to a stop beside them.

"A submarine?" said Artur. "Hold on now. Wait a fecking moment. Going on a boat is one thing, but ye can't seriously want us to go *under* the water – where all the monsters are, mind – in this mustard monstrosity?"

Dan nodded. "That's the idea. Doesn't matter if it's day or night up here. Soon as we get down a little, it's going to be pitch blackness."

"I have some very grave reservations about this, Deadman. I don't want to go into the details, but let's just say I've had some bad experiences underwater in my time. Some *very* bad experiences. Know what I'm saying?"

"Not a clue," Dan said.

"No. I suppose I'm being quite vague," Artur admitted. "But just take my word for it. No good can come of this, Deadman. No good at all."

He shrugged. "Still, I'm game if everyone else is." He was doing his best to sound more confident now, but Dan could tell he was worried. "I mean, what's the worst that could happen?" he asked.

Finn opened his mouth.

"Make any attempt to answer that question and I'll wedge meself in yer throat until ye suffocate," Artur warned.

Finn closed his mouth again.

"I like the color," said Ollie.

"The color is awesome," Finn concurred.

Ollie couldn't have looked more pleased. "You like it, too?"

"Are you kidding? I love it. It's like... when the sun shines through the gaps in the cities Up There, and hits the ground just right. You know?"

"Not really," Ollie admitted. "But it sounds awesome!"

Dan rolled his eyes and muttered something mildly disparaging just loud enough for everyone to get the gist of it without picking up any of the specifics.

"What do you think of the color, brah?" Finn asked him.

Dan fixed him with a cool stare. "What do I think? I think it's yellow."

"Yeah, no. I mean, I know it's yellow, but what do you feel about it? What does it say to you?"

"It says 'get in the fonking submarine,'" Dan told him.

"And how do ye propose we do that?" asked Artur. "I've been looking at the thing for the past minute and a half, and I've yet to see a door."

"Maybe we sit on top?" Ollie guessed.

"That would be impractical, Peaches," Artur said. "Not to mention suicidal."

"I thought it was a great suggestion," said Finn, smiling encouragingly at Ollie.

Dan grunted. "Because you're an idiot." He leaned over the edge of the jetty. "Open."

A line of four green lights illuminated on top of the submarine, and part of the roof folded in on itself like unnecessarily complicated Origami. A single pilot's seat was revealed at the front of the sub, with two padded benches lined up behind it. It looked like it was designed to carry eight or nine people. Three and one-tenth people would be no problem.

"Want me to drive?" Finn asked.

"No, I do not. Sit there at the back," Dan instructed. "Ollie, you go behind me."

"Ye ever driven one of these things before, Deadman?" Artur asked.

Dan peered down into the sub. The controls, from what he could gather, amounted to a single stick.

"No," he confessed. "But how hard can it be?"

THE SUB CRUISED ELEGANTLY AWAY from the harbor, blue light playing across its sleek curves as it banked down into the darkening depths. It found a current and let itself be carried onward into the ocean, its nose pointing forward, its course straight and true.

Artur whistled appreciatively through his teeth. "Nice driving," he remarked. "Sure, it barely even feels like we're moving."

"Thanks," said Finn, flashing a smile back over his shoulder.

"Better than this hopeless bastard, anyway," said Artur. He nudged Dan, who was sitting next to him on the bench. "I mean, how can ye crash before ye've even started the engines?"

Dan sighed.

"And into a wall, no less. We're underwater, and yet he somehow finds a wall to drive us into head-first!" Artur shook his head. "I mean, a wall! It was like ye were driving with yer eyes shut."

"OK."

"Like a blind suicide bomber, so ye were."

"I got it. Thank you," Dan grunted.

"On roller skates."

"Yes. OK. So, it wasn't my finest moment."

"Never mind *finest* moment, I thought it was me *last* fecking moment."

Dan chose not to continue the discussion, and instead

looked around the interior of the sub. Up front, Finn was holding the single steering stick, but was surrounded by the bewildering array of holographic readouts and touch controls that had led to Dan's collision with the wall, not to mention his collisions with the jetty, two boats, and a rusted shopping cart someone had rolled into the sea.

From the outside, the sub had looked like solid metal, but inside there were large windows taking up the majority of the walls and ceiling. Even the floor beneath the seats was transparent, giving the impression they were all floating in mid-air above a dark and watery abyss.

There were a couple of storage lockers at the back. One of the doors had kept flapping open, revealing a gray diving suit inside. On Dan's instruction, Ollie had wedged the door shut with a box they'd brought from the car. A box that contained – and this was really something of an understatement – a *fonkload* of guns.

The sub itself packed a torpedo launcher and a couple of robotic limbs. Neither would fare particularly well against any of the larger predators they might come across, but the back of the sub opened into an airlock, blasters worked underwater, and Dan didn't need to breathe. If anything came after them, he felt confident he could at least make it regret that decision.

Ollie sat on the bench behind Finn, her knees brushing lightly against his back. Dan had no heartbeat of his own, but he could practically feel both of theirs thumping through the floor.

He wasn't sure why it bothered him, exactly. If you ignored the 'brah' thing, then Finn seemed like a good kid.

It wasn't jealousy, either. He'd never thought of Ollie in that way, and even if it hadn't been for the whole 'being dead' situation, he was old enough to be her father.

He put it down to his deep-rooted distrust of people he didn't know. Although, in fairness, he trusted most people he did know even less. While he'd never admit it, he... felt responsible for the girl. He didn't want her getting hurt because it might trigger some outburst of demonic power that could level the whole city.

And, well, because he didn't want her getting hurt.

"So, what's the plan?" asked Artur.

Dan looked down at him, then gestured out into the depths of the ocean. The sub's powerful torch beams picked out a startled-looking fish in the middle distance, which quickly turned tail and zipped off out of the vessel's path.

"This is the plan. We're doing the plan."

"What, just drive around until we find it? That's yer idea? I thought ye'd have brought, ye know, some sort of fancy tracking gizmo, or what have ye."

Dan shook his head. "Well, I didn't."

Artur leaned back to look up at him. "So, ye mean we're just going to cruise around underwater all night, dodging assorted big monsters in the hope of finding the one specific monster that we're after? That's yer grand scheme?"

"Have you got any better ideas?"

"Yes!"

Dan pushed back his hat. "OK. Let's hear them."

"Well I don't know the details yet, exactly," Artur admitted. "But if ye give me five minutes I'm bound to come up with something."

Finn turned his chair so he could address the rest of the group. "I've been looking at the controls, and I think there's, like, a scanner thing that should show us anything nearby. Looks like we can set it to show only stuff over a certain size, too. Should I try that?"

"Aha! Now *that* sounds like a plan," said Artur.

Dan gave a begrudging sort of a grunt. "I guess that can't hurt," he admitted. "Sure. Go for it."

Finn faced front again. He poked hesitantly at the controls. "OK, so... Right. I think if I... And then..."

A fuzzy black and green image appeared in the air in front of him, partially obscuring the view through the front window.

"Bingo!"

"*Holy shoite, what's that thing?*" Artur cried, pointing to a ridiculously huge grainy green blob that took up the whole bottom half of the image. He jumped up, grabbed the cuff of Dan's sleeve, and shook it violently. "Look at the size of it! We're all going to die! I knew we shouldn't have come down here. I fecking telt ye!"

"That's the city," said Dan.

Artur stopped shaking him and studied the screen. "Is it? Ye sure?"

"Pretty sure," said Dan. "It's a million times larger than the sub and it's directly behind us, so either it's the city, or yes, we're all about to die, along with everyone else on the planet."

Artur scowled. "Ye know what they say about sarcasm, Deadman?"

"No. What do they say?"

"They say it's used exclusively by arseholes. Or words to that effect, anyway."

"I'll bear that in mind," said Dan, then he slapped his hands on his thighs and stood up. "Now, who wants to help me check out some guns?"

DAN SLID the battery pack into a blaster rifle, pulled a

variety of levers on the side of the weapon, then squinted down the sights.

"How's it looking?" asked Artur. He was peering into the barrel of another gun, though he hadn't really explained what, if anything, he was expecting to find.

"All good," said Dan. "Forty percent charge, so not perfect, but enough."

He added the rifle to one of two roughly equally sized piles of firearms on the floor beside him.

"So that's six that look likely to work, and six that are totally banjaxed," said Artur. "Not bad going."

Ollie had torn herself away from Finn long enough to come and see what was going on. She stood over them, scowling a little disapprovingly at the weapons.

"What's up wi' yer face, Peaches?" asked Artur. "Ye look like ye've stood in something nasty."

"They look dangerous," Ollie said.

"Kind of the whole point," Dan pointed out. "Not much use having a gun that isn't dangerous."

"I don't like them," Ollie said.

"Well, sadly we don't all have the power to blow things up using just our hands or our minds or what have ye," said Artur. "So, ye know, tough shoite."

"You'll be thankful for them if we get attacked," said Dan. "The weapons on the sub won't make a dent in that thing that almost pulled us under last time, let alone the toilet monster."

Ollie wrapped her arms around herself. "I just don't like them," she said. "I mean, I liked your old gun - that was fun. These don't look fun."

They all shared a moment of silence as they remembered Mindy.

Damn, Dan missed that gun.

"Yeah. That one was fun," he agreed.

"I loved the shoite-yerself mode," Artur reminisced. "That one fair used to crack me up."

"Brown noise," Dan said. He snorted a half-laugh. "Yeah. Yeah, that came in handy."

He gave himself a shake.

"But that gun's gone," he said. "These are the guns we have now, and they'll do the job we need them to do."

"Helloooo?" called Artur into the barrel of another rifle. He quickly put his ear to the opening, listened for a moment, then nodded.

"Sounds good to me," he declared, then he sat back on his haunches. "That's all very well ye saying they'll do the job, but that sort of depends on whether we get the chance or not, don't it?"

"What do you mean?" asked Dan.

"I mean we've been sailing for a while now."

"Not sailing," Finn corrected. "It's not a sailboat."

Artur sighed. "Fine. We've been *submarining* for a while now. Is that better?"

"Yeah, brah."

"And yet we've still found precisely feck all. We've seen some fish, a lot of green stuff, and - in case anyone's forgotten - that wall ye crashed us into, but not a whole lot else. This thing we're looking for..."

"Things," Ollie corrected.

"These things we're looking for, they could be on the other side of the planet by now. Or even five miles in any direction other than the one we're sailing in."

"Not sailing."

"Whatever it fecking is!" Artur snapped. "My point is, it's not just like looking for a needle in a haystack, it's like looking for a needle in a planet-wide ocean that's filled with other, much larger needles that could spring up out of nowhere and tear our eyes out through our arse at any given moment."

"We'll find it. Or them. We'll find it," said Dan. "We found it last time."

"It found us last time," Artur corrected. "Which isn't the same thing. And even if we do just happen to chance upon it, what then? I mean, I'm a fan of shooting things with big guns as much as the next man, but I'm not convinced how effective it's going to be."

"It'll work," said Dan.

"Well, I guess we'll just have to wait and see," replied Artur. "Although, we won't, because there's not a snowball's chance in Hell that we're going to come across the fecking—"

BUMP.

The sub rocked, just a little. A torrent of bubbles appeared at one of the windows closest to the back, blocking their view of whatever was out there.

"What was that?" Ollie asked.

"Something bumped us," Finn whispered.

"Yes, we worked that part out," Dan hissed. "What was it?"

Finn prodded at the controls. "Hold on, I'll see if I can..."

The black and green map appeared in the air again. Everyone stared at it for a while, nobody speaking.

"So..." began Artur. "We'd be the little yellow dot there, is that right?"

"Right," said Dan.

"And the black bit... that would be the surrounding ocean?"

"It would," Dan confirmed.

"Right. That's what I thought," said Artur.

There was silence for a while longer. The bubbles had all rolled up off the window now, but only darkness was visible beyond.

"I suppose, if I'm honest, it's the green parts I'm worried about," said Artur. "Ye know, the way there are five or six of them just sort of circling around the yellow dot there."

Dan nodded. Those were definitely a concern.

BUMP.

The sub shuddered again as something clipped it from below. Its frame creaked, the noise sounding oddly squeaky this far under the water.

This time, when Dan glanced down, he caught sight of a gray shape vanishing into the murk. The way it moved through the water immediately worried him. This thing was big enough to move a submarine, and swam like it fonking owned the place. Even from his brief glance, he could tell it had 'Apex predator' written all over it.

"What should we do?" asked Ollie. "What is that?"

"I think our best bet is to stay very, very quiet," Artur whispered, then he immediately screamed as a shark-like snout thumped against the closest window, its soulless black eyes staring hungrily at the occupants of the sub.

"We're lunch," Artur whimpered. "We're a fecking meal in a can in here. Oh, I so should've listened to me old mammy!"

"Why, what did she say?" asked Ollie.

"She said a lot of things, Peaches, and I'm pretty sure 'Don't get eaten by a big fecking shark-monster' was somewhere on the list."

"Wise woman," said Dan. He stood and moved to the front, leaning on the benches to support himself as the sub was nudged once again.

A squirming mass of fat gray tentacles oozed past the front window, before being swallowed by the murk again.

"What was that?" Dan barked. "Swing the light round on it."

Finn peered at the controls. "Uh... I don't know how to do that."

"Then turn the fonking sub!" said Dan, grabbing the stick and yanking it to the right.

The submarine lurched suddenly, throwing Ollie and Artur against one of the windows just as one of the shark-things hammered against the other side.

Out front, Dan and Finn caught a glimpse of teeth and tentacles. They got a very brief, yet deeply concerning impression of the thing's size, then one of the sub's lights blinked out, hiding it from view.

Something hit them from underneath near the back, turning the floor into a steep slope running down toward the nose. Ollie stumbled and Artur tumbled to the front, only for a tail or some other appendage to strike the sub like an open-handed slap, lurching it sideways.

Another of the spotlights flickered, then blinked out.

"What the feck are those things?" Artur whispered.

"Don't know, but they're intelligent," said Dan. He gazed out through the window, but saw mostly his own reflection looking back.

"Me arse. If they were that intelligent, they wouldn't be living in the fecking ocean," Artur said. "They'd have a house somewhere nice and dry."

"They're smart, all right," Dan insisted. "They're going for the lights. They want to leave us in the dark."

"The bastards!" Artur cried. "The dirty fishy bastards."

Dan charged to the back of the sub, grabbed one of the working rifles, and swung it onto his shoulder. Fishing in the pile, he found a blaster pistol, double-checked the charge, then wedged it into his holster. It didn't fit perfectly – not like Mindy – but it would stay in until he needed it.

The sub rocked. The final light blinked out.

The ocean became a gulf of darkness around them.

"That's not good," Finn muttered.

"Everyone wait here, stay quiet, and hold on," Dan said. "If you can turn out the inside lights, do that."

Finn turned out the inside lights and the blackness became absolute.

"I meant once I was out," Dan sighed.

The lights returned.

"Sorry, brah."

Dan hit the button that opened the rear airlock. The wall spiraled open like the shutter of a camera, revealing a small space beyond. It was barely big enough to hold two people, but that was good. Big things couldn't fit into small spaces, so as long as Dan stayed inside, he'd be safe from the sharktopii.

He hoped.

"Be careful," Ollie told him.

"I always am," Dan said, stepping through the opening.

"Well, that's *definitely* not true," Ollie began, but the airlock door had already closed, so Dan missed most of it.

There were two tether cords attached to a heavy metal hoop on the floor. Dan tied one around his waist, yanked on it a couple of times to test it, then tied on the other one, too, just in case.

The sub jerked. The single light in the airlock blinked out. Dan had now way of knowing if Finn had turned it off, or if the black-eyed fonks outside had done it. Either way, the darkness suited him just fine.

He slapped at the button that opened the outer airlock door, but missed it. He fumbled around for the next several seconds trying to find the thing, his eyes gradually adjusting to the complete absence of light.

He eventually found it. He still couldn't see that he'd pressed it, but was able to figure it out from the way the wall spiraled open and the ocean crashed in, slamming him against the inner door and holding him pinned. A lifetime of instinct made him gulp down a desperate – and unnecessary – last breath, before the water swirled around him and up over his head.

SEVENTEEN

THE WAY the sound changed was the first thing Dan noticed. The creaking of the sub sounded muted, yet somehow amplified at the same time, like it was bypassing his ears and kicking the shizz out of the aural receptors in his brain.

The second thing he noticed was the mouth. It was hard to miss, due to the way it opened wide in front of him giving him an up-close view of some very large and nasty teeth before they snapped shut again just beyond the outer airlock door.

The dead-eyed, pointy nosed head squashed into the gap, its mouth gnashing and gnawing at nothing but water as it tried to chew Dan up.

Dan had an urge to deliver a witty quip. Something along the lines of how you should never eat rotten meat - he hadn't fully workshopped the punchline yet - but the fact he was both fully underwater and mostly full of the stuff made him decide against the idea.

Instead, he shrugged the rifle off his shoulder, held it at

waist height, then pumped a couple of rounds into the octo-shark's gaping maw.

Even underwater, the rifle performed admirably. The shark-thing's internal organs and rectum, less so. They exploded outwards in a tumbling ball of blaster bolts and gore. The monster's mouth stopped with all the biting nonsense and fell open with a rubbery flop.

Placing a foot on its nose, Dan shoved the thing back from the airlock. It drifted away and sank down into the darkness, its blood blooming around it like a cloud of red mist.

One of the other shark monsters quickly homed in on the blood scent and set to work tearing the dead one apart. Dan watched, fascinated, as teeth the size of his hand chomped and hacked and tore at the dead monster's flesh.

He was so busy watching, in fact, that he didn't see another of the fonkers closing in until it was almost too late. He threw himself back against the inner airlock wall just as the octo-shark hit the sub at ramming speed.

The force of the impact shoved the sub on and spun it out to the right. Dan scrabbled for a handhold on the wall, but found none. He swung out from the airlock on his tether ropes and the battering-ram shark's tentacles all squirmed at once, propelling it towards him.

Roaring bubbles, Dan opened fire. He heard the *hiss* of the blaster bolts as they were spat one after the other from the barrel of the gun, followed by the *kersplurks* of the impacts as they slammed into the shark-thing's hide.

These things, Dan realized, were a whole lot softer on the inside. The blaster fire left deep glowing craters in the monster's side, but it was still alive, still moving, and even more angry looking than it had been a moment before.

Grabbing the tie-ropes, Dan yanked hard, heaving

himself back into the airlock. He felt the sub shudder again as the shark-thing slammed against the opening right at his back, but this time managed to avoid being thrown back out into the ocean.

Turning, he found himself almost pinned by the thing's head. It thrashed and wriggled, eyeballs larger than Dan's head staring him down as the teeth chomped at him. The mouth was too low down, the angle of the thing's head blocking a clear shot down its throat.

Dan went for the eye instead. He slammed the butt of the rifle against it, but the thrashing only became more frenzied. Metal groaned as the thing forced its way further into the opening, its nose inching ever closer to Dan, its teeth still doing their gnashing and gnawing thing.

Fishing in his coat, he found the pistol. The shark bucked and thrashed as Dan jammed the barrel of the gun deep into its bulbous eye and squeezed off several rounds. Its tentacles slammed against the sub and pushed, and the shark's head *popped* from the opening like a cork from a champagne bottle. The blaster, still wedged in the thing's eye, was wrenched from Dan's hand. He went back to the rifle and opened fire.

A crater erupted on the shark-thing's snout. Another on the side of its head, right beside its gills. Neither one stopped it. Its oily tentacles thrashed and wriggled furiously, launching it into another charge. Dan wedged his arms and feet against the sides of the airlock, trying to prevent himself from being knocked out into the ocean again when...

Oh.

Oh, shizz.

The thing that rose up from the depths was bigger than the octo-shark. If Dan had to put a number on it, he'd say it was probably bigger than four or five octo-sharks, although a lot would depend on how you positioned them.

Its head was long and crocodile-like, but disproportionately narrow for its smooth, shiny body that resembled some sort of slug.

Narrow or not, the thing's jaws made short work of the shark-thing. Dan both heard and felt the *crunch* of its bones snapping and, the *shhkt* of its tough gray hide being torn apart.

There was a rush of bubbles, a flick of a tail, and then both creatures – the living and the almost-certainly dead – vanished into the darkness beneath the sub.

Dan hoped the appearance of the *whatever the fonk that thing was* would scare off the other octo-sharks, but no such luck. He could clearly see two circling around, but got a vague impression of at least another two a little further out. He tried to remember how many green blobs they'd seen on the scanners, but 'too many' was the most accurate answer he could give.

He checked the rifle. The charge was dropping fast. It wasn't quite flashing a warning at him yet, but another shot should do it. After that he'd have three, maybe four more before the charge was fully depleted. Not enough. Not nearly enough. He could only hope killing a couple more of them would be enough to send the others a message. Although, considering they hadn't batted an eyelid when one of their number was devoured by something four times its size, Dan had some pretty serious doubts.

One of the shark-things curved towards him, its body changing direction without any apparent effort on its part. The tentacles coiled lazily then kicked out, firing the tooth-filled head and pointed nose at the sub like a guided missile.

Dan brought up the rifle, but didn't open fire. The hide

was too thick on the outside, and he didn't have the ammo to waste trying. He kept his finger on the trigger and waited... waited... waited for the mouth to open and the cavern of its throat to be exposed.

The sub lurched suddenly as something struck it at the front end. Dan catapulted forward, his finger instinctively tightening on the trigger. The blaster bolt hit the top inside lip of the airlock door, ricocheted backward, then rebounded off the wall and floor before streaking on up toward the distant surface.

As the rifle kicked, it jerked from his grip. Dan tried to grab for it and his rope at the same time, but the shark-thing was on him as he turned, all eyes and teeth and fins and legs. He swore creatively, though no sound emerged, and watched with a growing sense of horror as the shark's jaws unhinged until they were impossibly wide, then clamped shut across his thighs.

There was no pain. Not exactly. There was a certain level of discomfort, perhaps, which – coupled with the growing realization that he was being eaten alive by a fonking enormous shark – was causing him a not inconsiderable amount of concern.

He grabbed for one of its eyes, curving his fingers into claws, but it thrashed violently, throwing his arms out above his head as he was dragged left and right in the water.

The thing's saw-like teeth had just about reached his thigh bones when it spat him out and drew back, its tongue flapping around as if trying to wash the taste away.

"Too gamey for you, huh?" Dan said, although he had to say it in his head on account of the whole being underwater thing. Still, as quips went it was pretty poor, and as the octo-shark wouldn't have understood him, anyway, it was no great loss.

Black blood oozed from the ragged tears in his thighs. Seventy percent of his pants were hanging on by threads. He'd also lost a shoe. All things considered, it could've been worse.

He remembered the other shark-monsters who had yet to be put off by his taste, and realized there was still plenty of time for 'worse'.

Grabbing his tether ropes, he pulled himself back towards the sub.

Or tried to. The pulling part was easy. The 'back towards the sub' part was where the problem lay. The ends of both tethers floated limply in the water, neatly cut in half. At first, Dan put it down to a bite from one of the shark-things, but then he saw the end of each rope was scorched, and realized the blaster rifle ricochet must've been responsible.

Fonk.

Fonkity-fonking fonk.

Turning, he searched for the sub, but saw nothing but darkness, monsters, and an awkward-looking orange fish that was beginning to realize it had made a grave navigational error. There was a large shape looming off in the distance which *might* be the sub, but might equally be something mean and toothy, with a less-refined palette than the shark-things had.

Fonk it.

Dan started to swim. His coat didn't help with this. Nor did the fact his legs were only partly attached. He shrugged the coat off, figured there wasn't much he could do about the legs, and started after the submarine.

Blobs of congealed blood trailed behind him as he pulled himself through the water. He didn't look back. He didn't have to. He could sense the bamstons behind him, their lust for blood – even his blood – drawing them to him like flies to shizz.

One more bite and his legs would be gone. Without those he wouldn't be able to keep swimming. He'd sink and probably end up stuck down there on the ocean floor for years, until he either rotted away completely, or convinced some passing crustacean to cave his skull in with a rock.

Balls to that.

He swam, powering himself clumsily through the water as best he could. If those fonks were going to eat him, he was going to make them work for it.

Up ahead, the sub slowed. The shark-things behind him noticed this, and seemed to draw back. Dan burped out a bubble of triumph. They'd noticed he was gone. They were stopping. They were going to come back for him.

The submarine flicked its tail, and Dan's hope sank as he realized it wasn't the submarine at all. The glossy, slug-like body curled around in the water, revealing the elongated head and mouth that had snapped one of the octo-sharks in two.

Its eyes were two bulbous globes, each one the size of a beach ball but with none of the fun-factor. They worked independently, each one swiveling and rotating as they searched the surrounding water.

First one, then the other eye locked onto him. Tiny fins stood on end along the length of the gelatinous body, then all flicked at the same time, propelling it through the water. Dan stopped swimming forward and kicked upwards.

He wasn't sure how far he was from the surface, or what he'd do even if he got there. He just knew he wanted to be as far away from this thing as possible. There was no chance this thing would spit him out after a nibble. It would swallow him whole, and while the subsequent indigestion he might cause it would be of some small consolation, he'd much prefer not to wind up in its stomach in the first place.

The shark-things scattered, shooting off into the darkness with annoying speed and ease. Damn. He'd hoped they might try to take a bite out of the big thing and buy him time to escape, or at least a few more seconds of not being fish food.

He risked a glance down. If his heart had still been beating it would have stopped right there, right then. The thing's mouth was open just twenty or thirty feet below him and closing in fast. The ocean whirlpooled into its fleshy tunnel of a throat, and Dan knew that this, now, was it.

First his life, then his afterlife flashed before his eyes. He wasn't particularly happy about either of them.

He thought of his wife, Vanshie. Of their child that never was. He thought of the handful of people he'd helped and the vast crowds of those he'd hurt. He thought of dying and of coming back.

He thought of Artur, although not for long because he didn't want to give the little shizznod the satisfaction.

He thought of Ollie and took a little comfort from the fact that maybe she didn't need him now.

He hoped she'd be happy. The kid deserved that, at least.

Dan stopped swimming. What was the point? A few more seconds alive – or undead – weren't worth much if they were spent thrashing around in panic or being eaten up by regret.

He waited, hands raised. If this thing was going to swallow him, he was at least going to punch the shizz out of it on the way down.

The pressure of the water changed as it pushed in on him from both sides. Those gigantic jaws were closing. This was it. There was no escape, no way out. He was dead in the water. Literally.

The water around him was suddenly alive with a blinding white light. Even through his lifeless nerve endings, Dan felt a jolt of something like electricity as the big-toothed slug-fish was wrapped in a cocoon of crackling luminous bonds.

It bucked around for a moment, but the fight soon left it. Those jaws, which had been about to devour Dan whole, flopped all the way open. Its globular eyes rolled back until only the whites were visible, then it drifted down into the darkness and was swallowed by the darkness of the ocean.

Treading water, Dan turned, searching for the case of whatever the fonk had just happened. Was it the sub? Had Finn discovered another weapon they hadn't been aware of? That would've been an incredible stroke of luck, which told Dan it almost certainly wouldn't be the case.

Still, something had done it. He just wished he knew who or what it—

A cocoon of electrical energy wrapped around him.

Son of a... Dan thought, and then the bonds tightened, his skin *fizzled*, and his head was filled with an explosion of all-consuming white light.

EIGHTEEN

Dan became aware of a buzzing sound, but only dimly. It was loud, but far off. Or maybe close, but quiet. He didn't care enough to try to work it out. One of those, anyway.

There was something on his face. It partly covered one side, pressing down hard on his cheek, ear, and part of his forehead. It was rough, cold, and annoying. He tried to swat it away, but his arms were behind his back. Probably. They were somewhere, anyway.

He became aware of a buzzing sound. Then he became aware of a sense of Déjà vu.

His head hurt.

No, that was an understatement, he thought.

His head *really* hurt?

Better, but still not even close.

Fonk it.

There was something on his face. Was that new? He tried to brush it off.

No luck.

It was dark. Too dark for even his enhanced night vision to make anything out. Unless...

He opened his eyes. There was something large and gray very close to him. Too close for him to see anything but a vague, nondescript blur.

Several seconds passed before he realized it was the floor.

He flopped onto his back, waited for the world to stop spinning, then sat up. This, he concluded, was a mistake. His head, which had really hurt, now really, *really* hurt. He winced and tried to rub the pain away, but his hands were still... where? He looked for a shoulder then followed the arm until it vanished behind his back. He tried to pull the arm around to his front, but it pulled the other one with it and he concluded his hands must be shackled together.

An embarrassingly high-pitched "Yeurwargh!" burst from his lips as assorted teeth-and-throat-based memories rose like bubbles in his steadily growing consciousness. He remembered – with zero fondness – being partly inside a shark-thing.

He looked for the wounds in his legs, and discovered they had been coated with a poultice of dark slimy greens and crusty browns. The ends of some thick sutures poked out here and there, suggesting someone had sewn him back together.

The vast majority of his pants were missing. What was left resembled a pair of cut-off shorts that revealed his legs in their full horrifying glory.

He had no shoes or socks on. One of his feet was smaller than the other, but that had been the case for a few weeks now. If it weren't for the stitching marks around the ankle, Dan wouldn't even have been able to remember which foot was the original and which the replacement. After a while, you lost track of these things.

He was in what was unmistakably a cell. The floor,

walls and ceiling were all made of the same rough gray stone, mottled here and there with swashes of green. Despite his deadened senses, he could taste salt in the air. Of course, it could've been from his time in the ocean, but something about this place felt... fishy. In more ways than one.

Getting to his feet wasn't easy. It involved several aborted attempts, a face plant into the wall, and a lot of abuse hurled at nobody in particular. Finally, by pushing up with his feet and sort of 'hopping' up the wall with his forehead, he stood fully upright.

Now what?

"You are awake."

Dan spun away from the wall and searched the cell for whoever had spoken. This didn't take more than a second or two, since the cell wasn't very big.

"Looks like it," he said, his eyes darting to the corners of the room. It was octagonal-shaped, so there were quite a lot of corners for his eyes to dart to. They found nothing lurking in any of them.

"Someone shall attend."

The voice seemed to come from directly in front of him. Dan lumbered forward, half-expecting to collide with some invisible man in the center of the cell. Instead, he tripped on his own feet, stumbled, and was filled with that sinking feeling that comes with knowing you're about to smash your face against the floor, and the awareness that there's fonk all you can do about it.

Dan smashed his face against the floor. Technically, it was only his chin that took the full impact, but this wasn't of any particular consolation.

"You fell over," the voice informed him.

"Nn fnking shzz," Dan rasped.

After clicking his jaw back into position, he began the laborious process of getting to his feet again. Having already established a system, this time was easier. Still not exactly dignified, but easier.

"Someone shall attend," the voice repeated, and Dan grunted begrudgingly in reply.

The cell door was made of a dull copper-colored metal, with a small rectangular hole that was shuttered from the other side. There was no handle on the inside, although that didn't really come as any sort of surprise.

Dan put a shoulder to the door, not so much trying to escape as gauging its weight. Heavy. *Very* heavy. He wouldn't be kicking this fonker down anytime soon.

He pulled on the shackles that held his hands together. They held his wrists twisted together, the hands back to back. The bonds themselves were thick and clamped him from his wrists to halfway up his forearm. Even if he pulled hard enough to pop his new hand off, he still wouldn't be free.

There was nothing to do but wait and worry.

He wasn't worried for himself. Wherever he was, he wasn't being eaten alive by a sea monster, so his situation was a vast improvement on what it might have been.

He worried about Ollie. He worried about Artur.

Finn, not so much.

Under normal circumstances – basically any circumstances when they weren't thousands of feet under the water – he knew they could handle themselves. Trapped in a submarine that was being attacked by hungry shark monsters, though? That was more difficult. Ollie might be powerful, but that power would be the end of them all if she unleashed it inside the sub.

Dan sighed. What had they even been doing down

there? No one was paying him. No one would even thank him. He was an idiot for getting involved.

Ninety-six adults and thirty-eight children died before his eyes again in a crowded mall. They stared at him – desperately, imploringly – as the things tore through them, and spilled all that they were onto the polished shopping center floor.

"Fonk. OK, OK," Dan said, although to what or who he couldn't quite say.

The hatch in the door slid open and a rectangle of face was revealed. It was a mostly blue-green face that shone like scales, but with dark bruising around both eyes. A slimy poultice, like the one on Dan's thighs, was spread across the man's nose, presumably covering a wound that...

Wait.

"Hey. I know you," Dan said. "We met at Krato's."

"Met? Is that what you call it?" the man asked. His voice had a gargle to it, further emphasizing his fishiness. "You broke my nose."

"That was an accident," Dan claimed.

"You elbowed me in the face."

"No, I hit you on purpose, I just didn't think I'd done it hard enough to break your nose," Dan said. "You must have a weak face."

The man's weak face scowled, but this made pain flash behind his eyes, so he quickly adjusted his expression into something less contorted.

"You have been formally charged with the hostile invasion of our realm," he continued. "You and your accomplices."

"Accomplices? Wait. What accomplices? Are they here? Are they OK?"

"How do you plead?"

It was Dan's turn to scowl. "Plead? What are you talking about? My friends, do you have them?"

"How do you plead to the charge of hostile invasion?"

"Hostile invasion of what? I have no idea what you're talking about."

"Liar!" spat the man on the other side of the door. "You are an invader from Up There. Your actions are a declaration of war."

Dan shook his head. "Wait a minute, wait a minute. I'm not from Up There."

"You are to us."

If he were honest, Dan would have to admit that his brain wasn't yet functioning at full capacity. Being chased by sea monsters, zapped by an energy cocoon, then repeatedly battered against the cell floor had all taken their toll, and it took him a moment or two longer than usual for the man's words to make any kind of sense.

"Us? Hold on. Exactly where are we?" he asked.

"Do not feign ignorance, land-dweller. You know."

"Indulge me," said Dan. "Please."

"You are a prisoner of the greatest city below, on, or above the surface of this planet," the man replied. Even through the hatch, Dan saw him swell with pride. "You are now the property of Deeper Down."

Dan snorted. "Ha! Sure."

The man stared back at him, his face impassive and swollen. Mostly swollen.

"Funny," Dan said.

The man did not appear to be laughing.

"Wait. You're not serious?"

Dan had heard of Deeper Down, of course. Most

people had. But they'd heard of it in the same way they'd heard of *Floomfo Forest*, or the *World of Gnarls*, or Daddy Krosyh - the kindly-yet-creepy old man who visited the bedrooms of children on Kroyshuk Eve and methodically licked the dirt from their faces while they slept.

It was bullshizz. All of it. Make-believe nonsense designed to amuse infants and imbeciles alike.

There was no *Floomfo Forest*. There was no *World of Gnarls*. And Daddy Kroysh had been captured by the Magister and brought before the Intergalactic Court of Justice years ago.

Deeper Down was a myth, just like they were – a bedtime story about a legendary lost city beneath the waves, filled with magic and technology and wonders the likes of which no one on the surface had ever seen. It was make-believe nonsense for infants and imbeciles, of which Dan was neither.

"OK, is there somebody else I can talk to?" Dan asked. "I'd like to thank them for saving me, find my friends, then we'll all get out of here and leave you in peace."

"It is too late for peace," the man replied. "War is now inevitable."

"What? What are you talking about?"

"We did not wish to believe it at first. All we have ever sought is solitude. All we wished for was to remain hidden. Secluded. But recent events have shown us that we are not to be permitted this luxury. And so, war is coming. It will be terrible, it will be regretted, but it will *be*. And we shall endure. We shall survive. We shall be victorious."

Dan scraped his tongue against the roof of his mouth. "Well, good luck with that," he said. "Now, is there a supervisor or someone I can talk to? No offense, but you seem a little... I don't want to say 'batshizz crazy' but... Ah, what the fonk? You seem a little batshizz crazy. I'd like to talk to someone else."

"Soon."

"No, not soon. Now," Dan said. "Get me someone now."

"Soon," the man repeated, then the hatch slammed closed and Dan wasted his most intimidating glare on a rectangle of dull red metal.

"I'm working with the Tribunal!" Dan hollered. "That's what you are, right? I'm working with you. Check with Polani. Go ahead, ask him."

Silence answered him. It wasn't an expectant, breath-being-held sort of silence, but an empty no-fonker's-there sort of silence, and Dan realized he was wasting his breath. Metaphorically speaking.

"Damn it," he spat, giving the door a kick. It didn't so much as rattle.

Deeper Down. It was impossible. Hell, he was more likely to be a prisoner in *Grobin's Grotto*. At least a few people claimed to have seen that place. Granted, they had all recently consumed vast amounts of hallucinogenic drugs and weren't the most reliable of witnesses, but at least they *were* witnesses.

Nobody alive had claimed to have seen Deeper Down. The only accounts of the city came from centuries ago, and had been passed down via word of mouth ever since. Over the generations it had alternated between being a fantastical bedtime story and a dire warning for kids who misbehaved. Don't clean your room and you might get snatched away and taken to Deeper Down. Don't eat your vegetables and you could be forced to live among the fish people forever. It was a city-sized version of the Thumb Fairy legend, although Dan knew from experience that that scissor-wielding bedge was all too real.

"Hey!" Dan shouted. "Artur? Ollie? Can you hear me?"

If they could, they didn't reply.

Dan stepped into cover beside the door, ready to pounce if it should open. He had a plan. It involved kicking the living shit out of whoever stepped into the cell, then...

Actually, that was currently as far as it went, but he felt like the first part was solid enough that he could probably just improvise the rest. It would almost certainly involve a lot of kicking people, though, unless he could somehow find a way to get his hands free.

He heaved suddenly on the bonds, like he could somehow catch them off-guard. They held fast. There was no way he was getting his hands free.

Still, maybe he could make them more useful than they currently were. Dropping to the floor, Dan rolled onto his side and brought his knees up as close to his chest as he could get them. The tendons were tight and his muscles had become more rigid as they'd decayed, but the lack of pain receptors meant he was able to ignore both these issues.

He flopped around like a fish on dry land, jerking his bound wrists down over his ass-bone. This was more difficult than he'd hoped, and he spent almost a full five minutes hissing and spitting and cursing as he tried to tuck his bottom half through the gap in his arms.

At last, with a final yelp of effort and a distinct tearing of cartilage, his buttocks passed the event horizon and the shackles scraped along the underside of his thighs.

He'd reckoned that at this stage in proceedings, the battle would be all but won. This turned out, however, not to be the case, and getting the rest of his legs through his splayed arms quickly proved to be no small task.

Dan flapped violently, kicking his feet and slamming his shoulder against the floor in frustration. "Fonking... fonking *fonk-fonk!*" he spat.

He stopped thrashing, closed his eyes, and found some calm center.

That done, he went back to thrashing and swearing for a while, until it was clear that neither was especially helping.

He was, quite unarguably, in a much worse position than he had been before. If he could somehow stand up now, his wrists would be shackled halfway down the back of his thighs, and his forehead would be touching the floor. He could probably go back to his original situation, but then all this would've been for nothing.

Dan as halfway through another frantic rage-flap when he heard the snigger. Like the other voice he'd heard, it seemed to come from out of the air itself. Unlike the other one, this one was familiar.

"Holy shoite, Deadman," it said. "Why are ye all folded up? Are ye trying to do what I *think* yer're trying to do?"

Dan sighed. "I'm trying to get out of these cuffs."

"Ah. No. That's very much not what I thought ye were trying to do," said Artur. "Hold tight, ye bag o' spanners, we'll have ye right out."

OLLIE THREW her arms around Dan and hugged him. Due to the handcuffs – as well as some deep-rooted emotional and psychological issues – he was unable to hug her back.

"You're alive!" she cried.

"More or less," Dan confirmed.

When she pulled away, Finn moved in for a hug, too,

but Dan's scowl made him reconsider, and he managed to turn the move into a handshake, instead. Dan regarded the offered hand for a while and waited for the penny to drop.

"Oh. Right. You're tied up," said Finn. He patted Dan on the shoulder and stepped back beside Ollie. The backs of their hands brushed together, and their fingers very gingerly interlocked.

"We thought we'd lost ye," said Artur from way down on the floor. "We thought maybe ye'd been eaten or something."

"They didn't like the taste," Dan said.

They were still in his cell, but the door now stood wide open behind them. From what he could tell, none of them were any the worse for wear.

"Where are we? And why am I the only one in cuffs?"

"They cuffed us too, brah," said Finn. "We were all tossed into a cell together."

"And then someone came in and apologized," said Ollie. "They just came in all, 'Forgive us! We made a mistake!' and they let us out. I don't know why they changed their minds, but Artur said it was probably best not to ask."

"And what about the 'where are we' part? Do we know?"

Artur cleared his throat. "I think we're in Deeper Down," he said. "Don't go asking me how I know, because I can't tell ye."

"That's what the nose guy said, but there's no such place."

"I beg to differ," said Artur. He shifted uncomfortably, then jumped on the opportunity to change the subject. "And what 'nose guy'?"

"That nose guy," said Dan, as the blue-green man with the broken nose slapped into the room on his flipper-like webbed feet. He was dressed in an all-in-one silver swimsuit that covered him from neck to groin and clung to his torso like a second skin.

"My name is Cobia," he said, making no effort to hide his contempt for Dan. As he turned to the others, his expression changed into something much more welcoming. "You will all please join me in the auditorium."

"What about these?" asked Dan, turning side-on and highlighting his shackled wrists. Cobia made a dismissive waving motion with the elongated fingers of a webbed hand.

"Someone will remove them eventually," he said. "This way, please."

DAN STILL DIDN'T BELIEVE they were in Deeper Down as they passed through several security doors and then moved through a network of tastefully decorated corridors. The walls were adorned with artfully arranged paintings and carvings, all depicting underwater scenes.

He continued to not believe it as they crossed an immense ballroom with sweeping golden staircases and towering ice carvings of unfamiliar marine creatures.

It was only when they stepped outside that Dan's natural skepticism was forced to shut the fonk up and go sit somewhere at the back.

Technically, they weren't 'outside' at all. A vast semi-transparent dome covered the whole place, protecting it from the unwelcome attention of the oceans above. Through it, Dan could see a variety of fish and various other kinds of water-dwellers zipping around. A sizeable squid-thing clung to the barrier somewhere near the top, its suckers squashed against the glass, or whatever the dome was made of.

They were in a grassy plaza with a large fountain in the middle in which children were playing. All around it, more of the blue-green adults relaxed. Individuals sat up reading books. Couples lay together in the grass. Groups laughed and joked.

They all stiffened when they saw Dan and the others, but a reassuring nod from Cobia relaxed them again.

"Whoa," said Finn. "This is awesome."

Ollie melted a little as his fingers tightened around hers. "Awesome," she agreed.

Dan, who was plodding along at the back of the line with Artur on his shoulder, called up to Cobia at the front.

"So, this is really Deeper Down?"

"It really is. This way."

He stepped onto a moving path that immediately swept him in the direction of the fountain. Ollie stopped just before the walkway, but Finn gave her an encouraging smile.

"We'll go together, OK?"

Ollie nodded. "'K."

Finn stepped, and Ollie jumped on. She wobbled unsteadily for a moment, holding her free hand out at her side to steady herself, then she laughed with relief when she managed to keep her balance.

"You did it!"

"I did it!"

"Way to go!" Finn said, then – to his surprise, as much as hers – he leaned in and kissed her quickly on the cheek.

Ollie stiffened, relaxed, blushed, temporarily forgot how to breathe, then just sort of giggled as the moving path carried them along together.

"Love is definitely in the air wi' those two," Artur announced. "Ye can smell it a mile off. And, I might add, it makes a refreshing change from yer own revolting stench."

"I still don't trust him," Dan said. He stepped smoothly onto the walkway and lowered his voice so only Artur could hear. "This can't be Deeper Down. It doesn't exist. Right?"

Artur wriggled a little uncomfortably. "Well, I mean, I suppose it depends on yer definition, doesn't it?"

"No. It either exists or it doesn't."

"Right. Yes." He took a deep breath. "Well then I guess it exists."

"What aren't you telling me, Artur?" Dan asked. They were almost halfway across the plaza now. The children who had been playing in the spray of the fountain stopped to watch them as they trundled past, the smaller ones taking cover behind the bigger ones.

"Sure, I don't know what ye mean," Artur replied.

"Bullshizz. I know you. There's something you're not telling me."

Artur sighed. "Fine. OK. If ye must know, I *may* have been aware of this place's existence. I'd have told ye before now, but I was sworn to secrecy."

"By who?"

"I can't tell ye that, either. Not even if ye start with them puppy dog eyes of yours. My lips are sealed, Deadman, and there's nothing ye can do to make me change me mind."

From somewhere close on Dan's left there came a banshee-like screech. Dan had barely managed to turn his head before a blue, green and gold shape slammed into him, knocking him off the walkway and onto the grass. He rolled clumsily, his hands still fixed behind him.

Twisting, he kicked out at his attacker, but found only

empty space. A tall woman in golden armor was leaping around and stomping down on the grass. She'd have been strikingly beautiful if her face wasn't quite so contorted in foam-spitting rage.

Artur scampered and dodged in the grass, his red and white checked dress making him an easy target.

"Hey, steady now!" he yelped. "Whoa! Cut it out, ye crazy bedge! Ye don't want to do this!"

"Stay still, runt!" the woman shrieked, kicking and stamping at him as he darted this way and that. "I'll kill you!"

"Hey."

The woman spun just as Dan's bare foot crunched into her armored chest plate. Knocked off balance, she thumped onto the grass. Her attempts to get back up were thwarted when Dan placed a foot on the armor.

"Stay down," he warned her. He was aware of some commotion growing around him. Ollie and Finn had doubled back to help, but were currently jogging on the spot as they fought against the moving walkway.

"Steady on, Deadman!" Artur cried. "That was a bit harsh, was it not?"

"She was trying to kill you," Dan pointed out.

Artur scratched the back of his head and looked around at nothing in particular. "Sure, she was that. But, well, she may have had good reason."

"Too fonking right, I do!" the woman hissed.

Ollie and Finn finally figured out they could get off the walkway and hurried across the grass to join the others.

"Everything OK?" Ollie asked. "What happened?"

"Don't know," said Dan, narrowing his eyes. "Artur's about to explain."

Artur cleared his throat. "Aye. Well. Right. OK." He

took a deep breath. "Deadman. Peaches. Other fella whose name I can't quite put me finger on at the moment..." He gestured to the woman pinned beneath Dan's foot. "Say hello to me wife."

He smiled sheepishly, then winced. "Or one of them, anyway."

NINETEEN

DAN LOOKED AT ARTUR.

He looked at the woman below his foot.

"Your *wife*?"

"You have a wife?" Ollie gasped.

Finn frowned. "I didn't know you were married, brah."

"To be fair, ye don't know feck all else about me, either," Artur pointed out, then he looked up at Dan and shrugged. "What can I say? I'm a complicated man of mystery. I'm layered. And yes, that's me wife, so if ye'd be so kind as to take yer flapping great plate o' meat off her ample bosom, I'd greatly appreciate it."

"Release her!" Cobia warned. "Release her *this instant*."

Just for that, Dan kept her pinned there for a few more seconds.

"OK, *Artur*," he said, holding Cobias' gaze. "Since you asked so nicely, I'm going to remove my foot."

He waited until Cobias blinked, then looked down at Artur, who was hidden by grass up to the waist. "But don't blame me if you get stamped on."

"Ah, she'll do nothing of the kind," said Artur, then he

yelped and jumped back as Dan removed his foot and the woman's open hand *thwacked* down on the spot where he'd been standing. "Shoite, come on now, Marnie, quit acting the maggot. Joke's over, sweetheart."

"*Joke?*" Marnie hissed. "Do I look like I'm laughing, 'chaun?"

"No," Artur admitted. "Which is a shame, because ye look fecking gorgeous when ye laugh. The way yer nose all crinkles up and—Urk! Feck off!"

He legged it as she dived at him, both hands grasping like claws. "Look, can't we just talk about this like fecking grown-ups?" he cried.

"You made me look a fool!" Marnie spat.

"No offense, lady," Dan said. "But right now, the only one making you look a fool is you."

He gestured with his head to the gathered onlookers. Even the children had stopped playing in the fountain and were watching her with open mouths as she scrambled around in the grass.

Marnie looked from face to face. A set of gills or fins or something along those lines rippled on either side of her neck, then quickly folded flat. If Dan had to take a stab at what the gesture meant, he'd say it was some flavor of shame or embarrassment. She stopped trying to kill Artur, anyway, and jumped quickly to her feet.

"Fine," she said through gritted teeth. "Let's *talk*."

"I'm afraid not," said Cobia, stepping between them. "The prisoners are expected in the auditorium. We do not have time for... personal matters."

"Prisoners?" said Marnie.

"Wait. We're still prisoners?" asked Ollie. "I thought you let us go."

"We let you out of your *cells*. For now," Cobia said.

237

"That does not mean you aren't still prisoners here." He looked Dan up and down, his already wide nostrils becoming even more so. "Especially him."

He motioned for them all to step onto the walkway. Artur made a show of looking disappointed.

"Ah, really? Well, that's a shame, that is. I'd have loved to stick around and catch up wit' ye, Marnie, but what can we do? Still, great to see ye. Give me love to yer da'."

"He wants your head on the end of a pencil," Marnie said.

"OK, well maybe not *love* then, exactly. Me best regards, maybe."

He hopped up onto the walkway and waved as he was carried along. "Bye now, b'bye!"

"Screw you, 'chaun!"

Ollie and Finn stepped on the walkway beside him. "Why does she call you 'Con'?" Ollie asked.

"What can I say? She's a complicated woman," Artur said, still waving. "Cracking old pair o' tits on her, though. Real beauties."

Finn grinned, but then stopped when he saw Ollie looking at him. "Inappropriate," he murmured, trying to look disapproving.

"Nice to meet you," said Dan, stepping onto the moving path.

"Fonk you," Marnie retorted.

Cobia shot her a stern look, but said nothing as he joined the others on the walkway. Barging past Dan, he made his way to the front. He stood straight and upright, his hands crossed behind him as the walkway curved towards an open doorway just ahead.

"Now, assuming no further interruptions," he said, "we shall be there momentarily."

As they drew closer, Dan saw six women all bunched together, their expressions ranging from 'anxious' to 'grief-stricken' and covering pretty much the full range in between. They hugged, supported and consoled each other, a few of them turning to gaze imploringly at Dan and the others as they trundled past.

The path carried them through the door and into the most mind-bogglingly confusing room any of them had ever seen. The ground on either side of the path fell away, revealing a deep chasm-like space beneath them. More paths crisscrossed through the empty space, connecting other doorways on hundreds of different levels.

Looking up, Dan saw easily another forty or fifty walkways trundling along above them. Like the one they were riding, most of them fed directly into a wide central column that ran from somewhere far below to somewhere high above. The whole place was like a complex spider's web, and they were currently stuck on one of its strands.

They weren't the only ones. Hundreds – thousands – of blue-green people rode the walkways. Some chatted freely to friends. Others rode in solitude, their heads down as they tapped the screen of some handheld gizmo or other.

The ocean was further away here, like a dome had been placed on top of the original dome. Through gaps in the walkways, Dan caught glimpses of distant lights moving smoothly through the water. Submarines, he guessed. A *lot* of submarines.

"Please stand clear of the edge," Cobia intoned.

"No shoite," Artur muttered.

Ollie and Finn shuffled into single file, though they managed to keep holding hands. "What is this place?" Ollie said. She said it in a whisper in case her usual volume would somehow make the whole complex structure come crashing down around their ears.

Cobia ignored the question. He glanced back at them as the walkway trundled them towards the central column. "This may initially seem... unpleasant," he warned. "But there is no cause for alarm. I assure you it is quite safe."

"*Quite* safe?" asked Ollie. "Can you make it very safe?"

"I meant 'quite' as in 'very,'" said Cobia, visibly irritated. "Not 'quite' as in 'partially.'"

They rolled in through an opening in the central column then staggered as the path unexpectedly shoved them off onto a spongy floor. It was the color of kelp, and emitted a faint bio-luminescence, not unlike the moss in the sewers, only fainter. It swallowed the sound of their foot-steps as Cobia led them into the center of the circular room.

"Stop here. Stand apart," he instructed. He motioned to Ollie and Finn. "You two, step away from each other."

"Good luck with that," Dan muttered, but Ollie and Finn did as they were told. Their fingers remained entwined as they side-stepped in opposite directions, their touch lingering for as long as possible.

"Good," said Cobia, although he looked far from impressed. He nodded. "Now then. Try to relax."

This had the opposite effect to the one intended. Dan tensed immediately. "What do you mean? Why do we need to—?"

Some gloop fell on him. A lot of gloop. It hit him from above with a *sploosh* and cascaded like gunge down over his shoulders, back and chest.

He tried to shout his objections, but the stuff had covered his face, trapping his words in there with him. His hearing became muted, but because the goo was transparent, he could see reasonably clearly.

Cobia, Ollie and Finn were all in the process of being coated, too. Whoever had dropped the stuff obviously hadn't made any allowances for size, and Artur was current trapped beneath a gelatinous mound of the stuff. He was completely frozen in place, like a prehistoric man perfectly preserved in a block of ice. His eyes darted around freely. They briefly met Dan's, then Artur's blob rocketed up towards the ceiling thirty feet or so overhead.

Dan couldn't move his head enough to follow Artur's flight. He struggled against the gloop, but it had cocooned him fully now, just as it had done to Ollie and the other two. Dan watched helplessly as first Ollie, then Finn streaked upwards.

Before he had a chance to figure out what the fonk was going on, Dan felt his center of gravity shift. He lurched into the air and saw the floor fall away from him. Raising his eyes, he saw no sign of Ollie or the others. What he did see was the ceiling. It was approaching really rather rapidly and had a worryingly solid appearance that didn't bode well for the next few seconds or so.

Instinctively, Dan tried to close his eyes, but the gloop held them open. He hissed as his head collided with the ceiling. Rather than come to an abrupt spine-shattering stop, though, he felt himself speeding up.

There was a *schlomp* sort of sound as he passed through the ceiling and the floor above. To his surprise, this part of the column looked nothing like the one they'd just left. In fact, from what he could gather it wasn't part of the column at all.

He was rocketing along a water-filled tube that was barely wide enough for his goo-covered frame. The hardened gunge made a series of echoing screeches as it bounced off the tube's narrow walls, rocketing him around its many twists and turns.

The tube itself was clear, but he was moving too quickly to really grasp what was outside it. More water, he guessed, although it could equally be outer space, or even the Malwhere. It was dark, mostly, with the occasional glimpse of light or suggestion of a shape. Nothing helpful, anyway, and nothing that told him where or when he was likely to emerge from the pipe.

He didn't have long to wait. He hit another barricade with the same *schlomp* sound as before, then his momentum was replaced by a sense of sudden deceleration.

The solid gloop became just plain old gloop. He scraped enough of it out of his eyes to see that Ollie and Finn were both standing in front of him in relatively the same position they had been before. Down on the ground, Artur clawed and gasped his way free of the sludge mound, then spent several seconds bemoaning the fact that his outfit was, "Fecking ruined!"

Dan wasn't really listening. No one was. Instead, they were gazing up at the roof of the dome which was now just twenty feet or so above their heads. It felt closer, like the ocean was suspended right above them within touching distance.

Clouds of colorful fish streaked by like fireworks. Vibrant glowing eels rippled through the water, sparks flickering from their dancing bodies. Tiny specks of light zipped this way and that like shooting stars, painting trails behind them.

Beyond all this, the darkness was layered in blues and blacks, suggesting the immense scale of the ocean, and the promise of everything it held.

"It's beautiful," Ollie whispered.

"You get used to it," said Cobia. He had appeared behind them, and only his head had so far emerged from his gloopy coating. "Dissolve."

Dan blinked. "Huh?" he said, but then all became clear when the transparent slime that currently clung to them all became water and fell away. It seeped into the floor immediately, and Dan noticed his clothes – what little was left of them – were bone dry.

"Impressive," he said, fixing Cobia with a glare. "But spring something like that on us again and it won't just be your nose I break."

"You are prisoners. Suspected war criminals," Cobia reminded him. "I can do whatever I wish."

"I'd like to see ye try," Artur warned, but Cobia ignored him.

"Were it up to me, you'd still be rotting in your cells. I do not approve of this... *meeting*," he said, spitting the last word out like someone had slipped poison in between the letters.

"Meeting? Who are we meeting?" Dan asked.

"That would be me, Mr Deadman."

Dan and the others turned to see a red-skinned man descending some ornate gold steps that led down from a doorway in one of the dome walls. He had a pointed abomination of a beard curving out from the bottom of his chin, and was flanked on both sides by a squadron of six heavy-set Deeper Downians, all carrying long-handled tridents. His expensively tailored suit seemed out of place among their armor and weapons. His grin, even more so.

The guards stopped at the foot of the stairs and fanned out, forming a solid wall of muscle and metal. The man in the suit kept walking until he was just three good lunges and a headbutt beyond Dan's reach.

There was more movement from the top of the stairs. Six children shuffled out through the doorway and stopped at the top of the steps. From the other side of the door, Dan heard the soft lilt of music.

"Krato," Dan growled. His brow furrowed as his mind set to work trying to figure out what the arms dealer's presence here meant. His mind, however, came up blank. "What are you doing here?"

"Same as you. I'm here on business." He gestured around them. "And, you know, to admire the view. Spectacular, isn't it?"

He inhaled deeply, as if he could somehow smell the ocean on the other side of the dome. "Spectacular," he said again, and there was a note of sadness in it this time. "It upsets me that we would threaten such a place."

"Threaten? Who's threatening?"

"Why, we are. Up There. Or Down Here, depending on where you're from," Krato said. "An attack is imminent. We're going to obliterate this whole place."

Ollie looked from Krato to Dan and back again. "We are? That's horrible."

"I know. Utterly beyond contempt."

"First I've heard about any of it," Artur said. "Deadman?"

Dan shook his head. "Far as I knew, this place didn't even exist. Never met anyone who believed otherwise."

"And he's met some real crazy bastards," Artur said. "Trust me."

Krato raised a black-nailed finger and tick-tocked it admonishingly. "Now, now, you two. Let's not tell fibs. The good people of Deeper Down deserve better than that."

Since returning to life, Dan's sense of smell had deteriorated. This was probably just as well, given the stench he gave off. There were two things his nose could still be relied on to detect, though – bullshizz and trouble. Whatever was going on here carried the distinct whiff of both.

It was all connected. It had to be. Krato. The sewer monsters. The mall. Hell, even the music playing behind the kids. It was the same lullaby-like tune that had been playing back at Krato's office.

It was all linked, Dan just couldn't yet see how. He decided to take a stab at it and hope for the best.

"You're selling them weapons. This place, I mean. You're selling them weapons to fight a war that isn't coming."

"Oh, it's coming, Mr Deadman," said Krato, and the way his eyes blazed told Dan the guy believed what he was saying. "It's coming. And soon. That's why we're striking first."

"Wait, what?"

Krato looked past Dan to Cobia. "Bring him in, would you?"

Cobia bristled. "You have no authority over me."

"Well, technically I do," Krato said. "Your boss's boss's boss – you know, the Prime Minister? - has given me authority to manage the war effort. Or did you miss the announcement? Since you're here assisting with these prisoners of war – emphasis on 'war' – then that gives me complete authority over you."

His smile, which had been steadily growing, suddenly fell. "Now go over to that door, open it, and go fetch him."

For a moment, it looked as if Cobia might resist, but then he gave a single curt nod of his head and about-turned. Dan watched each resentful footstep until he reached a squat stone building a little larger than a garden shed. The door swung inward at his approach and they heard his footsteps scuffing down a set of steps on the other side.

"He's gone," said Dan, turning to Krato. He glanced over at the row of guards before lowering his voice. "So how about you tell us what this is really all about? You're giving them guns and sending them to invade the surface? That's insane."

Krato snorted. "Guns? No. Guns are so old-fashioned. All that *pew-pew*, *chow-chow*. It's... and speaking as someone who made a lot of money from them... it's all a little *embarrassing*, you know?"

He smoothed his beard with both hands, sharpening the point. "War has evolved, Mr Deadman. And the weapons we use to wage it must therefore evolve also."

"What's he on about?" asked Artur.

"The usual monologuing bullshizz," said Dan. "Like they all do."

"Ha! Yes, maybe, but indulge me," Krato said. "You see, war has always provided society with the opportunity to develop and grow. To overcome challenges it might never have otherwise anticipated. It allows us to push the boundaries, and – without blowing my own trumpet – I've pushed them further than anyone has ever pushed them before."

He held a hand out and it took Dan a moment to realize he was gesturing past them. "You know our guest, I believe?"

Everyone turned to the squat stone building. Cobia had emerged, leading a small rat-faced figure with him. "Wait a minute," said Dan, recognition dawning.

"Bonbo?" said Finn. His face lit up. "Bonbo, brah! Oh, man, I heard you were dead!"

"He was dead," Dan said.

"He doesn't look dead," said Ollie.

"She's got ye there, Deadman," Artur agreed.

"He died in that bathroom stall," Dan insisted. "I saw a fonking tentacle rip right through him."

"Did you?" Krato asked, his face a mockery of concern. "Did you really?"

He raised both eyebrows and a finger, as if an idea had suddenly occurred to him. "Or did you see a tentacle rip right *out* of him?" He stroked his beard and nodded sagely. "Because that would explain a *lot*."

"Ye're fecking right it would," Artur agreed. Then: "In what way?"

Something dark and sinister slithered deep down in Dan's guts as everything – or lots of it, anyway – slotted into place. His thought process went something along the lines of:

But that would mean...

Of course.

But then...

Oh, *fonk*.

"It was the stress, you see?" said Krato. "That fight or flight instinct when you had him cornered in that stall. No way out. Nowhere to run. That's what triggered it."

Bonbo wasn't meeting Dan's eye. He wasn't meeting anyone's eye, in fact. Instead, he was just staring at the floor directly ahead of him, hands clutched in front of him, fingers twisting together. He had literally been an empty skin sack last time Dan had seen him, and Dan wasn't sure how much of him had come back.

Bonbo's scrawny arms were bare from below the elbow. The scars of old scratches stood out as red lines against his skin.

"It was you. The mall. It was you," Dan said, turning to Krato.

Krato bit his lip to stop himself grinning, but couldn't contain himself. "Ack! OK, you got me. Yes, it was me. It was a test. A proof of concept, if you will."

That slithering thing in Dan's gut coiled tight as his fears were confirmed.

"Ollie," he said. "Step away from Finn."

Ollie blinked. "What? Why?"

"Just do it. Trust me."

Ollie looked at Finn, who shrugged.

"What's going on, brah?"

"I'm sorry, kid. I really am," Dan told him. "But if you care about her – and I think you do – then step away. Now."

"You're scaring me," said Ollie. "What's wrong?"

"Kid, I mean it," Dan said, ignoring her and focusing on Finn. "Step back. Step away. I'm asking you nicely."

"Deadman? Ye've lost me here. What's the problem."

Krato cackled. "The problem is he's figured it out. I knew you'd get there eventually."

"Two of them. At the mall, there were two of them," Dan said. He nodded in Bonbo's direction. "He was one of them."

"He don't look like one of them," Artur pointed out.

"It's temporary, somehow. He changed back," Dan said. He ran his dry tongue across his chapped lips, then nodded at Finn. "He was the other one."

"*What?!*" Ollie cried. "No! That's not... I don't... He's not... Are you?"

Finn shook his head. "Huh? No! I don't know what he's talking about. I don't know what you're talking about, brah."

"I know you don't, kid," said Dan. "For what it's worth, I'm sorry."

Finn laughed. It was a worried, fearful chuckle that

bore no relation to his current amusement levels. "Sorry for what? I don't know what you're talking about!"

"The drug test," Dan said. "That's what he was testing. He injected you with something that turned you into one of those things."

Krato tutted. "'Injected'? Oh, please. It was substantially more complicated than that."

"That's how the thing found us out on the ocean. That's why it looked different. It wasn't the one we saw in the sewers. It was him."

"What was me? I still don't follow, brah," Finn insisted.

"It's good you don't remember," Dan told him. "This is going to be hard enough on you."

He turned to Krato, his face darkening. Dan had lost count of the number of times he'd been tied up or shackled over the years, but never had he wanted his hands free more.

"You're a monster," he said.

"No, I make monsters, Mr Deadman," Krato corrected. "Although... maybe you're right. Maybe I am. But all's fair in love and war."

He looked taken aback by the phrase, like he hadn't been expecting it, and gave a little satisfied nod. "I like that. I may use it again."

"Why are you doing this?" Dan demanded. "What's in it for you?"

Krato looked offended. "Why, the knowledge that I've helped one of Parloo's greatest civilizations protect itself from an act of aggression!" he said. "And money, of course. A lot of money."

"What are ye going to buy with it? Fish?" Artur asked. "As far I know, there's not really an exchange rate between Down Here and... well, down here. Good luck spending it."

"Not their money," Krato said. "See, the beauty of these bio-weapons is they'll kill indiscriminately but leave most of the property intact. You see, in return for helping them protect their city..."

"They're letting you keep whatever's left of ours," Dan finished.

"Got it!" said Krato, winking. "Good job."

"I hate to break it to you, shizznod, but two of those things aren't going to take out the whole place. The Tribunal will stop them."

Krato's eyes gleamed. "Who said I only have two?"

Dan remembered Krato's office.

He remembered the children, all lined up and anxious-looking. He looked at them now, their eyes glassy and emotionless, like they weren't fully here in the room.

Treatment, that's what he'd said. They were there for their *treatment*.

"I'm going to kill you," Dan told him. "I want you to know that."

"What are you going to do? Dangle me from the roof again? I don't think so, Mr Deadman. I don't think you're going to do anything."

Krato waved to his guard. "Return them to their cells. Keep the blond one. We need him."

Ollie, who had been struggling to keep up with everything that was going on, became suddenly animated. "What? No! What are you doing?" she demanded.

She raised her hands as Finn was yanked away by one of the guards, but a downpour of transparent gloop plastered them to her sides again.

"No!" she shrieked. "No, don—"

Wherever the sentence ended up, no one heard. As the

cocoon closed around her, Ollie sank through the floor and out of sight.

Dan kept his gaze fixed on Krato as the sludge hardened around him. Krato smiled and waved his fingers, then Dan felt the bottom fall out of the world, and plunged downward into the dark.

TWENTY

"Hrmf fckn mm!"

Dan flicked his eyes open and, for the second time that day, found himself locked in a cell all alone.

"Fckn ft eeit!"

OK, maybe not alone. He rolled over a little and heard Artur gasp with relief.

"Finally! I thought ye were never going to fecking move!" he wheezed. "I thought me final resting place was going to be stuck between the floor and yer armpit, and that would've been a very disappointing way to go."

"Where's Ollie? What happened?" Dan asked.

"Again, I was trapped under yer armpit," Artur said. "My grasp of the current situation has been kind of hindered by total darkness and yer overpowering body odor."

Dan sat up. This proved tricky, partly because of the slime that still coated him, but mostly because his hands were still shackled behind him.

"Take care of these, will you?" he said, angling himself in Artur's direction.

"A 'please' wouldn't go amiss," said Artur, but he shoved an arm into the locking mechanism, bit his tongue as he searched for the release mechanism, then gave a sharp yank. The cuffs sprang off and clattered onto the floor.

"Don't mention it," he said.

"I was going to say thanks."

"Me arse ye were."

They both got up, their feet slipping and sliding in the transparent sludge.

"Dissolve," Dan said. The sludge continued being sludgy. "Fonk it," Dan muttered.

He carefully picked his way over to the door, his arms held at his side to steady himself.

"Careful now," said Artur, then his feet shot in opposite directions and he yelped as he did the splits. "Ooh, me lads," he groaned. "Me precious lads."

With some wobbling, a few sharp intakes of breath, and at least one, "Fonk," Dan finally reached the door. He hammered a clenched fist against it, spattering the copper colored metal with flecks of slime.

"Hey! Open up!" he demanded.

He continued to demand variations on the same theme for several minutes, before accepting that nobody was coming to let them out.

"Damn it!" he grunted. He turned his back on the door, forgot about the slime situation, and had to grab the wall for support while his legs kicked frantically as his feet tried to find purchase on the floor.

"Dissolve!" he said, more forcefully this time.

Still nothing.

"So, what now?" Artur asked, once Dan had successfully found his footing. "Have ye a plan all worked out?"

"Not yet," Dan admitted.

"What, nothing at all?"

"I've got 'Escape,' but it's a pretty broad heading and I haven't worked out the details," Dan said, mostly through gritted teeth.

He thumped the door behind him a few times, but got the expected 'nothing whatsoever' in response.

Artur, who had fallen over three times before deciding he was better off just staying seated, scooped some gunk from his beard and scratched his chin through it. "Explain something to me," he said.

"Explain what?"

"Just, ye know, all of it. The whole thing with the monsters and what have ye. I mean, I think I've got a fair grasp of it, it's just certain bits that I'm... Actually, no. I don't have a clue about any of it. What's going on?"

And so, Dan explained, as best he could, based on what he'd figured out. Krato had devised a way of turning people into living weapons, and had used it on Bonbo and – Dan was almost certain - Finn. The attack on the mall was a test, or maybe a demonstration. Either way, it had been done for the purpose of convincing the government of Deeper Down to go along with Krato's scheme.

"He convinced them they were going to be attacked, then sold them the weapons to defend themselves with," Dan concluded. "Only what they think is a defensive action will be the opening salvo in a damn war."

"Bollocks. That's not good," said Artur. "How's that plan coming along?"

"Get out of here, get Ollie, get up to the surface," Dan said, listing the points on his fingers.

"Now ye're talking!"

"As for how we actually achieve any of them? I'm open to suggestions."

Artur gave this some thought.

"Someone's bound to come eventually, right? If ye keep making a racket, I mean. They can't just leave us in here forever."

"We hope."

Artur shook his head. "Nah, they wouldn't. They're a pretty fair lot. Quite nice, really."

"Still can't believe you're married to one."

"Technically, I'm married to two," said Artur. "Possibly three. It's complicated. The point is, they're not going to leave us in here to rot. Someone is going to come."

"And then what?" Dan asked.

Artur grinned. "And that's when the fun part begins."

———————————

KELPO AGWA HATED PRISONER DUTY. Admittedly, this was his first experience of it, and he was less than twenty seconds into his first shift, but he already hated it.

If they were prisoners, then why did he have to run after them? Why did he have to give up his morning to deliver their food? Why were they even getting food? Cobia had said they were war criminals on a mission to infiltrate Deeper Down, so why were they in a cell rather than in pieces? 'Better chopped up than locked up' – that was his motto. Granted, it hadn't been his motto for more than the last minute or so, but he felt confident he was going to adopt it long-term.

At least the bowls of gray gunk looked utterly unappetizing. That was some consolation, but it still seemed too good for them.

Pausing at the end of the corridor, Kelpo *hocked* up a mouthful of phlegm, then carefully deposited half into each bowl. He stirred them both with his finger, gave a satisfied nod, then continued on in the direction of the cell with a spring in his step.

Halfway to the door, he heard the shouts.

"Help! We need a doctor in here!"

The voice was loud, and Kelpo guessed it had to be the larger of the prisoners doing the shouting. He hesitated, not quite sure what to do.

"Please! Anyone! He needs his medication. He'll die without it."

Shizz. As well as, 'Quit complaining and deliver the fonking food,' Kelpo's only instruction had been to make sure nothing happened to the prisoners. This included, he reckoned, dying.

"Artur! Artur, wake up, buddy. Wake up, help's coming!"

Kelpo glanced around, hoping to see a medical team rushing towards him, ready to take charge of the situation. He was alone in the corridor, though. It was down to him.

"Fine. Hold on, I'm coming," he called back. "What's all the noise about?" he demanded, sliding open the hatch.

A little gunge-coated figure crouched just inside the opening, his hair plastered to his face, his dress pulled up over his knees. The tiny shiny man winked back at him through the gap.

"Surprise," Artur said, then he pounced.

Dan waited by the door, listening to the shouting, screaming and swearing from outside. The shouting and swearing were mostly Artur. The screaming mostly wasn't.

Something heavy shook the door in its frame.

A tray *whanged* against something boney-sounding.

"Did ye gob in these, ye nasty bollocks?" Artur

demanded. It was followed by some howling, some sobbing, and something going *crack*.

"I'm sorry! I'm sorry!"

"I'll fecking 'sorry' ye."

Dan couldn't see much through the gap in the door other than a blue-green shape occasionally being thrown past it at high speed. This was usually followed by a crunch and a whimper, until the last time, when the whimper never came.

"Artur?" Dan whispered. "What's going on? I can't see."

The door clunked and swung a few inches inward. Artur leaned on the door frame right down at the bottom, his arms folded across his chest and a smug expression plastered on his face.

"Get out of here," he said. He made a ticking motion in the air. "Check. Now, what's the next item on our agenda?"

IT TOOK them just a few minutes to do a sweep of the other cells. With each empty room they came across, Dan felt the knot of worry further tightening in his gut.

"She's not here," he announced, after checking the final cell.

"Then where is she?" Artur demanded.

"I don't know!"

"Shizz. What if they've killed her? The bastards. I bet they have, an' all."

"What? I thought you said they were nice?" Dan hissed.

"I said they were *quite* nice. I never said they were fecking saints." He threw up his arms. "So that's it, then. They've killed her."

"Let's assume they haven't until we find proof," Dan

said, waddling back along the L-shaped prison corridor and trying not to slip on his own slime trail. "Besides, I don't think she'd go easily, and I haven't heard anything being blown up."

"Fair point, Deadman," Artur conceded, scurrying along behind. "Ye're right, she's *definitely* alive. And yes, I'm aware that was a quick turnaround, but I can be very fickle."

"Shh," Dan urged. He had stopped at the bend in the corridor, and was pressed against the wall. He made a complicated hand gesture, then nodded in the direction of the cell they'd escaped from, which neither of them could see from their current position.

"What?" Artur asked.

Dan tutted and gestured again.

"No, that's what ye did last time. I don't know what it means," Artur said.

"For fonk's..." Dan sighed. "There's someone there," he whispered. "Outside the cell."

"Our cell?"

"Yes! That's what I was signaling."

"Ye were waving yer hands around and jerking yer head all over the place," Artur argued. "How I was supposed to get 'There's someone outside our cell' from that, I've no idea. I'm not a fecking mind reader."

A foot stamped down, flattening him against the floor and pinning him beneath its webbed toes. Dan lunged for the blue-green figure, but the other foot swung up and heel-smashed him across the jaw. He spun, then his gloopy coating made his legs slide out from beneath him and he hit the floor hard.

Dan and Artur both looked up into a face that was positively contorted in rage.

"Give me one good reason why I shouldn't kill you, *'chaun*," spat Marnie.

Artur smiled nervously up from between her toes. "Old time's sake?" He gulped as the foot pressed down. "OK, OK, wait, wait! Let me explain."

Dan made it to his knees and swung a punch at Marnie's stomach. She pirouetted on Artur, and Dan grimaced as her heel smashed into the back of his head, *clunking* his face against the wall.

"Listen, darlin', listen to me!" Artur pleaded. "I know we've had our differences. I did some bad things, you did some bad things..."

The foot pressed down harder until Artur's eyes almost bulged out of their sockets.

"Fine, fine, *I* did some bad things," he wheezed. "And I'm sorry, darlin'. I'm genuinely, fully, one hundred percent, heart-on-me-sleeve sorry that ye found out, but right now we've got bigger fish to fry. No pun intended."

"You escaped your cell!"

"Krato lied to you," Dan said. He got up slowly in the hope of avoiding another roundhouse kick to the skull. "The surface isn't going to attack you. They don't even know this place exists."

"Ha!" Marnie spat. "Of course they know. *He* would've told them. No way he'd have kept his mouth shut."

"I didn't, darlin'. I swear."

"He's telling the truth," Dan said. "He didn't even tell me."

"And he's me best mate!" Artur said. "I mean, more through lack of choice than anything else, but still. I haven't spoken a word about ye. Not to nobody. I swear on me ma's grave."

Marnie's eyes narrowed. "Your mother died?"

"That old cow? Chance'd be a fine thing," Artur said. "But the point still stands. I didn't say nothing to nobody. I kept it secret, just like ye asked."

"But it's not going to be secret for long," Dan told her. "This place is about to draw a lot of attention to itself."

"We... He said we need to protect ourselves."

"That's just what Krato wants you to think. See, war is his business. He makes weapons and then he finds idiots like your people to buy them," Dan told her. "And you know the funny thing? When Down Here – my city, I mean, up there – when it starts shooting back, it'll be using weapons he sold it. A lot of people are going to die on both sides, and the only one who's going to win is him."

Marnie's jaw tightened, but she said nothing.

"He's being on the level wit' ye," Artur said. "Yer people have been duped, darlin'. Ye need to help us stop this before it gets out of hand."

Marnie's jaw tightened. Artur's face turned a worrying shade of purple as the foot pressed down. Dan tensed, but Artur stopped him before he could intervene.

"Don't, Deadman," he gasped. "Let her do what she needs to do. Sure, she's got every right."

"You're damn right I do!" Marnie hissed.

"Whatever ye decide to do, I just want ye to know," Artur said. He smiled benevolently. "I forgive ye."

"What?! You forgive *me*?" Marnie spat. "*You* forgive *me*? Oh, that's rich! That is... That's just like you, 'chaun. That's just like..."

She sobbed. It snagged at the back of her throat and almost choked her. A tear rolled down her cheek and plopped onto the floor by Artur's head.

"They're using children," she whispered, her voice cracking apart. "They told them it was a great honor, that they were the future of Deeper Down. But they're *children*."

"We know," said Artur. "So if ye won't help us, then at least help those poor skiddlers."

Marnie peered down at Artur like he was something unpleasant she'd trodden on. Mostly because he was.

"Why do you think I'm here?" she asked, then she lifted her foot away and Artur gulped in a generous lungful of air.

"That's my special lady," he said, winking up at her.

She raised her foot up high.

"Don't tempt me."

"OK, OK! I was just being friendly, like," he said.

"Wait a minute," said Dan. "What do you mean *that's why you're here*?"

"They shouldn't be sending children. I don't know about that other stuff, about Krato and what you said, but they shouldn't be sending children. It's not right," Marnie told him. "I want you to help us stop it. I want you to help bring them home."

"I reckon we can lend ye a hand, alright," said Artur. He gestured up at Dan, then down at the snail-trail of slime that covered him. "But first, any chance ye might be able to get this shoite off us and help us find our friend?"

"Dissolve," said Marnie, and the gunk became two puddles of liquid on the floor around them.

"Ta very much."

"That was the easy part. The second bit will be more difficult," Marnie said. "Your friend is being held in a stasis cell. She knocked out eight guards before they were able to subdue her."

"Only eight?" said Artur. "Count yerself lucky she went easy on ye. She could've brought this whole place down around yer ears if she'd been of a mind to."

"Where is she?" Dan demanded.

"Like I said, stasis cells."

"Yes, but we don't know where that is."

"Oh. Right. Well, it's not far," said Marnie. "But she's heavily guarded. You won't be able to fight your way through them all."

"Ye'd be surprised," Artur said. "Me and Deadman? When we get going? We're a force to be reckoned with, and that's a fact. Sure, I took out yer guard fella earlier single-handed."

"He wasn't a guard. He was a fourteen-year old-intern," Marnie said.

"Was he? Shoite. Is that why he kept crying?"

"What did you do with him?" Marnie asked.

"He's in our cell," said Dan. "He's fine, but he'll be out for a while."

"The guards around the stasis cells, they're... different. They're not like the rest of us. You won't be able to fight them on your own. Not all of them."

"What about weapons?" Dan asked. "You've got guns, right?"

Marnie shook her head. "We've never needed them."

"Well, we need them now," Dan said. "There's seriously nothing? Not one single blaster?"

"No. Like I said, we've never... Wait. There may be some in Salvage."

"Salvage?"

"We have automated clean-up sweeps of the ocean around us. I pick through it sometimes looking for sculpting materials. I'm sure I've seen some guns there before. Don't know if they work, though."

"Sculpting materials?" asked Artur. "So ye're still at the

old art, or whatever? Good on ye. I always said ye had a fantastic eye for—"

"Shut up," Marnie told him. "I'm still not talking to you."

Artur held up his hands. "Fair enough."

"Can we focus?" Dan asked. "The guns. Salvage. Where is it?"

"You'll never get in without being spotted," Marnie said. "I'll go. They're used to me going in and out."

"Mind when ye were used to *me* going 'in and out' back in the day?" Artur asked, his beard parting to reveal a growing grin. "By which I mean—"

"I know what you mean," Marnie barked. "But if you mention it again, I'll crush you beneath my heel."

"Right ye are. Receiving ye loud and clear," Artur said. "I'll come with ye. To the salvage, or what have ye. It's not that I don't trust ye, mind, it's just that—"

"Fine. Whatever," Marnie said. She pinched Artur's hair between a finger and thumb and hoisted him off the ground. Only then did she realize there was nowhere obvious to hide him, with the possible exception of...

She sighed. "Don't get any ideas," she warned, then she stuffed him down the neck of her armor and wedged him below the breastplate.

"God, I've missed these!" said Artur in a voice that suggested he was being smothered, but wasn't about to complain about it.

"Don't get used to it," Marnie told him. "And quit wriggling around down there."

"Sure, that's not what ye used to say. Just the opposite, in—"
Marnie banged a fist on her breastplate.
"Ow!"

"We'll be back," she told Dan. "Don't go anywhere."

"Don't be long," Dan said. "Or there's no saying where I might wind up…"

"SERIOUSLY, Marnie? Now? With everything that's going on?"

The man sitting behind the desk was much older than Marnie, as evidenced by his dried-out scales and graying moustache. He was short, overweight, and had swapped the traditional golden armor look for a comfortable shirt and slacks combo.

Marnie smiled and shrugged. "You ask me, Bool, times like these are when we need art more than ever. All that war stuff? Creativity is the best antidote there is."

Bool's bushy eyebrows knotted above his flat nose. "Marnie, that's a load of fishshizz," he said. He held her gaze for a moment, then chuckled. "Ah, get out of here," he said, waving her over to a door marked 'Salvage.' "But when you get rich and famous, I want my ten percent."

"You got it, Bool!" Marnie said. She blew him a kiss, which he made a show of catching, then she hurried on through the door before he changed his mind.

"OK, quick question," said Artur from inside her armor. She waited until the door had clicked closed behind her before answering.

"What?"

"Are you having sexual intercourse with that man?"

"*What*?!" Marnie spluttered. "Who, Bool? He's, like, a hundred and forty."

"Avoiding the question, I see," Artur said.

"No, I'm not avoiding the question, I'm refusing to acknowledge it."

"I'm yer husband. I deserve to know."

"No, I'm not having *sexual intercourse* with Bool. He's old enough to be my grandfather."

"So am I, and it never stopped us," Artur said.

Marnie looked down into the shadow beneath her breastplate. "*What?!*"

There was a moment of awkward silence.

"Look, can we just focus on the matter at hand?" Artur said. His head emerged from beneath the armor, and his eyes widened when he saw what they'd walked into.

It was impossible to tell how big the salvage room was. This was mostly due to the towering piles of junk that loomed like a mountain range around the small clearing where Marnie stood. They stretched several stories high, and if Artur squinted he reckoned he could just make out a layer of cloud around some of the higher peaks.

"Holy shoite. Ye fished all this out of the sea?"

"Not me personally, but yes," said Marnie. "You land people dump a lot of stuff."

"So it would seem," said Artur. He whistled through his teeth, then hopped out of the armor and landed beside a coil of fencing wire, half a street sign, and a bucket mostly eaten by red-brown rust. He picked up an old bolt, turned it over in his hands, then tossed it back into the pile.

"How are we meant to find a gun in all this?"

Marnie strode over to the pile on the left. It curved steeply at the bottom, before rising straight up into a cliff face of metal and plastic. "This is the latest stuff," she said. "I'm sure I saw a rifle or something here a few days ago. It might be buried a little deeper now, but we can find it."

She began to dig through the scrap, tossing aside unrecognizable bits of car engines and fried-out old circuit boards.

Artur scrambled up onto the junk pile and began heaving some of the smaller pieces aside. "So," he said, rolling the word around in his mouth. "How've ye been?"

Marnie stopped digging and glared at him. "Seriously?" she sneered, then she went back to shoving the scrap aside, more forcefully this time.

"I'm getting the impression that ye're still a little upset."

"Upset? *Upset?* No, I'm not upset!"

Artur's face brightened. "Aren't ye?"

"I'm *furious!* She was my sister, Artur. My *sister!*"

"Shoite. Ye knew about that, did ye?"

"Yes! I knew!"

"Right. Yes. I can only apologize. I was out of line. I should never have taken advantage of yer little sister like that."

Marnie stopped digging. "Wait, my *little* sister?"

"Oh. Ye meant the other one." Artur winced, then held his hands up in surrender. "They both came onto me, it wasn't my fault."

Marnie's face darkened. She kicked out at a piece of buckled wall cladding, dislodging it from the pile. The mountain creaked ominously above them.

"Steady there, darlin'," Artur warned. "Ye don't want to bury us both alive now, do ye?"

"Not us both, no," Marnie spat. She shoved aside the shell of a TV, revealing the smooth butt of a blaster rifle sticking out through a gap in the trash.

"Ye found it!" Artur said. "Well done."

"Shut up," Marnie hissed. Grabbing the rifle, she gave it a tug. It didn't budge, and her scales turned an angry shade of purple as she pulled and wrenched it more violently. The mountain visibly teetered and Artur slid down in a cascade of nuts and bolts.

"Careful. Ye'll bring the whole thing down," he warned, but Marnie ignored him.

"Come... out!" she hollered, giving the rifle a final heave. There was *kerack* as something snapped. She staggered back, half a rifle clutched in her hands, a look of triumph already fading on her face.

A blaster bolt screeched from the broken weapon and slammed into the foot of the salvage mountain. The whole place rumbled as part of the cliff face collapsed.

"Oh bollocks," Artur muttered. He covered his head with his arms as several tons of junk fell on him from above.

Marnie, who had staggered clear, dropped the rifle, her face turning a pale sky blue. "Oh no," she whispered. She clambered over the debris and frantically began to dig. "Artur? Artur, where are you?"

The only reply was the groan of the junk settling.

"No, no, no. Shizz, shizz, shizz," Marnie hissed. She shoved aside some sort of spaceship canopy and part of a garage roof. "Artur? Speak to me, 'chaun! Don't you be dead. Don't you dare be—"

She discarded a few car parts and an old shopping cart. And there, pinned beneath a rusted vault door, was Artur. His eyes were closed, his legs trapped, his upper body bent unnaturally.

Marnie wasn't quick enough to catch the sob before it escaped from her throat. "Fonk! Artur! Artur, I'm sorry. I'm sorry. I'll get help. You're going to be OK." She raised her voice. "You hear me? Please be OK!"

Artur blinked. "Holy shoite, there's no need to shout,"

he said. "I'm half-dead, not half fecking deaf." He grinned at her. "Is that us even now?"

Marnie picked up a scorched and blackened piece of metal and covered him again.

"I'll take that as a 'no,'" he said, his voice muffled.

With a grunt, he pushed his way free from beneath the junk and dusted himself down. "That was close," he said, looking up at an overhang of salvage still teetering above him. "Sure, I could've been..."

His voice trailed off. He cocked his head and squinted at the outcrop of scrap. Slowly, a smile emerged from somewhere inside his beard. "Well now," he said. "What do we have here?"

TWENTY-ONE

DAN SWUNG out from around the corner, fist drawn back.

"Wait, stop, it's us!" Marnie cried.

Dan lowered his arm. "About time."

"Ye're an ungrateful sack o' shoite, ye know that, Dead-man?" Artur said. The voice didn't come from inside Marnie's breastplate, but rather from a bulky canvas bag she dragged along beside her. A couple of buckled pipes poked out through the partially fastened opening.

"What's that?" Dan asked. "Doesn't look like a gun."

Marnie released the bag's strap and knelt beside it. "I had to take a few things or Bool would get suspicious."

"Who's Bool?" Dan asked.

"He's my lover," Marnie said.

Artur almost choked in the bag. "I fecking knew it!"

"He's no one. Doesn't matter," said Marnie.

"I don't care," Dan told her. "Did you get a gun?"

"Get *a* gun? No," said Artur. Marnie opened the bag, revealing the shizz-eating grin on Artur's face, and some-thing else. Something incredible. "We found *the* gun."

"No fonking way," Dan muttered. He reached into the

bag and practically groaned with delight as his fingers slipped into the indents of a pleasingly familiar grip. "Mindy," he said, raising the hand cannon and savoring her weight against his palm. At the sound of her name, the lights on Mindy's chamber pulsed in readiness. "Am I glad to see *you*."

DAN AND MARNIE stood on either side of the doorway leading into the stasis cell block. Despite quite a bit of protesting and pleading, Artur was in Dan's breast pocket, rather than his preferred option of between Marnie's breasts.

"How many?" Dan asked, as Marnie peeked around the corner.

"I make six," she whispered. "Two at the door to her cell, four patrolling." She looked across the gap at him. "What's the plan?"

Artur snorted. "Heh. 'Plan,' she says."

Stepping out of cover, Dan raised his gun. Two stun-shots pulsed from the barrel, hitting the two door guards squarely in the face. They spasmed as they fell, their trident weapons clattering to the floor.

All six of the guards were large and heavy, like eighteen regular Deeper Downians had been condensed three-a-piece into these hefty fonks.

They moved surprisingly swiftly for their size. Two of the other guards even had time to tighten their grips on their tridents before Dan shot them. They dropped immediately. The remaining two quickly met with the same fate.

"That was the plan," Dan said, striding to the door of the cell the Deeper Downians had been stationed outside.

The door had the same slide hatch set-up as the door of his own cell. He *clanked* it aside and saw Ollie floating in the center of the room, her eyes rolled back in her head, her limbs spread like she was frozen midway through a star-jump.

"How do I open this?" Dan demanded. "There's no handle."

Marnie grabbed the arm of one of the stunned guards and slapped the webbed hand against the door. It *bleeped*, then slid into the wall beside it.

The inside of the cell danced like water reflecting on a swimming pool wall. Marnie grabbed Dan's arm before he went charging in.

"You need to disable the stasis field first," she told him. "Or you'll get caught in it, too."

"OK, so how do I do that?" Dan asked.

Marnie peered into the cell, her eyes darting across the floor and ceiling. "I don't know."

"Ye don't know? Now ye fecking tell us!"

Dropping to her haunches, Marnie patted down the closest guard. "There should be a remote. It can only be switched off from the outside, so there has to be a remote."

The lights on the ceiling became swirling red beams as the echo of an alarm tore through the complex.

"Shoite. Guess they know what we're up to," Artur announced. He hopped out of Dan's pocket, slid down his front, then set about searching the second door guard.

Dan was about to start on another of the guards when a blaster bolt screamed past several feet above his head. A Deeper Downian stood in the doorway, a comically over-sized blaster rifle balanced awkwardly against his hip.

"I thought you said you didn't have guns!" Dan barked.

"We don't!" Marnie said.

A second blast hit the wall a few arm-lengths off to Dan's left, blackening the mossy stone.

"At least he can't shoot for shoite," Artur commented. Dan took the guy down with another stun shot, but a flurry of movement in the corridor at the man's back suggested more were right behind him.

"Fonk," Dan spat, as a squadron of anxious-looking Deeper Downians filed in, rifles clutched in their webbed hands. "Krato must've armed them. That son-of-a-bedge."

Mindy kicked twice in Dan's hand, dropping two more of the weapon wielders. They almost looked relieved as the rifles slipped from their grips and they sank to the floor.

One of the guards on the floor became a sudden blur of movement. His hand clamped around Dan's bare ankle, his eyes wide awake and filled with rage.

"Shizz, he woke up fast," Dan muttered. He fired off another stun shot, sending the guy back to sleep. Around them, the other five fallen soldiers began to stir.

"Bollocks. This isn't good," Artur yelped.

"Found it!" Marnie declared, holding up a slender silver rod.

She tapped and slapped it as if it were some sort of percussion instrument. The swirling light in Ollie's cell dimmed, and she hit the floor with an "Oof!"

"Uh... hello?" she called.

"We're out here," Dan said.

Ollie stumbled into the doorway, looking like she'd woken up with a hangover. She yelped and ducked as a blaster bolt screamed past her.

"Oh yeah, and we're being shot at," Artur said. "We probably should've mentioned."

"Where's Finn?"

"Not here," Dan said, firing a volley of stun-shots into

the growing crowd of Deeper Downians. "Marnie, how do we get to our sub?"

"You don't," Marnie said. "It'll be scrap by now. I mean, it was practically scrap to start with. And who paints a submarine yellow, anyway?"

"So how do we get to the surface? How do we get out of here?" Dan demanded. He put a stun-bolt in the back of a rousing guard's head before the man could wake up all the way, then sent a few more in the direction of the reluctant gunmen. "I'm going to be out of battery real soon at this rate."

"There are subs. Proper subs, I mean. Ours," Marnie said.

"Which direction?" Dan asked.

"Out the door, then we'll have to—"

"I wasn't asking how we got there, I asked which direction."

Marnie frowned, then pointed at the wall behind him. "Uh, that way, I guess."

"Mindy, explosive round," Dan barked. He spun on a bare foot, raised the gun, and spat out a warning. "You might want to get down."

The wall erupted at a squeeze of the trigger, filling the room with dust and smoke and a high-pitched ringing that might have just been in Dan's ears.

There was a large hole where the wall had been. Through it, Dan saw a grassy plaza, not unlike the one Cobia had led them across earlier. Several dozen shocked-looking Deeper Downians stood frozen to the spot, not quite sure what the fonk was going on. One by one, they began to run – away from the hole, thankfully, rather than towards it – and Dan beckoned for the others to follow him through.

"Go. Lead the way," he urged, shoving Marnie ahead.

For a moment, she looked like she might hit him with another of those heel-kicks, but then she was off and running, shouting at any stragglers on the plaza to get out of their way.

They jumped onto a moving walkway, but kept running, using it for a speed boost. A single blaster shot scorched the air above them.

"Those idiots! There are people here!" Marnie cried.

"Ye ask me, they're starting to like their new guns a little too much," Artur said.

"This way!" Marnie instructed, jumping onto a second path that had branched away from the first. It swept them towards another tall column like the one they'd been in earlier. Just like that one, the inside of this one was filled with hundreds of intersecting walkways both above and below their own.

"You're going to have to trust me," Marnie said.

Dan didn't like the sound of that. Trust wasn't his strong point. "Why?"

"You just are," said Marnie, then she shoved Ollie off the walkway, grabbed Dan by the shirt, and threw herself over the edge.

They fell for what felt like a while and yet, simultaneously, no time at all. Artur managed to fit in a lot of swearing, and yet Dan had barely had time to raise Mindy and take aim at Marnie before they were swallowed by a cloud-like mist that seemed to push back against them, slowing their fall.

The water met them at quite a leisurely pace. Despite the height he'd fallen from, Dan barely dipped below the surface before bobbing back up again. Artur coughed and spluttered in his pocket while, somewhere through the fog, Ollie *whooped* with delight.

"That was fun!" she said.

"Speak for yerself," Artur hollered back.

"This way."

That was Marnie's voice, somewhere just ahead of them. "Come with me. Hurry. We don't have much time."

"Time for what? Are ye going to shove us off something again?" Artur asked. He quickly held his breath as Dan began to front crawl, forcing Artur under the water.

Ollie flapped her way through the mist and arrived beside Marnie just about the same time that Dan did. Artur exhaled sharply as Dan straightened and his head was raised above the surface again.

"Bit o' warning next time," he grumbled, adding: "Ye great big bastard," as an afterthought.

"Where now?" Dan asked.

"How the feck should I know?"

"Wasn't asking you."

"Oh. Right."

"We wait here," Marnie said. "Stay close together."

Ollie looked around, but the fog made it impossible to see more than a few feet in any direction.

"I don't get it. What are we waiting for?"

Bubbles burbled to the surface all around them.

"For this," said Marnie, then the water became a whirlpool and they were all dragged down together beneath the rolling, foaming waves.

TWENTY-TWO

HANDS GRABBED at them through the murky water. Dan felt fingers wrap around an ankle and instinctively jerked his leg free. Marnie appeared through the gloom in front of him, her cheeks puffed out. She shook her head, pointed down, then let herself be pulled down into a gaping mouth-like opening that had appeared below them.

Fonk it. It wasn't like he had a lot of options.

The hand caught him again. Dan surrendered to it but kept Mindy ready as he was pulled into the hatch. Ollie and Marnie were both in there, Ollie's already purple-pink skin turning red with the effort of holding her breath.

A door slammed closed above their heads. There was a gurgle, then a hiss, as the water was ejected from what Dan now realized must be an airlock.

When the water cleared, five women stood around the group, their blue-green scales shiny and wet.

"OK," Dan said. "So, who the fonk are you?"

"These are the mothers of the children they sent to the surface," Marnie explained.

One of the woman stepped forward and caught Dan's

arm. Her eyes blazed with a hopeful intensity that would've taken a breathing man's breath away. "Help us bring them home. Please."

Dan could only hold the woman's gaze for a moment or two. He looked around at the other women, their faces just as desperate and pleading. "Sure." He shrugged. "Why not?"

Marnie slammed the door release button and an interior door slid aside. The inside of the main sub looked like some kind of military dropship, with a row of seats running down each side of the narrow interior, both rows facing the other. Various straps and harnesses were attached to the chairs, and Dan and Ollie were both carried along as Marnie and the other women hurried to strap themselves in.

"Get a move on!" instructed a female voice from inside a partially walled-off cockpit area. "They're going to be onto us if we don't hurry."

Shoving Mindy back in his holster, Dan pulled the harness across his chest, almost squashing Artur in the process.

"Hey, watch what ye're doing there!"

"Sorry."

Dan removed Artur from his shirt pocket, fastened the harness, then looked around for somewhere safe to put him.

"Over here," called Marnie. She sat directly across from Dan, her hands splayed like a Boomball player waiting for a pass.

"Hey, wait a fecking minute!" Artur protested, but then he was hurtling through the air, his arms and legs frantically flapping as he tried, with very little success, to fly.

Marnie caught him, fumbled, but managed not to drop him. Artur huffed and puffed in her hands.

"I have never felt so violated in all me life," he protested, then Marnie shoved him down the gap at the front of her breastplate and he immediately changed his tune. "Actually, it's fine," he said, his voice echoing out from her cleavage. "I totally support the previous course of action."

"Everybody strapped in?" called the woman in front. From the way she said it, Dan knew she had to be another mom, and suspected she'd asked that same question many times before. He wondered if she'd ask if anyone needed the bathroom, too.

The Deeper Downians gave two short tugs on their harnesses. Ollie did the same, but Dan felt confident enough in his ability to fasten two clips together that he didn't feel the need.

The sub didn't move. Dan felt the women's eyes on him. He sighed.

"Fine."

He tugged the harness, albeit quite sarcastically.

"Happy?" he asked, then everyone was thrown sideways in their seats as the sub went from 'stopped' to 'moving stupidly fast' in one sudden eye-watering lurch.

There were no windows in this section of the sub, and Dan couldn't see into the cockpit from his seat. From the way the sub banked and turned, though, he got the impression they were either maneuvering through somewhere, or dodging something. Possibly both.

"Are they onto us?" he asked.

"Not yet," the pilot replied. "But they could be waiting for us on the other side of these turbines."

"Turbines?"

Dan leaned forward in his chair and managed to see a corner of the sub's windshield. A series of enormous spinning blades were chewing up the water just ahead. Dan leaned back again and tried to pretend he hadn't seen it.

"Once we're through – once we're at the surface," one of the mothers began. "What then?"

Dan frowned. "Huh?"

"What's your plan?" Marnie asked.

"My plan?" Dan looked around at their expectant faces. "I thought you must have a plan."

There was some concerned murmuring from the moms.

"What? No," Marnie replied. "That's why we broke you out. That was our plan."

Dan closed his eyes and gently thumped the back of his head against his head rest a few times.

"OK, fine," he said, once he'd finished. "I've got a plan."

"That was quick," said Artur.

"We're going to go up there, get your kids back, and stop a war," Dan said. He held up a hand before anyone could respond. "I know, it's a little light on detail, but we'll flesh each part out when we come to it."

"And save Finn."

Dan turned to Ollie. "Huh?"

"And save Finn," she said. "You forgot to mention that part."

If the look of desperation on the mothers' faces had stung, the look on Ollie's cut him all the way open.

"Sure, kid," he told her. "And save Finn."

There was an ear-smashing *bang* and a brief but worrying *screeeeeech* as one of the spinning turbine blades nicked the back end of the sub, throwing the occupants around in their seats.

"Assuming we make it there in one piece."

"Sorry, that was close," the pilot said.

"Me arse. 'Close' means 'that thing almost hit us,'" called the voice in Marnie's cleavage. "Whereas what actually happened was that thing actually fecking hit us."

"Well, we're through," the pilot said. "And the coast's clear, so I'm going to start speeding up."

Dan blinked. "Wait. *Start* speeding up?" he asked, but the words went mostly unheard as they were lost to the whine of the sub's engines.

It felt, Dan would later recall, like all his atoms switched places at the same time. Their previous speed, which he'd considered to be stupidly fast, suddenly felt reassuringly sedate as the sub took off like a warp-enabled missile, and his teeth tried to retreat back into their sockets.

Through his watering eyes, he saw the other occupants of the sub shrink a good three inches, their faces contorting as the immense G-Force stamped its authority all over them. He tried to blink, but his eyelids were pinned open, his face was ten percent flatter and thirty percent wider than usual, and it was all he could do not to black out.

He blacked out.

He woke to the tinny echo of Artur throwing up, which was very quickly followed by a squeal from Marnie.

"Urgh! What the fonk?"

"Oh, shoite. Sorry, about that, me darlin'," Artur said.

He threw up again.

He was still throwing up when Marnie yanked him out from beneath her breastplate and tossed him onto the floor.

Sunlight streamed into the sub through the gap in the cockpit wall. In the distance, Dan could hear the *squawking* of seabirds on the mooch for food. They were on the surface.

Oh sweet, glorious Krosyh, they were on the surface.

Ollie was sitting bolt upright in her chair, her hair slightly tousled, her eyes wide with wonder. "Whoa. That was awesome," she whispered.

Artur threw up on the floor. "Speak for yerself, Peaches," he said, punctuating every other word with a violent retch.

The side of the sub bumped gently against something solid. "We're here," the pilot announced. She appeared in the doorway, looking much shorter and frumpier than Dan had expected. She wore a green shawl across her shoulders that might well have been made of seaweed, and looked more like a grandmother than a mom.

"This is where they came up," she said. "The other subs are on the next jetty over."

"I can't hear shooting or screaming or any of that stuff," Artur pointed out. He swallowed and wiped his beard on his sleeve. "That's a good sign, right?"

"It is," Dan confirmed, unfastening his harness.

"So, what now?" asked another of the moms.

Dan unfastened his harness and stood up. "Same plan as before. We get your kids back. And we stop a war."

"And save Finn," Ollie added.

"And that, too," Dan confirmed.

Marnie unclipped herself and stood beside him. "And do you have any more detail yet?"

Dan thought for a moment. "No," he admitted. He drew his gun and nodded at the women. "So, let's go improvise."

DAN, Ollie and Marnie hid behind a stack of cargo crates, barely able to believe their luck. Krato stood at the other end of a long jetty at an industrial-looking dock, pacing back and forth like some military commander. The six children stood in a line before him, wearing headsets that encircled their heads like oversized halos that had slipped down so they almost covered their eyes. Bonbo flanked the group on one side, with Finn at the other. Bonbo's eyes were still pointed at the ground, while Finn struggled against a set of cuffs that locked him together at the wrists and elbows.

"We made it in time," Dan whispered.

"At the rate that mad cow was driving, I'm surprised we didn't get here first," Artur replied. He was perched on Dan's shoulder, holding onto an ear for support.

"There's Finn," said Ollie. She stepped out and raised a hand to wave, but Dan quickly clamped one of his own hands across her mouth and pulled her back into cover.

"What are you doing?" he hissed. "You almost gave us away."

"But it's Finn. He's right there."

"And right now, we have the element of surprise," Dan told her. "If you let them know we're here, this could all go to shizz."

Marnie, who had been scowling in the general direction of Krato's back for the last minute, finally spoke.

"This isn't right."

"What do you mean?" Dan asked. "We're going to get the kids back. That's what you wanted."

"No, I mean something's wrong. Why is Krato there by himself?"

"He's not by himself," Ollie said. "Finn's there. And all those other people."

"I mean there were a dozen subs docked down there. So where is everyone else?"

From behind them there came the sound of a throat being cleared.

"Drop the weapon," Cobia instructed.

Dan turned, gun-arm whipping around to take aim. Before he could level the weapon at Cobia's head, a trident moved to intercept. His wrist wedged between its prongs, and Mindy was flung from his grip as the trident was twisted.

Grabbing the trident's long handle, Dan wrenched it out of the Deeper Downian's hands and smashed the butt into Cobia's face, further shattering his nose. Cobia howled and covered his face with his hands, his blood quickly pumping out through his webbed fingers.

Another of the weapons cracked Dan on the back of the skull, turning the solid jetty to a squidgy putty. Stunned, Dan realized he and the others were now surrounded by a number of identical twins. Either that or that last head injury had fonked up his vision.

Two partially conjoined troops moved in perfect unison, and a single fork speared his left side. Another pierced the flesh on his right, pinning him in place.

Marnie caught one of the spearmen by the back of his armor, but he was considerably larger than she was, and he shrugged her away.

"Water," Dan told her. His eyes went to the ocean behind them, then to Ollie.

It took just half a second for Marnie to get the point. Grabbing Ollie, she raced for the dock edge.

There was a splash as Ollie and Marnie hit the water and vanished below the surface. A couple of the Deeper Down soldiers moved to follow, but a shout from Cobia stopped them.

"Forget them. Keep the dead man pinned. He's the danger."

"You have no idea," Dan said. "Mindy, rapid fire."

Down on the jetty, Mindy's chamber rotated and locked into position.

"Mindy, fire!"

Dan jumped and caught the top of the crate stack just as the weapon kicked into life and spun across the dock, spraying blaster bolts like ankle-height fireworks in every direction.

There was screaming. A lot of screaming. It was quickly followed by a lot of falling over, and then a not-inconsiderable amount of death as Mindy's pinwheel of pain tore through the toppling bodies, obliterating any heads and torsos unlucky enough to stray into its path.

"Mindy, cease."

The torrent of blaster fire died away. Mindy's frantic spin became an increasingly sedate series of rotations, then stopped.

Dan dropped back onto the dock. Artur regarded the sizzling corpses and the groaning *not-quite-yet* ones. There was no sign of Cobia, but then some of the bodies had been obliterated to the extent that only a DNA sample, or a particularly skilled psychic medium would be able to identify them.

"Brutal," Artur said, then he jumped when Ollie broke the surface of the water, gasping in a deep, desperate breath.

Marnie appeared beside her. Dan retrieved Mindy while they climbed up onto the jetty.

As their heads drew level with the dock, both women paused.

"Whoa. What happened?" Ollie asked. "Are they dead?"

"The ones without heads definitely are," Artur told her. "And, I mean, those three are just legs, so they're done for, too."

Marnie ducked out of sight. Dan and Artur tried to ignore the *HUUURK* of her throwing up into the water.

"She's being sick," said Ollie.

"Is she now?" asked Artur.

RRRRUUMG! HWOOAGH!

"Yes."

They waited until the vomiting episode had ended. Marnie groaned, then raised her head again.

"Ye alright there?"

BLEUWGH! GRUURGH!

Artur rocked on his heels on Dan's shoulder. "Let's give her a minute."

"No time. We've lost our element of surprise. She'll have to catch us up," said Dan. "Mindy, stun shot."

He stepped out from behind the crate to find Krato waving at him. With the other hand, he held a gun jammed against the side of a boy's head. The kid hadn't flinched, and none of the other children seemed to have even noticed. Whatever the halo thing was, it seemed to be keeping them in some sort of trance-like state. Bonbo was still staring at the ground, while Finn continued to wrestle with his bonds.

"Hello, Mr Deadman," Krato said. "Please, don't try any heroics. I'm not in the mood."

Ollie appeared beside Dan, water pouring off her onto the dock. "He's got a gun," she gasped.

"He has that," Artur confirmed.

"Toss your weapon into the water," Krato instructed.

Dan hesitated. Krato pressed the barrel of his gun against the kid's head. While the boy's expression didn't change, Dan saw a single tear glisten as it ran down his face.

He tossed the gun. Krato waited for the splash before nodding his approval.

"Good. Now come over. Join the fun."

Ollie started to look back over her shoulder, but a hiss

from Dan stopped her. "Don't. He doesn't know she's there. Eyes front," he instructed.

Placing a hand in the small of Ollie's back, he led her along the jetty. Finn's face lit up when he saw her, and he immediately redoubled his efforts to wrestle his arms free.

"We don't have all day," Krato said, adding a theatrical sigh to emphasize his point. "Hurry, please."

Dan and Ollie picked up the pace, closing the gap until they were less than fifteen feet away.

"Far enough," Krato instructed. "Look down. Imagine there is a line right in front of you. See it in your mind. If you cross that line, someone dies. Understood?"

"What the Hell are you doing, Krato?"

Krato's red face twisted in rage. "Is that *understood*?"

Dan gritted his teeth, then nodded. "Don't cross the line. Understood."

The villain's smile returned. "Good."

"Finn. Are you OK?" Ollie asked.

"Oh, and no one talks to my... what? Associates? Prisoners?" Krato tapped a finger against his stupid beard. "Weapons. No one talks to my weapons or *BLAM!*"

He shouted the last word, making Ollie and Finn both jump. None of the kids so much as blinked.

Krato laughed, then gestured over to the stack of crates. "So, did you kill them all?"

"Most of them," Dan admitted.

"And it wasn't fecking pretty," Artur added. "So ye might want to think about that before ye start giving us any of yer shoite."

Krato looked positively delighted by this news. "Thank you. That helps me out a *lot*. That's going to buy me a round two at least."

"What's the scrawny little bollocks talking about now?" Artur asked.

"Well, since you've taken out our fishy friends, there's no harm in telling you," said Krato. "And frankly, this is all too damned clever not to gloat about."

He placed a hand to the back of his mouth as if imparting some great secret. "The thing is, I don't give a shizz about Deeper Down."

"You don't say," said Dan. "You want to take over the city. You explained that already."

Krato snorted. "Take over the city? Please. With Geronimus Krone about to move in? How long would I be in charge for? A day? A week?" He shook his head. "No. *Take over the city*. Ridiculous."

He gestured around at the smoke-spewing factories behind them, and the dirty high-rise housing blocks just beyond. "Besides, it's a horrible place. What would I even want with it? No."

"Well... what, then?" Dan asked.

"You tell me, Detective," Krato said. His eyes sparkled. "In fact, let's make it a game. I'll give you... let's say one minute to figure it out. If you don't, I'll pull this trigger."

"What? No!" said Ollie. She started to take a step forward.

"The line!" Krato screeched. He pressed the gun harder still against the boy's head, bending his neck. The headset tilted a fraction, and Dan heard a brief snatch of that same lullaby tune he'd heard before. "Don't make me remind you."

Dan caught Ollie by the arm and felt a crackle of energy that stung even his nerve-endings. He held on, ignoring the pain until she stepped back over the imaginary line.

"Good girl," Krato said. He eyeballed her for a while, then shifted his gaze to Dan. "Forty seconds."

"What? Now wait a fecking minute!" Artur protested.

"Thirty-five."

Dan felt his fingers ball into fists. The kids still hadn't flinched, but three of the six had hot tears streaming down their silent, unmoving faces. Bonbo was shuffling anxiously from foot to foot, his mouth moving as he whispered something only he could hear. Finn, for his part, was still struggling pointlessly against his shackles. He might not be the brightest, but he was a tryer, Dan would give him that much.

"Twenty-five. Tick-tock-tick-tock."

Behind him, a blue-green figure slid silently out of the water and onto the dock.

"Look, just fecking tell us, alright!" Artur bellowed, waving an arm to attract Krato's attention. "We don't want to play yer stupid game. There's no need to hurt the skiddlers, just tell us and we'll all pretend to be impressed or whatever it is ye want from us."

Without looking, Krato swung the gun around and squeezed off a single round. The bolt hit Marnie in the chest, crumpling her armor and launching her a dozen or so feet along the dock. She rolled awkwardly to a stop, one arm pinned beneath her, the other flopped over her face.

"Marnie!" Artur yelped. "Ye bastard! I'll feckin' kill ye!"

The gun pressed against the boy's head again. "Ten. Nine. Eight."

"Hold on," Dan urged.

"Seven. Six. Five."

"For fonk's sake, just give me a—"

"Four. Three. Two."

"An enemy! You made them the enemy!" Dan blurted.

Krato's mouth began forming the first 'W' sound of the number one, then stopped. He cocked his head. "Go on. But be quick."

Dan's mouth started talking before his brain had filled in all the blanks. "Krone. You said you got out of the weapons business because there was no money in it. You'd been selling planetary defense weapons, and with Krone moving into the sector no other planet would risk waging war on us, or he'd wipe us both out."

"And...?"

"And so, if you couldn't convince the Tribunal they had to prepare for threats from other planets, you thought you'd scare them into believing there's a threat here on this one. Deeper Down. You're making them look like the big bad monsters from the deep so you can keep selling guns to the Tribunal."

Krato smirked. "Bingo! Well figured out, Detective. I mean, you've barely scratched the surface, but you've got the general idea. See, once I send the broken bodies of their people back down to them – and show them the footage of their children being cut down in the streets – how do you think Deeper Down will react?"

"They'll want to arm themselves," Dan said. "They'll want to retaliate."

"And around and around we go," Krato said. "Beautiful, isn't it? I'd love to take the credit for it, but we've been doing this sort of thing for centuries, all across the galaxy. Give people guns, make them hate each other, then get rich from the escalation. It's timeless, really."

This time it was Dan who shuffled forward. Krato spotted the movement right away. He screwed his gun into the side of the kid's head. "The line! Cross it and he dies!"

"He's going to die anyway," Dan said. "They all are, right?"

"But they have to die *correctly*, or what's the point?" Krato spat. He quickly adjusted a knob on the side of the weapon. "Ah, fonk it," he said, then he turned the gun on Dan and shot him between the eyes.

TWENTY-THREE

THE IMPACT SNAPPED Dan's head back just as a second gunshot hit Ollie in the chest. Neither of them fell. Instead, the world raced into fast forward around them. Krato's movements became cartoonishly quick, his voice emerging as a high-pitched series of cheeps and squeaks.

"Cool, huh?" he chirped, his voice so sped up Dan had difficulty understanding the words.

Dan looked down at his hands. To him, they appeared to be moving at their regular speed, but the rest of the world was racing ahead of him, with the exception of Ollie.

"What's going on?" she asked. "Everything's going fast."

Dan shook his head. "Slowdown rounds. The son-of-a-bedge has slowdown rounds. He's dropped us into slow motion."

"C'mere, ye bastard," cheeped Artur, then he bounded off Dan's shoulder with relatively superhuman speed, roaring as he hurtled through the air in Krato's direction.

A third slowdown round hit him, mid-fall. From Dan and Ollie's point of view, Artur's movements slowed to normal speed. To everyone else around, Artur's descent became a laborious crawl, like he was gradually sinking into thick honey.

Dan and Ollie could only watch as Krato shoved Finn and Bonbo inland toward the factory gates looming in the distance. The children followed robotically behind him as he scurried off in the direction of the city.

By the time Artur hit the dock, he, Dan and Ollie were alone.

"So this is what it feels like," Dan grunted.

"Can't we speed up?" Ollie asked.

"Not until it wears off," said Dan.

"And how fecking long will that take?"

Dan shrugged. "Depends on how much power he used. And on the gun. Besides Mindy, I've never seen one that can do this."

He looked up and watched ships streak across the sky like shooting stars.

"Marnie!" Artur cheered.

Dan lowered his head just as Marnie jerked upright like she had been spring-loaded. Her head whipped left and right, her face flitting through a range of comically accelerated expressions. Dan blinked, and she was suddenly right in front of him, arms flailing, voice chirping out like a rodent in distress.

He couldn't make out all of what she was saying, but he got the general, "What the fonk is going on?" vibe.

"Find my gun," he said, spitting the words out as quickly as he could. Marnie's head snapped briefly into a nod as she looked him up and down.

"What's wrong with you?" she asked. Or Dan guessed that's what she said, at least.

"Find my gun!" he said again, pointing to the water. From Marnie's point of view, this was quite a lengthy process, and by the time he'd finished pointing she was standing in front of him with Mindy.

"Here."

She thrust the gun into his hands. "Mindy. Slowdown cancel," he said.

The gun's lights remained dark, his voice imprint not recognized. *Fonk.*

"Mindy-slowdown-cancel."

Nothing.

From somewhere in the distance came a high-pitched scream. Dan had never seen an episode of the cartoon series *Alvin and the Chipmunks* before. If he had, and if said episode featured one of the chipmunks – Theodore, maybe – being lowered feet first into a kitchen blender, he would almost certainly have noticed a distinct similarity between those screams and this one.

A series of crashes followed, although they sounded to Dan's ears like corn popping.

"Mindyslowdowncancel. *Mindyslowdowncancel!*"

The gun's chamber spun with such speed and ferocity it almost jumped out of Dan's hands. Lights illuminated on the weapon's side, but only two of them. Fonk.

Dan jammed the gun under his jaw and pulled the trigger. The world around him immediately jolted back to regular speed.

He looked from Ollie to Artur, who were both still in the process of reacting to him shooting himself. One shot left, then he was out. He might need both of them, but one of them he could carry.

He shot Ollie in the stomach. She yelped and stumbled back, clutching at the invisible entry wound. "What the...? Oh. Oh!"

She wobbled her arms, jumped, then contorted her face. "I'm normal. Everything's normal speed!"

Artur glowered up at Dan. He began to say, "Ye no-good traitorous bastard," but by the time he'd finished he had been stuffed inside Dan's shirt pocket, and they were halfway to the factory gates.

A scene of chaos awaited them when they emerged through the gates and out into the city. A multi-vehicle pile-up smoldered at the side of the road, dozens of other cars abandoned in both directions. The throngs of pedestrians Dan would have expected to see on a street like this one had all fled. Only a handful remained, and the only reason they hadn't legged it was because they were quite emphatically dead.

Two squirming armored balls of spikes and tentacles stabbed and swiped at the few vehicles that hadn't yet been abandoned. Krato watched them with paternal pride as they hacked and slashed and killed and maimed their way along the street.

The kids were still lined up in front of him, still staring blankly ahead. There was no sign of Bonbo or Finn, aside from the broken shackles on the sidewalk at Krato's feet.

Still, at least they weren't too late to save the kids.

Mindy didn't have enough juice left to cancel out another slowdown round, but he could tease a single stun shot out of her. He only had one chance to make it count.

Krato still hadn't seen them. Dan raised the gun and took aim. The kids were in front of Krato, but he was tall enough that Dan had a clean shot of his head.

"Night night, you piece of shizz," he growled.

He squeezed the trigger. The gun kicked. A yellow bolt streaked through the air, closing quickly on Krato's head.

There was a *pew* as it ricocheted back out of the

doorway and streaked back over Dan's head. The air around Krato became a swirling pattern of colors, like oil on water, and he jumped back in surprise.

His eyes briefly widened when he spotted Dan, then that fonking smirk of his returned. "Personal shield," he announced. "Nice try."

Krato raised something roughly the size of a cigarette lighter. He winked and laughed as Dan broke into a lumbering run.

"Too late, Detective," he said, as his thumb pressed down on the top of the device. Dan stopped running as a number of terrible things all happened at the same time.

The halos around the children's heads all lit-up in blinding shades of white. The kids screamed and clawed at the devices, their rigid, trance-like demeanor replaced by a frantic thrashing and screeching as pain tore through their insides.

Krato gave a little wave, then stepped through the door behind him and closed it.

The children staggered into the street, their skin blistering and bulging, their limbs bending like tree branches in a thunderstorm.

Marnie made a move to run to them, but Dan stopped her. "Get the others," he told her.

"Others? What others?"

"Those kids are about to *seriously* start misbehaving," Dan said. "Go fetch their moms."

Marnie nodded, then raced back in the direction of the dock, her webbed feet *paff*ing on the hard sidewalk.

"Whaaaaaaat aaaaaaaaare weeeeeeee—" Artur began.

"Sorry, Artur, no time," said Dan. He ran toward the children, waving his arms and trying to shape his face into something resembling a smile. "Hey, kids! Over here. It's OK, calm down, fight it. Think happy—"

A spiky black tentacle erupted from one child's mouth. Another doubled over and screamed as she split open, revealing a tumbling ball of tentacles within.

"Ah, fonk," Dan spat. "So much for that."

One by one, the children fell, their bodies unfolding and rearranging themselves into something larger and infinitely more terrifying. It was almost impressive in its own way. Horrifying, but impressive.

"What do we do?" Ollie asked. She waited a little over a second before asking again. "What do we do?"

"I don't... I don't know," Dan admitted. Finn and Bonbo were much further along the street now, tearing open storefronts and stabbing frantically at anyone taking cover inside. Sirens screamed from a few different directions in the distance. The Tribunal, no doubt heavily armed.

The war was about to begin.

"Krato must have some way of stopping it," Dan reasoned, although he had nothing whatsoever to base that on. "I'll go after him."

"What should I do?" Ollie asked.

"Nothing. When the moms arrive, get them to try to calm the kids down."

Ollie looked over to where the children had been. In their place were six glistening balls of fury, each one protected by a shiny exoskeleton. They flapped their deadly limbs, as if testing them for the first time.

"How are they supposed to do that?"

"I don't know," Dan said. He headed for the door Krato had gone through, but stopped almost immediately. "Tell them to sing."

Ollie frowned. "Sing?"

"Sssssssssssiiiiiiiiiii—?" began Artur.

"There's a lullaby or, I don't know, a nursery rhyme." He had a half-hearted stab at the melody. "Like that. Tell them to sing that."

Ollie nodded. "What about Finn?"

Dan glanced along the street to where the two monstrous wrecking balls were thrashing their way through a line of traffic.

"I'm working on it."

DAN BARGED through the door and into the hallway of a neat, if a little run-down, family home. He found the family themselves in a room through the back, cowering behind an overturned sofa. Two children recoiled in terror at the sight of him, while a wizened old woman with two extra eyes on her forehead pointed silently at the back window.

"Thank you," said Dan. He leaned out through the window, then jumped back as a blaster bolt disintegrated the frame. "Shizz!"

He waited for a moment, then quickly thrust an arm out and back in. Another hail of blaster fire screamed across the house's backyard, burning holes through a line of washing that had been hung out to dry.

Dan gave Mindy a shake, then slammed her twice against his hip. The lights remained dark. The charge was fully depleted.

"Fonk!"

Shoving the gun back in its holster, he took a step back from the open window and readied himself to jump through it. If he moved fast enough, maybe he could get clear before

Krato opened fire. Maybe he could find cover. Maybe Krato wouldn't score a direct hit to his head.

Lot of maybes, but what other choice did he have?

"OK," he muttered, psyching himself up.

Just before he started his run, something heavy slid across the laminate flooring and stopped at his feet. It was a gun. A small gun, but a gun all the same.

He looked across to the sofa. The old woman nodded, and he nodded back.

Snatching up the gun, Dan approached the window. There was a lamp on a table just beneath it. It had been knocked over, presumably by Krato. Dan lifted it, turned it over in his hand, then tossed it out through the window.

It was shot to pieces before it hit the ground. As it exploded, Dan vaulted through the gap, opening fire in the direction Krato's shots had come from. The gun made a little *pwing* sound every time he pulled the trigger, launching disappointingly cute-looking marbles of fire across the backyard. They hit the fence Krato was taking cover behind, throwing out a few clumps of splinters, but otherwise doing no damage.

Dan tucked himself into cover behind a large trash can. Garbage sprayed out as Krato blasted holes in the metal, and Dan knew he only had seconds before the whole thing disintegrated.

He studied the old woman's gun, hoping for some sort of slider or dial that could crank up the firepower. No such luck. He had a peashooter against a man with a portable shield generator. Sure, the battery readout said it was almost fully charged, but what good was that when the shots it fired were so pitifully weak? He may as well be throwing Funplings.

Wait. The battery.

Dan ejected the clip and caught it. It wasn't the same size as Mindy's, but the connection...

Mindy's own battery popped free. Dan compared the terminals and came very close to smiling. It took some fiddling – not helped by the crescendo of blaster fire screaming around him – but the battery eventually slotted into Mindy's grip.

The chamber spun. Lights illuminated.

"Mindy, explosive round," he said, then he stood up, ignored the hole that was blasted through his stomach, and the damp *splat* of innards hitting the wall behind him, and fired.

The explosive round turned the fence to matchsticks, while also turning the previously stationary Krato into anything but. His shield flickered as he tumbled across an alleyway and crashed through another fence.

Dan stalked across the yard through the flapping sheets drying on the line.

"I'm coming for you, Krato," he warned, keeping Mindy raised as he approached the smoking hole in the fence. "Put down your gun and let's talk."

There was a buzz like a chainsaw and dozens of blaster bolts cut what was left of the fence in half. Dan ducked for cover, firing blindly at the source of the gunfire. The first explosive round detonated with no apparent effect, but the second brought a pained *"Urk!"* from inside the other garden and the rapid-fire assault sputtered to a stop.

"Diiiiiiiiiiiiiiiiiiiidddddddd yeeeeeeeeeeeee geeeeeeeeet...?"

"Don't know, Artur," Dan said. He jumped to his feet. "Let's find out."

"SING? WHAT DO YOU MEAN *SING*?"

"Sing!" said Ollie. "You know. Laaaa! Like that."

"Sing what?" Marnie demanded.

They were surrounded by all six mothers. The women gaped in horror at what had become of their children, watching helplessly as they squirmed and rolled off along the street, limbs swiping and slicing at anything that moved.

"A song. You know, like... I don't know," Ollie admitted. "Dan said there was a song. A lullaby or something? He said you should sing it."

The mom who had been piloting the sub looked round at her. "Wait. The Tidesong?"

Ollie shrugged. "I don't know. What does it go like?"

The mom cleared her throat and sang a couple of faltering notes. Ollie yelped. "Yes! I think that's it! That's what Dan sang. Only his was all..." She lowered her voice into a gravelly growl and almost choked on the notes that emerged. "Like that."

"And what's it supposed to do?" Marnie demanded, but before Ollie could give an answer, one of the other moms began to sing. Her voice was high and piercing, yet smooth like velvet.

There were no words to what she was singing, but somehow the tune itself told a story that Ollie instinctively understood. It was a story of home and of hope and of snuggling up safe. It was a story of a mother's love – pure, unconditional love – that wrapped around Ollie's shoulders and swaddled her like a blanket.

Another mom joined in, then another loaned her voice to the harmony. The sound rose as all seven Deeper Down women sang as one, their voices carrying along the street to their monstrously mutated children.

And doing absolutely fonk all.

"It's not working," Marnie said.

"They can't hear us. We have to get closer," the pilot mom said, but Marnie blocked her path.

"It's too dangerous."

"Get out of my way, Marnie. That's my son!"

"Not right now it isn't," Marnie said. "I'm sorry, Torus, but if you get any closer you could be killed. I can't allow that."

"We just need to get their attention," said Ollie.

"And how do you suggest we do that?" Marnie asked her.

Ollie's forehead creased as she tried to come up with a solution. She wished Dan were here. Dan would know what to do. Or Artur.

Or Finn.

Finn.

Her eyes scanned the row of partially-destroyed storefronts. They stopped on one that was no more or less damaged than the others, yet somehow managed to look worse in every conceivable way.

"Wait here," she said. "I think I have an idea."

———

DAN KICKED through the debris of the second fence, but found no trace of Krato. A nightdress whipped at him from another washing line, snapping so quickly he almost obliterated it with an explosive round.

"No point running, you piece of shizz. I'll find you," Dan warned. "Come out now and I'll only make you eat one of your own balls."

"Tempting, but no."

Krato's voice echoed around the yard, like it was being

projected from several places at once. It screeched a little on the higher notes, suggesting whatever was projecting the sound had taken damage.

"How's your shield holding up?" Dan asked, his eyes darting between gaps in the fluttering laundry. "Still got charge left, I hope? I'd hate for the next shot to put a hole through you."

"It's completely gone," Krato said. "If you want me alive, I'd put your gun away."

"Nice try," Dan said.

He opened fire in one of the many directions Krato's voice had come from.

"Cold," said Krato, once the dust had settled. There was a sneering tone to his voice that bugged Dan immensely. He fired off another two rounds in opposite directions.

When the dust settled again, the garden was deathly silent. It stayed that way for several long, drawn-out seconds, until:

"Warmer."

"This could all be over with, Krato," Dan said. "Just come out, help me change the kids back, and I'll make sure everyone goes easy on you."

"Mmm. Let me think about that," Krato said. "No. No, I think I'll pass."

Dan's voice became an angry growl. "I'm going to find you, you piece of shizz. You should've killed me when you had the chance."

"Kill you? Why would I want to kill you, Detective? I made you."

Dan hesitated. "What did you say?"

The voice broke up like a bad radio signal as Krato continued, but Dan heard enough to piece it together.

"Not the original you, of course, but this new incarnation. This... thing you are now. That was my doing."

"Bullshizz," said Dan.

"It wasn't deliberate. I had no idea your colleagues were going to murder you in cold blood and bury you in the exact spot where my company had disposed of some pretty unsavory toxins, but when they did, I thought... What the Hell? Let's wait and see what happens."

Krato's voice became a slightly awed whisper. "And then you emerged. Reborn into something better, something new. Just like those children. You were instrumental to my research, in fact. Without you – without having witnessed your comeback – I doubt I'd have cracked the necessary code that allowed me to put my current plan into action."

"You're lying."

"I really am not," Krato whispered. "Without you, Mr Deadman, those children would not currently be tearing up the streets. In many ways, this is all your fault."

He gave that a moment to sink in.

"Oh, and you're right. I should've killed you when I had the chance. After all, I brought you into this world."

Dan saw movement through the billowing sheets on his right. He turned, too late. A spray of rapid-fire blaster bolts turned his gun hand to pulp from the wrist down. Dan tried to twist away, but the blaster carved a trench through his ribcage and cut off his other arm at the elbow.

Krato released the trigger and the gun *whined* as it stopped firing.

"And I can take you out of it."

"Yyyyyyyyeeeeeeeeeeeeeeee ffffffffffffeeeeeeeeeeeeeeeccc-ccckkkkkkkk—"

Krato moved his gun so the barrel was half an inch from

Artur's face. "And I have zero emotional attachment to you, you little fonk. So just try me."

He cracked the butt of the gun against the side of Dan's head, staggering him. "Now, let's go watch all the excitement, shall we?"

TWENTY-FOUR

THE THINGS that had until recently been children thrashed their armored limbs, stabbing and pouncing at anything that moved on the street below them. They were twenty feet tall now, but with tentacles fully extended much larger still. They were growing, although they didn't really understand that. They understood very little now, other than the compunction to maim and kill and destroy that burned through them like cold fire.

One of them punched its pointed limbs through the front of a building and pulled. There was a roar of breaking brickwork as the wall collapsed out into the street, revealing a room full of terrified people beyond.

Two of the monster-children pounced like jumping spiders, their tentacles snapping and stabbing, their blood boiling in their blackened veins.

A child – a real one – howled in terror. Six armored shapes turned toward the sound as one. Thirty-two blade-like limbs drew back to strike.

"Loopy-Loopy-Loopy-Loopy-Loo-pee Lou's, it's fun for me, and it's fun for you!"

Thirty-two blade-like limbs froze.

"Come bring your friends. Meet you-know-who! Loopy-Loopy-Loopy-Loopy-Loo-pee Lou's!"

The monster-kids turned away from the house with the broken wall and peered down at a furry shape in a satin yellow shirt that jerked around erratically in front of them. From their high vantage point, they couldn't see the things dangling genitals, which was probably just as well really.

Loopy Lou's mouth flapped open and closed in time with the audio blasting from somewhere inside the suit.

"Hey-hey-hey, kids! It's your old pal, Loopy Lou! Say 'Hi Loopy Lou!'"

There was a heavy, oppressive silence.

"That's it!" Loopy Lou continued. "Hi right back atcha!"

A high nasal laugh screeched from inside the suit. "Now, who wants to play a game?"

The monster-kids regarded the furry figure with quite intense levels of bemusement.

"Everybody?" Loopy Lou laughed. "Well, OK, then. Let's play!"

A black tendril swatted Loopy Lou aside. Ollie screamed inside the suit, then briefly giggled as yet another electrical charge tore through her. She smashed into an abandoned car, flipped over it, and then crunched onto the street on the other side.

The car crumpled as one of the things stabbed a limb through its roof and hoisted it aside. Ollie spasmed as the suit zapped her again. "Uh, I think I have their attention!" she hollered.

Even through the heavy costume and the random *bzzzt* of electricity coursing through her body, Ollie heard the song come drifting along the street. It rippled over her like warm water, seeping through the seams of the suit, steaming up the eye lenses and filling the costume with the smell of...

No.

Wait.

She'd wet herself.

In her defense, that last impact had really hurt.

The suit gave her another shock, but this time something inside it went *pop* and began to smoke. Ollie pulled the headpiece off and saw one of the spiky monster-kids looming above her, two of its many limbs raised and ready to deliver a killer blow.

It never came. As the music swelled around them, the monsters' limbs first became limp, and then became smaller. Their armored black flesh rolled like boiling tar, then collapsed in towards each monster's center.

Scraps of skin appeared in the bubbling black, fusing together like the pieces of a jigsaw puzzle wherever they met. It was one of the most mesmerizingly horrific things Ollie had ever seen, and considering the shizz she'd spent her entire childhood being forced to watch, that was really saying something.

She sat up and backed away on her padded elbows, her stuffed penis waggling as she shimmied back toward the singing moms.

Four of the monsters had faces now. Their expressions would probably haunt Ollie's nightmares forever, but they had faces. Faces were an improvement on a moment ago.

It was working. It was actually working.

And then, just like that, it wasn't.

One of the two bigger monsters bounded through them, scattering them all like skittles. Its spear-like legs stabbed at Ollie, shattering the ground wherever she dodged clear.

"Wait, wait, don't. Stop!" Ollie protested, holding her

hands up in surrender. "Finn? Finn, is that you? It's me. It's Ollie!"

The children, stuck between forms, began to squirm and twist again. Their mothers raised their voices, singing their song of soothing that promised an end to all pain and all fear.

Pointy tentacles dug into the ground around Ollie, fencing her in. She had no idea where the thing's face was, but she could feel its eyes boring into her. She felt her own eyes fill with tears.

"Finn, if that's you, I know you won't hurt me. I know you won't. I know you're still in there. And I know you can come back."

She smiled up at the monster. She didn't flinch as it raised an arm, or a leg, or whatever the fonk it was above its head. Didn't blink as the blade stabbed down. Didn't scream as she heard the tearing flesh and felt the hot blood spatter across her face.

The monster howled and thrashed, spraying more of its blood across the street. At first, Ollie didn't notice that it had an extra limb, or that the limb was protruding through a wound in the thing's chest. It was only when the blade withdrew and the creature was violently knocked aside that she realized what had happened.

The second of the two larger monsters appeared above her. She knew him right away. Although she still had no clue where its eyes were, this one looked at her like Finn did.

Like it loved her.

"Hey," she said. A tentacle capable of tearing through solid steel reached down and tapped her lightly on the shoulder. Ollie felt herself laugh and cry at the same time, and couldn't decide which reaction was correct.

She got up slowly, so as not to startle him. The mothers' chorus continued to echo around them. The monster-kids had gone limp again, their panic subsiding, their transformations reversing.

"You look terrible," she said.

Finn nudged the discarded Loopy Lou head. "Totally suits me better," Ollie told him, and she swore she heard the thing snort.

Taking a breath, she stepped forward and placed a furry hand on his armored frame. "Come back to me," she urged. "Please."

The Finn-thing tensed, and for a moment Ollie thought he was going to run away. But then he slumped down, his tentacles flopping loosely around him. Ollie forced herself to watch as the black shape collapsed in on itself, and pieces of Finn's skin began weaving themselves together.

She almost cried again when she saw his face. There was so much pain and suffering written there, and she wondered if he remembered all the terrible things he had done. She hoped not. God, she hoped not.

It didn't take long for all his various pieces to reconnect. He stood before her, naked and bleeding, his whole body trembling in shock.

He blinked a few times, like he couldn't quite figure out how his eyes worked, or even what they were supposed to do. The pupils swam vaguely for a moment, before finally fixing on her. His face lit up when he saw her, like a kid on Kroyshuk morning.

"Hey, you," he said, then he frowned and looked down. "Uh, I'm naked. Why am I naked?"

"Long story," said Ollie. She, too, looked down. "Mine's bigger," she said, pointing to her impressively large artificial penis.

Finn blushed. "Harsh, brah," he said, then his chest erupted outwards and his throat ejected blood as Bonbo skewered him through the back.

Ollie grabbed for him as the blade withdrew. "No, no, no, no, no," she babbled, catching him in her furry arms. "Finn? Finn! No, no, no."

He gargled what would be the last sound he ever made. His final breath formed a bloody spit-bubble on his lips. And then it, and he, were gone.

The air around Ollie hummed. Loopy Lou's fur stood on end as sparks crackled between the coarse strands.

The other monster – Bonbo – loomed over her again, lining its limbs up for another strike.

"No," she said, and it squirmed in pain. She glared up at it, fire and fury burning behind her eyes. The markings on her face twisted and intertwined like serpents at an orgy, then a wave of heat radiated from her, stripping the monster's exoskeleton and revealing its dark, gelatinous center.

Ollie raised a hand and the thing rose from the ground, flapping and gasping like a fish out of water. She scrunched up a fist and watched as its mushy middle ignited, sending its limbs into a frenzy of movement.

A light exploded from within it, rapidly consuming its quivering, exposed flesh, blackening it and turning it to ash. It fluttered away as fine black flecks, leaving nothing behind but a dark stain on the road surface, and a dead man in Ollie's arms.

She breathed for what felt like the first time.

The singing had stopped. When had that happened? She couldn't say.

Six children hugged their mothers, sobbing as they were held close, deep welts clearly visible on their bare skin. But they were children again, that was the main thing. And they were alive.

Ollie held Finn for a moment longer, then lowered him to the ground. She flinched when Marnie's webbed hand rested on her shoulder. "You OK?"

She didn't answer right away. She didn't know how to.

"Not really," she admitted. She looked across the street just as Dan was shoved out of an alleyway, one of his hands and a sizeable part of the other arm missing.

"What the fonk is this?" demanded Krato. He had the gun jammed against the back of Dan's head, but his eyes were darting in all directions as he tried to figure out how his plan had gone so terribly wrong. "Did the Tribunal do this?"

"Do you see the fonking Tribunal here?" Dan asked.

"FONK!" Krato spat. The sound of approaching sirens was closer, but nowhere near close enough. "Fonk!"

He inhaled deeply through his nose and shook his head. "It's fine. I can still salvage this," he said. "I'll bring the bodies back to Deeper Down. I'll tell them Down Here did this. Killed all its soldiers. Killed its children, and their fonking interfering mothers."

Another crack to the back of Dan's head sent him staggering. Krato turned the gun on the closest of the moms. "They're going to be *so* upset when they see what happened to you all," he said.

Then, just before he could pull the trigger, a tiny transvestite punched him in the eyeball.

"Didn't see that coming, did ye, ye shoitebag?" Artur spat. He sank his teeth into Krato's eyelid while stamping down on the bridge of his nose hard enough to splinter the bone. "Yer fecking slowdown thing wore off. Not so tough now, are ye?"

Krato smashed the gun into his own face, knocking the wind out of Artur while fully destroying his own already broken nose.

Artur managed to wheeze out a brief, "Ye bastard," before Krato tore him off and tossed him onto the ground.

A bare foot *thwumped* into Krato's groin, doubling him over. He fired wildly with his gun, but Dan knocked it aside with his one remaining forearm and followed up with a headbutt when Krato tried to straighten up.

"S-stay back!" Krato babbled. He held up the same cigarette lighter-sized device as earlier and waved it around for everyone to see. "You think I didn't prepare for this?" he shrieked. "You think I wasn't ready for you fonking people? Ha! I've prepared for this for months! For *years!*"

He pointed to the kids. "Ask them about the implants. Hmm? About the devices I put in their heads."

He stumbled past Dan and into the street, blood spurting from his now utterly ravaged nose. From the way he kept gagging and coughing, even more of it was flowing backward down his throat.

"Explosives!" he said, his face twisting in glee. "There are bombs inside their heads. All I have to do is push this button and *KABOOM!* It's raining kiddie-brains."

Artur growled and clenched his tiny fists, but Dan shouted him down before he could do anything stupid. "No one moves," he said. "Artur, Ollie? No one moves."

"Listen to him," Krato suggested. "He's shizz-ugly and he fonking stinks, but he knows what he's talking about here. Anyone moves and the kids are dead. Hell, the explosions might take out all of us, I don't even know."

He backed off further, waving the device in front of him like a shield, which it was, more or less. "I'm going to go now," he said. "I'm going to go before the Tribunal arrives.

They've already paid me for the first delivery, you see? Enough for me to get off this planet and start again somewhere new. Somewhere fresh. It's a shame that things didn't work out exactly how I wanted, but I guess even I can't win them all."

He shrugged, then grinned through his mask of blood. "Still, compared to you guys, I'm king of the fonking world. Say hello to the Tribunal for me," he said. "You know, before they execute you all for—"

A spaceship landed on him.

It came down suddenly, and with enough force to make Krato's insides become his outsides. And vice versa.

Dan grabbed for the detonator as it was thrown into the air, but his lack of hands made catching it impossible.

"I got ye!" Artur cried, lunging for the device and wrapping his arms around it before it could hit the ground. "Oh, thank feck," he sighed, sinking to the ground and letting the detonator clatter harmlessly onto the asphalt beside him.

The kids were safe. Krato was spectacularly dead.

That just left the ship.

"Sorry. Our fault," called a man's voice from inside. "We totally didn't see that guy."

There was some whispering from the ship's speakers.

"Uh, I mean we totally aren't aware of *any* guy who may or may not have been under the ship when it – and I use this term generously – landed."

"Who the feck is this now?" asked Artur. He looked across to Marnie and the moms. "Ye got anything to do with this?"

Marnie just shook her head, transfixed by the greenish-gray ship before them.

"Peaches? Ye got any idea?"

"I think it's a spaceship," Ollie said.

"Points for observation, at least," he said. "Deadman? Do ye know who this is?"

"Guess we're about to find out," Dan said, gesturing with a stump to where a ramp at the back of the ship was descending.

For a long time, nothing happened. And then, just when it looked like nothing *was* going to happen, something did.

A ball of green slime trundled down the ramp and stopped at the bottom. Two wide and worryingly human-looking eyeballs gazed out from inside its gelatinous body. They flitted from Ollie to Artur, before finally settling on Dan.

"Well, I was not expecting that," Artur said. "Ye think he comes in peace? Should we take him to our leader? I don't know the official protocol here, like."

A man in a tan leather jacket descended the ramp, waving like a rock star and grinning at... well, everything. "There he is!" the man said, pointing at Dan. "There's my number one zombie detective guy."

"Ye know this arsehole, Deadman?"

Dan shook his head. "Never seen him before in my life."

"Aha! See, that's where you're wrong. Name's Cal. Cal Carver. We've met."

"We haven't," Dan insisted.

"We have. You gave me and some of my friends fake ID when we got stuck on this shizzho... On this fine planet a while back. But there were some time travel shenanigans that messed with the past, which messed with the future, and blah, blah, blah. The point is, we've met. I like to think we became pretty close friends in our own way."

Dan sighed. The Tribunal sirens were getting closer. He didn't have time for this shizz.

"I don't have time for this shizz," he said, making that point very clear.

"I know, I know," said Cal. "You're clearly in the middle of..." he gestured at the chaos around them. "...whatever this is. But here's the thing."

He beckoned up into the ship. "Come on, Ronda. Don't be shy. You already know what happens."

An elderly woman with permed gray hair and yellow skin descended the ramp with a surprising amount of grace. Cal tried to take her arm to lead her over to Dan, but she sidestepped past him and strode across unsupported.

"This is Ronda. She's a nun," Cal explained.

Dan glanced down at Artur, then across to Ollie. "Uh, OK."

"But, like, a *magic* nun," Cal said.

"I'm not magic," Ronda corrected. "I have limited precognitive abilities, and I am able to see damage to the timeline."

"Maaagic space nuuun," Cal whispered, waggling his fingers mysteriously. "She also makes awesome spit nibbles."

"I can help others see that damage, too," Ronda said. "Would you like me to show you?"

"Not really," Dan said.

Ronda smiled. "Yes. I knew you were going to say that," she said, and then her hands were suddenly on his head, her thumbs pressing into his eyes.

For a moment, Dan saw nothing but color, and then the inside of his head became a gloopy puree of thoughts and feelings he had absolutely no understanding of. Things that had been, but shouldn't, or hadn't been, but should. It all swelled up inside him, and he screamed as he felt like his head was going to crack open and it was all going to come spilling out.

And then Ronda was standing beside Cal again, and Dan was still screaming. It died in his throat when he saw the others all watching him. If he'd had any blood flow, he'd have blushed.

"Ye alright there, Deadman?"

Dan coughed. "Fine."

"It's just, ye were squealin' like a little girl for a moment or two."

"I'm aware of that."

Cal hadn't stopped grinning at him. "Well?"

No, not Cal. That wasn't his name.

Cal tapped on his chest and spoke slowly, as if addressing a caveman. "Me Cal Carver. Recognize me now?"

Dan nodded, just once. "Nob Muntch," he said, remembering the name he'd given the guy on his fake ID. Cal's face fell. "To what do I owe the pleasure?"

"Kind of a long story," Cal said. He jabbed a thumb in the direction of some approaching sirens. "And sounds like we're about to have company. We can explain on the way."

"What's this eejit talking about?" Artur demanded. "On the way where?"

Cal finally noticed Artur properly, and let out a gasp of delight. "Hey, is that a Leprechaun?" He looked back over his shoulder. "Mech? Loren? You're not going to believe this. They have a Space Leprechaun!"

He gave Ollie a quick once-over, checking her out. His eyes lingered briefly on the Loopy Lou suit she was still wearing. "And a furry woman with a purple face who smells of urine. Should we bring them, too?"

"How the Hell should I know, man?" demanded a voice

from inside the ship. "Just get a motherfonking move on."

"I'm going to take that as a 'yes,'" Cal called back. He rested a hand on Ollie's shoulder, then gave Artur a thumbs-up. "Good news, guys. You're in!"

"In?" asked Ollie. "I don't understand."

"What's all this about, Nob?" Dan asked.

"Cal. Please," said Cal.

Dan gave a brief shake of his head.

"OK, well we'll work on that," Cal said. "And as for what's happening...?"

The green blob rolled up his back and onto his shoulder. It rippled gently as he stroked it under the chin.

"We're going to kill the King of Space," Cal said. He glanced between them. "You in?"

Dan looked to Ollie and Artur, then around at the carnage in the street. For the first time, he saw Finn's body lying on the road, and felt an overwhelming urge to put an arm around Ollie's shoulders. She was standing on his left, though, and he didn't have enough arm on that side to reach her.

The Tribunal was coming.

This was all going to take a lot of fonking explaining. He was pretty sure he could kiss goodbye to his new office, too.

Dan shrugged.

"Fonk it," he said. "Could be interesting."

"Great! Although you may want to find some arms before we set off."

"Wait? What's happening?" asked Artur.

Cal squatted and smiled kindly down at him. "Well, *hey there*, little guy, don't be afraid," he said. "We're going on a big adventure in outer space. There'll be lasers and bad guys and we'll probably crash a lot. But don't worry, Splurt's little, just like you. He'll look after you and keep you safe. He'll make sure nobody hurts you."

Artur became remarkably still. One of his eyebrows raised. "Ye landed a ship on someone who deserved to have a ship landed on them, so I'm going to give ye one free pass," he said. "Ye've now used that up. That's gone. No more. So, here's the thing – if ye talk to me like that again..." He pointed to the green blob on Cal's shoulder. "...I will shove that thing up yer arse until ye sneeze it back out." He smiled, showing off his yellow teeth. "How does that sound for a fecking adventure?"

Cal's eyes became two circles of surprise. "Holy shizz. You even *sound* like a Leprechaun! This is going to be so awesome!"

Artur clenched his fists, but then shook his head. "Not yet. I'll wait until ye're least expecting it," he said. "I'd sleep with both eyes open from now on, if I were you."

He held Cal with a threatening glare for a moment, then raised his nose in the air and marched over to where Marnie was standing with the other Deeper Downians.

"Marnie, me darlin'," he began. "I was just wondering, is there any chance we might—?"

"Fonk off, 'chaun," Marnie said. She ushered the moms and their children in the direction of the dock. "If I see you again, I'll squash you."

"Right ye are. Fair play," Artur replied, tapping a finger to his brow. "Take care, now."

He waited until they were through the factory gates before turning back to Dan and the others. "Fecking dodged a bullet there, didn't I?" he said. "Looks like I've got nothing keeping me around here, so if Deadman's going, I'm going."

"To be sure, to be sure," said Cal, taking his life in his hands.

Dan rested a congealing wrist-stump on Ollie's shoulder. "You OK, kid?"

Ollie's eyes filled with tears. "Uh-huh," she said, but it came out as an unconvincing squeak. Her gaze flitted to the motionless Finn, but quickly returned to Dan. "I feel... sad."

"I know," Dan said.

"It's not fair."

"I know."

He awkwardly put both stumps around her and pulled her into a hug.

"You smell," she said, her voice muffled against his chest.

"I know."

"Uh, excuse me, sir," crackled a voice from the ship. It had a pronounced English accent, and might well have been some sort of butler. "Quite a large number of law enforcement vehicles are heading our way."

"I'm aware of that, Kevin," Cal replied.

"Should I destroy them?"

"Fonk, no! Don't do that. We're just coming." Cal looked across the faces of Dan, Ollie, and their adorable little Space Leprechaun. "We *are* just coming, right? Adventure awaits."

Ollie stepped back from Dan.

"What kind of adventure?" she asked.

"The best kind," said Cal, his grin somehow widening further. "Galaxy-saving seat-of-the-pants *space* adventure."

Ollie inhaled slowly. She took one last look at Finn, then wiped her eyes on her enormous furry hand.

"OK," she said. "We're in."

THE END